Clay

Also by Franck Bouysse

Born of No Woman

Wind Drinkers

Clay

Franck Bouysse

Translated from the French
by Lara Vergnaud

Other Press | New York

Originally published in 2018 as *Glaise* by La Manufacture de livres, Paris

Published by arrangement with Marie-Pacifique Zeltner, Agence Bibemus

Production editor: Yvonne E. Cárdenas
Text designer: Patrice Sheridan
This book was set in Chaparral Pro by
Alpha Design & Composition of Pittsfield, NH

1 3 5 7 9 10 8 6 4 2

Printed in the United States of America on acid-free paper. For information write to Other Press LLC, 267 Fifth Avenue, 6th Floor, New York, NY 10016. Or visit our Web site: www.otherpress.com

Library of Congress Cataloging-in-Publication Data
Names: Bouysse, Franck, 1965- author. | Vergnaud, Lara, translator.
Title: Clay / Franck Bouysse ; translated from the French by Lara Vergnaud.
Other titles: Glaise. English
Description: New York : Other Press, 2025. | "Originally published in 2017 as Glaise by La Manufacture de livres, Paris"—Title page verso.
Identifiers: LCCN 2024039771 (print) | LCCN 2024039772 (ebook) | ISBN 9781635420555 (paperback) | ISBN 9781635420562 (ebook)
Subjects: LCGFT: Novels.
Classification: LCC PQ2702.O9845 G5313 2025 (print) | LCC PQ2702.O9845 (ebook) | DDC 843/.92—dc23/eng/20241016
LC record available at https://lccn.loc.gov/2024039771
LC ebook record available at https://lccn.loc.gov/2024039772

She was a hunk of sculptor's clay,
My secret thoughts were fingers:
They flew behind her pensive brow
And lined it deep with pain.
They set the lips, and sagged the cheeks,
And drooped the eyes with sorrow.
My soul had entered in the clay,
Fighting like seven devils.

—EDGAR LEE MASTERS
"FLETCHER MCGEE," SPOON RIVER

We have a few old mouth-to-mouth tales; we exhume from old trunks and boxes and drawers letters without salutation or signature, in which men and women who once lived and breathed are now merely initials or nicknames out of some now incomprehensible affection which sound to us like Sanskrit or Chocktaw; we see dimly people, the people in whose living blood and seed we ourselves lay dormant and waiting, in this shadowy attenuation of time possessing now heroic proportions, performing their acts of simple passion and simple violence, impervious to time and inexplicable.

—WILLIAM FAULKNER
ABSALOM, ABSALOM!

Whatever was to happen that night would be decided by the heavens alone. The first signs had appeared the previous evening, when the swallows began flying low to the ground. Now a warm wind was walloping the branches of a tall chestnut tree in the courtyard as a mountain range of black clouds formed in the charcoal sky. Thunder rumbled and bolts of lightning flickered in the distance, illuminating the summit of Puy Violent.

Marie was waiting, seated on the edge of the bed, dreading the moment the storm would pass over the farm. She lit the wick of the oil lamp on her bedside table and put on her round glasses with the rusted frame, then stood to cover the distance between the bed and the oak dresser: seven steps heavy with age. Opened the top drawer and took out a locked metal box. All of which she could have done with eyes closed.

She left the bedroom carrying the box and lamp, closed the door to avoid a draft, and entered the kitchen, set both items on the table, and sat, annoyed to find that the others weren't awake yet. The wrinkles on her wizened face were dancing in the pale light, but her small eyes, discernable through the lenses of her glasses, remained fixed on her clasped hands.

The rolls of thunder became increasingly distinct, words tumbling into one another in a single sentence stripped of punctuation and repeated ad infinitum. Now that the storm had crossed the river, nothing could stop it. Marie's shoulders slumped at every reverberation, as if struck by an invisible violent force, confusion and fear battling in her mind.

Victor and Mathilde walked in, stepped over the bench, and sat beside the old woman without a word. Marie looked at her son, face stern.

"Why isn't he here?" she asked coldly.

"We didn't want to wake him," said Victor.

"You should have."

Victor gave his mother a weary look.

"He's sleeping. There's plenty of time," he said.

Marie unclasped her hands and thrust out her chest, perhaps to give greater weight to her words.

"What would you know?" she asked.

"It... it can't strike the same spot twice. Everyone knows that."

Marie gripped the box, her fingers like fraying strands of knotted rope.

"So it's you who decides where it strikes?"

"That's not what I'm saying..."

"If he was sitting at this table, I'm not sure you'd be so bold."

"I'm sorry."

Mathilde said nothing, wasn't listening, seemingly oblivious to the storm now hanging over the farm. Her pretty face was marred by fear, a different kind of fear provoked by a different looming storm. A first bolt of lightning through the window. Everyone hushed. Others followed in a series of deafening flashes that intermittently lengthened the shadows in the kitchen, then reduced them to nothing, then revealed them once again. Dazed faces, illuminated then extinguished. Waxen figures frozen in prayer, seeking an omen, some hint of salvation, beyond the thunder.

A deafening explosion set the walls shaking, and in the next second, rain began pounding the windows like stones being cast. The storm passed. The grave danger avoided. Victor watched his mother slowly come back to life. The old woman's hands were still trembling when she took a key out of her pocket, inserted it into the box lock, and turned it twice. Then she slid off the lid, glanced inside only to shut the box again, and placed the key back in her pocket as she leaned slightly to one side, her head struggling to find balance, like an air bubble in a level.

Victor kept his eyes on his mother.

"Go on back to sleep now," he said.

She didn't move.

"This storm," she said, raising her voice over the rain beating down on the roof.

"It's fine, it's over."

"It'll be the same where you're going," she said, as though she was talking to the box.

Victor flung his hand in the direction of the lamp, and the flame flickered in the sudden draft.

"Don't you worry. It won't take us long to send the Krauts packing with their tails between their legs."

"Bet the Krauts are thinking the same thing."

"The recruiting sergeant said it'd be a few weeks," Victor added, forcing a smile.

Marie lifted her head, and the way the light reflected in her glasses made empty sockets of her eyes.

"And your sergeant knows the future, is that it?!" she snapped.

With a single glance, Victor looked at both his mother and his wife. He wasn't smiling anymore.

"I don't have a choice," he said.

The old woman instinctively brought the box closer to her chest.

"Just don't get yourself banged up. That's all we're asking."

"I know..."

"And watch out for lightning."

Marie took a deep breath.

"You'll send news," she continued.

"I'll write as soon as I can."

"And you leave tomorrow."

"I have to be at the train station in the morning, with Caesar."

Marie pressed her fists against either side of the box.

"As if it wasn't enough already, they have to take our horse too."

"Leonard said he'll give you a hand with his mule."

"An old mule can't replace a draft horse. If they didn't want her, it's 'cause she can't be of much use."

Victor allowed silence to settle in, hoping that his mother would continue expelling her legitimate anger, which was the same that he had inside of him. But she didn't.

“They don’t have a clue. Old mules are awful hardy . . . and they’ll give us back Caesar when the war’s over,” he said.

Marie scornfully shook her head.

“Because you think he’ll find his way home all by himself, that it?”

“They’re going to mark him, that way they’ll know he’s ours.”

She shrugged.

“I suppose they’ll go round all the farms to bring us back our property,” she said in a cynical voice.

Victor raised his arm and let his hand slam onto the table.

“This isn’t of my making, you know.”

“Did you talk to the boy?” asked the old woman, disregarding her son’s comment.

Victor shuddered, giving his mother a look thick with incomprehension.

“He knows where I’m going,” Victor said coldly.

“You ought to take a little time with him.”

“I know what I ought to do.”

“Very well, but I still have the right to tell you what I think.”

Marie looked up at her daughter-in-law, who had yet to move.

“What do you think?”

Mathilde slowly turned her head toward Marie and clasped her hands as if she was about to applaud or pray; it was hard to tell which.

“I don’t know what’s best,” she responded.

“Certain things need to be said so people can hear them.”

“That’s coming from you?” interrupted Victor.

"And? I'm allowed."

"You really think I need a lecture on top of everything else?!"

Marie hefted the box in her hand, preparing to stand.

"Anyways, you two will do what you want," she said.

"As best we can," Mathilde retorted in a solemn voice.

Victor was still staring at his mother, defiance in his eyes.

"You've never told me what was in that box."

The old woman stopped short.

"All the things that must never burn."

Then she rose to avoid having to provide further explanation and returned to her room. She put the box back in the dresser drawer that squeaked when it rubbed against the solid wood base.

Sitting on her bed, Marie listened to the rain letting up a little more every second, waiting for the sun to rise. The rain stopped well before dawn. A glimmer of light skirted through the shutters and froze, unable to penetrate the house. A turtledove began to sing somewhere on the roof, in chorus with the dripping water.

Marie was beset by dark thoughts sloshing around her mind like an icy mudslide. If Victor wasn't to come back from the war, she would lose everything, cut down like a weed by a scythe, and there would be nothing that could lessen that pain, not even the presence of her grandson so like her, and whom she cherished unabashedly. Perhaps such demonstrative feelings skip a generation. She thought of Mathilde too, so unassuming, so fragile. Marie didn't sense that her daughter-in-law was equipped to confront an empty spot in the bed, the despair that would overwhelm her, a despair with which she herself was well acquainted. Her true fear had nothing to do with a void, but rather with her own falling apart, as a mother. An internal paralysis that she was adamant on hiding, and that had been building inside her since the bells of Saint-Paul had begun to ring out of time.

Marie felt old. Far too old to fend for herself. Her weary heart and body alike could have used a respite, but she loathed inaction and would loathe it even more once her son had left for the front. She knew what a wife could accept in the end. A mother, never.

On stormy nights, they usually woke Joseph so he could get dressed quickly and be ready to leave in case lightning struck, in case of fire. That's how his grandfather had died—struck by lightning in the middle of the courtyard as he was placing tarps over the wells he had just constructed. Ever since that day, his grandmother had been terrified of the slightest clap of thunder. Joseph was seven when she told him what had happened, without emotion, and without specifying the date or any details of the accident. That had been eight years ago. Though he'd never dared ask, Joseph had always wondered what remained of his grandfather after he was struck, what of him they had been able to place in the coffin. He had seen, more than once, what lightning could do to a tree, and so he could imagine the devastation it might wreak on a human body.

That night, Joseph rose silently, resisting the desire to join the rest of his family in the kitchen. Ear glued to the door, he listened to their conversation, certain they wouldn't have said as much in his presence. A succession of words marred by the rumbling thunder.

After the storm had passed, Joseph heard the feet of a chair scraping across the warped wood floor, followed by those of the bench, and rushed back to bed. Hushed footsteps neared the door to his bedroom, slowed, then continued past. His parents returned to their bedroom. From the other side of the wall, he could barely make out their muffled voices. His mother began to sniffle and cry, whimpering like a distressed animal.

Then silence again, but Joseph couldn't fall back asleep. The storm was far, sweeping across other regions along the volcanic mountain chain. He detected a box spring creaking, imperceptibly at first, then increasingly distinct, his father's hoarse breathing, his mother's restrained gasps, the swell of their compressed bodies, as if they were each fighting the night in their own way at the center of the same loud and unmistakable fire. In such moments, when he was younger, Joseph had often wanted to run to his mother's aid, but for the first time he wanted to save his father.

A draft animal, more accustomed to pulling a plow than carrying the slight man on its back. A placid creature seemingly created whole: a centaur with massive hindquarters bulging with muscle, its fragile chest covered by a cotton button-up freshly washed and dried in the previous day's searing heat.

Victor had mounted bareback, one hand holding the greasy hemp rope attached to the bit and which served as reins. As far as he knew, they weren't requisitioning saddles. His gaze ran over and past the three figures standing in the shade of the house. Three generations forever imprisoned inside the skeletal box of his skull, a vision that would nourish his memories wherever he might find himself.

The farm buildings suddenly struck him as insubstantial despite their heavy slate-stone walls and sloping roofs covered with thick tiles. He remembered the struggle to obtain even a meager harvest, the sense of impotence before a dying animal, the unforgiving elements, and not a single past triumph was enough to allay the pain of his departure. Everything he was leaving in their hands, unwilling though he was. He took a deep breath, held it as long as he could, and exhaled as he looked back at his family. Managed a smile in this tragic moment, but his weak smile was a lousy liar: *Don't worry, I'll be back, no doubt about it.*

The sun in his eyes, Joseph frowned, nervously scratching one shoulder. A timid response, it would seem, to his father's smile, the son squinting from the overwhelming brightness that was disintegrating the silhouette in his eyeline, like an impressionist painter who uses small, repeated brushstrokes so that nothing remains apart from the revelation of space between daubs of paint. So that the heaviness of the mortal coil lifts and only an essential source of light remains.

Joseph turned to look at his mother, who was staring at her knotty fingers. Then, with no warning, he ran toward his father. Mathilde threw up her hands, but her feet didn't budge from the beaten earth of the courtyard. Joseph grabbed the horse's neck, pressed his cheek against his nose, and spoke to the animal of the future, of homecomings, not daring to mention reality, for fear of inviting bad luck. Victor leaned sideways, clenching his thighs so he wouldn't fall, placed one hand on his son's head, and then withdrew it.

"I'm counting on you," he said.

Joseph took one step back. He blinked as he tried to meet his father's gaze.

"Bring me with."

"That's not possible, son."

"I'm old enough, you know."

"I'm sure you are."

"So then please."

"With all the work there is, you'll be of far more use here."

Victor leaned over even farther, as though he wanted to tell his son a secret.

"If I had any say in it, I'd be staying, believe me," he added.

"When are you coming back?"

The Percheron raised his heavy head, the bit clicking between his jaws. Victor sat back up to stroke him.

"It won't be long," he said.

"'It won't be long' doesn't mean anything..."

"If ever I'm not back by autumn, remember to pick the ripe potatoes and sunchokes, and to plant plenty of winter cabbage and turnips in their place."

Joseph's mouth struggled to retain a swell of emotion.

"We'll do it together."

Victor swallowed and tightened his grip on the rope.

"You're the man of the house for a little while," he said.

"I won't let you down."

"I know."

"Papa..."

"Go on, off you go, now."

Joseph obeyed, dragging his feet. Turned back a few times before reaching the women. Marie said nothing, face solemn. Mathilde raised one hand to her brow, and it would have been hard to say whether it was a wave or an attempt to block the sight of her husband leaving her. Even for her. Since that night's storm, her movements were no longer her own.

Victor took a final look at his family, lowered his eyes, and gently dug his heels into the horse's flanks. Caesar lifted one foreleg, bent a hoof blanketed with thick, reddish hair, and extended it to strike the ground in a cloud of ocher dust. The man and his mount made their way across the streams of light between the shadows cast by the tall cypress trees along the path, slender as dark, unmoving flames and planted by someone long forgotten. From a distance, the horse appeared to be walking alternately across black water and crystal-clear water. Finally, the centaur's hazy outline melted one last time into shadow and emerged farther on in an explosion of light to then be slowly swallowed by the sloping terrain, until all that was left was the sound of hooves chanting a muted prayer. The world taking a breath. And not the slightest trace left behind.

Marie lifted her hands to hip level. They floated there without purpose, or as though she was gauging the weight of something infinitely heavy. Shadows had taken refuge on her impassive face, charcoal marks that swallowed her eyes. Mathilde was still staring at the empty path, still seeking some godly meaning for this calamity. Joseph wished she would speak, would rage, that she would shout words never spoken aloud but that might have been, finally, to this man who was leaving, this husband, but she remained silent and so did he.

In the middle of Bélier Meadow, Victor spotted the tree struck by lightning in the night. He pulled on the rope to stop his horse. A sole poplar tree, whose trunk now resembled a large tibia bone cracked in half thirty feet above the ground. A flock of crows approached, hesitating briefly over the wreckage before continuing, thrashing the air with their jagged wings, to the edge of a nearby wood, where they landed in silence. Later, they watched the man pass on his mount as one crow stuck out its pointed tongue, cawing. Mournful notes, like dropped capitals noisily ripped from the book of the dead.

Victor crossed valleys, dells, meadows, and forests, rode along hedges and low walls built of stones gathered from the fields during plowing, absorbed the smells of these natural surroundings to which he had never, it now seemed to him, allotted enough attention. Everything that he passed at the Percheron's calm and resigned pace bringing them to foreign land to enter an abstract war. As he crossed the forest, he sobbed quietly beneath the branches of the tall beech trees. It wasn't that he truly felt like crying, but rather that he didn't want there to be a single tear left to shed when they took Caesar from him.

Victor reached the Salers train station a little before noon. There were others already waiting for the train to arrive, some accompanied. He recognized a few. Greetings were exchanged. Victor brought the two ends of the rope together, leaned over, and dismounted, sliding down the horse's flank, which he stroked for several moments, then patted his neck, placing his own cheek in the same spot where his son had glued his. Then he led Caesar to a patch of yellowing grass adjoining the station and set him freely grazing with the other horses; his cut a fine figure, rope dragging on the ground like a snake responding to a charmer's haunting music.

Victor joined the thirty men scattered in front of the station, boys for the most part. A few were joking around, trying to outdo one another with a bravado as yet untested, emphasizing their local accents, but most were silent. There were some women solemnly accompanying their husbands, fiancés, or brothers even, all holding back any demonstration of sadness, however legitimate. The other recruits watched Victor walk toward them, then returned to their conversations, or their silence, once he sat down, back against the station wall, facing his grazing horse.

Early in the afternoon, a whistle echoed in the distance, followed by others. Eyes met, and in those stunned gazes there was an infinite range of human emotions, as if these enlisted men hadn't truly believed they were leaving until that moment. No one said another word; everyone was listening. Victor hadn't touched the bread he'd been fiddling with. He looked up at Caesar and put the bread back in his pocket.

The train entered the station a few minutes later, welcomed by a kaleidoscope of twirling blue, white, and red fabric, which went limp once the convoy came to a halt. Uniformed soldiers got off the wagons. A noncom checked service books. One last kiss and the gravity of the occasion crept in, despite the promises made: all vestiges of pride gone, gazes now averted. Victor climbed into the first wagon, immediately headed to the open window, and stuck out his head. He had time to glimpse Caesar, who was being led to the end of the convoy. The horse lifted his heavy head and swung it in the opposite direction of his master, as though he didn't want the moment to drag on. And then Victor couldn't see him anymore. Would never see him again.

When the passengers disembarked at the Aurillac station, they were dumbfounded to find a swarming town, an indescribable theater of chaos and noise. Victor followed the crowd. Walking along the train platform, he heard neighing behind him, coming from the cattle cars, and quickened his pace without looking back.

They were taken to the barracks of the 139th infantry regiment. A jubilant throng accompanied the future heroes. Items flew through the air, falling and then taking flight again amid the hurrahs. Hysterical girls came up to touch the soldiers and in some cases kiss them. Huddling in the shade of shops and houses, a few old women were gravely observing the troops with the lucidity of those who know but don't dare speak.

Victor didn't react when someone called him "soldier" for the first time. This way of designating these men as brothers, of ripping away their pasts, appeared to stream right past him. It was only once in uniform that he truly realized that he was being stolen from himself and from all those he loved.

The heat at Chantegril was so relentless that the slightest exertion wrung out their bodies, forcing them to drink often to keep from hardening and cracking like dried clay. Unburdening themselves of a few leaves, the trees too battled dehydration, and the thick air absorbed any smells, porous as egg whites. Even the shade burned.

The day passed. They ate, exchanged at most a few glances during the meal, just as quickly looking away for fear their gaze would catch on the woeful snag of a memory or a simple image. They chewed loudly and pretended as though their every gesture required all the concentration they had at their disposal, so that there would be no space for anything except the carrying of food to their mouths and the movements of their noisy jaws.

After dinner, they gathered in front of the house. The night was beginning to extinguish the sun above the mountains—an invisible force pulling on a woolen string to unroll a skein. In the distance, a large cloud had descended upon the peak of Puy Violent, and it almost looked as if that ruin of a volcano was still expelling its three-million-year-old steam, in the same way that the light of dead stars continues to this day to reach the eyes of the living. A vestige of the fury of the earth that had shaped this world by offering it life, starting with the underground algae, and all the way to these two women and this young man now contemplating the streams of fossilized basalt. Then the sun slowly disappeared, a perfect circle ingurgitated by one mountain, and which another would spit back out in all its splendor come morning.

It was as if the trio had convened by silent agreement to await some heroic return, though it was simply the coolness and the breeze that had drawn them, and nothing more, or so they wanted to believe. And yet, every so often, they would glance toward the path, like sentries questioning lookouts stationed somewhere in the tall cypress trees. Though each took care not to let the others notice this irrational reflex orienting their gaze.

When night fell, they cloistered themselves inside the house's large walls, exhausted, ravaged, and silent. Waited for evening to chase away the day's torpor, trying to fall asleep, to get as much rest as possible, windows wide open, in various stages of undress on stripped-down beds, largely indifferent to the mosquitoes and their stings, to the cries outside. They simply wanted to breathe without having to think about it.

Joseph rose at dawn. He left the house carrying his fishing rod and a satchel containing a chunk of bread and some lard. He knew he wouldn't have another chance to go fishing anytime soon. He felt the need to be alone.

He crossed yellowing meadows crowded with stiff nard and sheep's fescue ruffled by the morning breeze, and heavy with gentian flowers. Heard the bells of a flock tinkling in the higher summer pastures and echoing across Bélier Meadow. He collected several dazed grasshoppers from the sedge bordering the forest and placed them inside a small iron box with a few holes hammered into its metallic lid, along with some blades of grass. Then he plunged beneath the cover of the forest of gigantic beech trees that led to the valley at the bottom of which the river was flowing like an open-air drain. As he hurtled down the steep slope, his feet occasionally slipped, prompting him to grab hold of the frail trunks emerging from the humus. The Maronne River would reveal itself soon; he could hear the current crashing against the rocks. When he reached the river, Joseph felt his heartbeat quicken. He entered the cold water and made his way upstream toward his favorite fishing spot, aware of every pitfall, kicking his feet to move a stone, weaving to avoid a hole. Rocks formed high walls along both riverbanks, like a magistral construction in perpetual evolution.

Joseph finally reached a first pond full of clear water and sufficiently deep to house trout, and from whose surface emerged several large mounds of whitish stone that bore visible marks of the dropping water level. He approached cautiously, hunching over to shorten his shadow. Once he had observed the river at length, identifying the fish's new hiding spots, he pulled down the leader at the tip of his bamboo rod, then attached a hook to a grasshopper by its back, taking care not to rip open the abdomen of the insect now persistently extending its hind legs in search of a nonexistent foothold. Joseph swung the rod back and forth a few times in a row and delicately set the grasshopper on the water in such a way that it wouldn't drown and would continue to move.

Joseph fished for two hours, caught five good-sized trout, their backs darkened by the shade of the rocks and skin adorned with viscous stars. They all bravely put up a fight, and he cracked their spines by twisting their heads backward with the aid of one thumb shoved just under the mouth, to forestall rigor mortis, the way his father had taught him. A single trout unhooked itself, flopping onto his leg and then, before he could grab it, disappeared quick as a flash.

Seated on a rock, in the shade of a large willow tree with golden, panting branches, Joseph grabbed a piece of bread from his bag and took a few bites. Didn't touch the lard. A hummingbird hawkmoth was swirling around the foot of a foxglove, its indefatigable, powder-covered proboscis dripping with nectar, a tiny drunkard powerless to abandon the source of its pleasure. In the distance, an oriole was singing, invisible. Another responded, also invisible. Then they hushed. Ordinarily, these simple lives, whose functions were so clear, so directly linked to nature, would have struck Joseph as the opposite of mankind, but now that his father was gone, they no longer did. He was beginning to realize that he would have to find a different way of taming a world amputated from the soft flesh of childhood. Become a man before the age of manhood.

Marie heard muffled footsteps as she got dressed. Through the half-open shutters, she watched Joseph walk toward the meadow. The sun was rising like a golden loaf of bread. She cleaned the lenses of her glasses with a fold of her dress, then hung open the shutters and went to the kitchen. Made a fire beneath the three-legged stool by placing a few twigs on a page from an old newspaper, and added three logs on top. Set a flat stone in a pot and heated some milk. Then she remained motionless for several minutes, facing the fire, hands deep in her pockets and resting against her jutting hip bones, while the stone danced inside the pot, clanging against the walls.

Mathilde entered the kitchen without a word. The sleepless night was visible on her face. Marie wrapped a rag around the pot handle and approached the table.

"He went out," she said as she poured the milk into a bowl.

"So early?"

"He needed to, I s'pose."

Mathilde approached the window, cast a brief glance at the courtyard, and closed the shutters.

"It's already sweltering," she said, turning toward the fire.

"You want some milk?"

"Now that it's warm."

Mathilde grabbed a bowl from the sideboard and set it on the table. Marie, visibly impervious to heat, poured out the remainder of the pot's contents using one finger to keep the stone from falling. Mathilde sat down, and Marie placed the pot on a large pitted slab in front of the smoky hearth.

"It'll go out soon," said Marie.

Then she sat down at the table, gripping the bowl.

"We'll need to get organized," she added.

"You're used to that," said Mathilde with more bile than she intended.

Marie lifted the bowl and blew on the milk, watching the steam writhe in front of her.

"Dear girl, I never had a choice," she said coldly.

"I know."

"If you have a better idea."

Mathilde lifted the bowl to her lips. Marie waited for her to drink before continuing.

"We'll need to tackle the harvest first. Joseph'll do the reaping, he's strong enough for that. Meanwhile, Leonard will help you tie up the sheaths and the pair of you will bring them in bit by bit with his mule and wagon. Then it'll be high time for the threshing. I'll stay here and take care of the farm, the sun doesn't bother me anymore."

"I'll go let Leonard know," said Mathilde wearily.

Marie took another gulp.

"Already did. He'll be here tomorrow morning."

Mathilde placed her bowl back on the table, hands still around it, eyes on the old woman.

"I can reap too," she said confidently.

"We'll see. If there's need."

"Of course, we'll see..."

"We need to conserve our strength. We don't know what the future holds."

"I have plenty of strength, and certainly more than you think."

"I don't doubt it."

They finished their milk in silence as light piled up in the room, revealing whole worlds hanging in the air.

The sky wove its way between leaves and branches as the midday sun, beaming down on the tree canopy, slowly incinerated the meager coolness that had accumulated in the undergrowth overnight. Mathilde found herself on the overgrown paths she used to scramble along barefoot as a child, following the warblers and the martens and, on one occasion, her father, on the way to Chantegril to be presented to her future husband.

And it was a child's emotion that rose in her throat when she heard frogs croaking, their guttural voices accompanied by the music of a stone scraping against the blade of a scythe, on one side and then the other, *zip-zip, zip-zip*... Mathilde spotted her father in the field, not far from the pond. She looked around and her eyes slowly filled with sadness at seeing only him, arm extended on the curved blade as if it were the shoulder of a woman with whom he was preparing to dance. *Zip-zip, zip-zip, zip*... Then he placed the whetstone in the leather sheath on his belt and resumed cutting the tender grass, his movements deliberately broad, slow almost, so he could work into the evening without tiring, without ever pausing with the tip of the scythe planted in the ground.

Mathilde had arrived too late to say goodbye to her brother and was now abandoning the idea of asking her father for help. Hidden by the trees, she watched the grass fall, the next phase desiccation, which would make for crisp feed for the animals come winter. She didn't approach her father, convinced that no words would come to their aid, and yet secretly hoping that he would meet her eyes and pause in a shared reassuring gaze, midway between them. But nothing of the sort. She watched him move farther into the distance and disappear, as if the sunlight were disintegrating him with each step.

Behind the barn, Leonard was sitting on a low wall, carving a piece of hornbeam, hat tilted slightly up. A single, mismatched button held his jacket closed, in the way of a fibula, and his coattails dangled like two wings at rest. A cane with a snake head was resting against the stones near him. Deep in concentration, he was making precise cuts that would bring him closer to the final shape, as though the fox head already existed within the wood and the old man's role was simply to bring it forth without damage. Nothing more.

"Hello, Leo!"

Leonard didn't look up. "Hello, my boy!"

Joseph sat beside the old man, not taking his eyes off his agile hands.

"That's damn beautiful," he said.

"I think I'm just about done."

Leonard folded back his knife, leaned to the side with one leg outstretched, and placed it in his pants pocket. Then he ran the palm of his hand over the carving to brush off any remaining splinters. This coarse hand, too, resembled wood fissured by time. A sculptor who had amused himself by carving out bits of skin with little flair and no apparent intention to stop there.

Leonard held out the fox head, observing it from every angle, then set it down between him and Joseph.

"I'm guessing the trout were out, this early in the morning," he said.

"I brought you two."

"Go on, keep 'em for your family."

Joseph cast a dark look at his satchel. "There'll still be plenty."

The old man let the moment pass, closing one eye as he looked up at the perfectly blue sky.

"He left," he said, letting his voice fall like an inert mass.

"Yesterday morning."

"He'll come back."

Joseph felt his heart racing.

"That's what he said."

"No reason not to."

"Might not be up to him."

"The man I know, your father, he'll fight like hell . . . though maybe he won't even need to."

Joseph looked toward the crimson prairie that extended to a wall of scrawny oak trees, their crooked branches entangled as if they were holding hands in preparation for an odd farandole lit up by the sun.

"He's counting on me," he said.

"We'll do what we need to so that everything's in order the day he gets back."

Joseph abruptly lifted the flap of his satchel, stuck his hand inside, and took out two brown trout, which he laid on the gray stone, near the sculpted head.

"He took Caesar," he said.

Leonard placed one hand on Joseph's leg and immediately withdrew it.

"Don't you worry. My mule's not the kind to run away, and neither am I."

"I know. Thanks, Leo."

"No need to thank me..."

"You ever been to war?"

Before he answered, Leonard took a moment to shake flakes of wood off his pants.

"Long time ago," he said.

"Did you kill people?"

The lines on the old man's face froze.

"That's what they expect you to do," he said after another pause.

"But you came back."

"I had the best reasons in the world to come back."

Leonard sucked air into his mouth, as though he wanted to pull back the words that had slipped out.

"And what were your reasons, then?" asked Joseph.

"Folks who were counting on me."

Joseph squeezed his satchel against his chest.

"I'm afraid, Leo."

"It wouldn't be normal if you weren't."

"I'm afraid of what might happen to him... and I'm afraid that... that we'll be alone."

"You need to have faith in the ones who left, and in those who stayed... I sure do."

Joseph tilted his face toward the old man, without looking at him.

"You don't want to tell me what happens," he said.

"Happens where?"

"At war."

Leonard placed his hand back on Joseph's knee, but this time he kept it there, tenderly observing the young man. Then he tilted his hat forward, the shadow formed by its brim like a trail of soot covering his forehead and eyes.

"Anything I could tell you wouldn't help you, and it wouldn't help me much either."

"We learned about the wars before, at school."

"Things have changed an awful lot, I'm sure."

"Maybe not for the best."

"It's not in the officers' interest not to take care of their soldiers."

The old man hawked and spat to the side, then took out a handkerchief to wipe his mouth.

"Where'd you catch those nice trout?" he asked.

"Above Pierres Blanches."

"Not the easiest spot to fish."

"Well, I guess there wouldn't be as many fish if everyone went there."

"Can't imagine what they like about those rocks."

Joseph forced a smile.

"Maybe there's something magical about them," he said.

"Magic can explain lots of things."

"Have you ever gone fishing?"

"Like everyone, I guess. Back when, I used to go there too."

"Why don't you anymore?"

Leonard slid a finger across one trout's gleaming flank.

"I wouldn't be able to make it up to Pierres Blanches."

"Trout are everywhere mostly."

"Sure, but when you can no longer get to a spot you always used to go, there's no point keeping at it, in my opinion . . . You lose something that you'll never get back, so it's best to make it so you don't lose anything else."

"I don't understand."

"It'd be a shame if you did, at your age. You see, even if I got brand-new legs, I wouldn't go back, seeing how I'd be too afraid not to find things the way I left them."

The river wove its way through Joseph's memory.

"It's as beautiful as ever," he said.

"I'd like to believe you."

"Ask me, nothing and no one could change that."

Leonard nodded.

"There's one thing that could," he conceded, as if talking to himself.

"I'm guessing you're not only talking about Pierres Blanches?"

Leonard was watching the rocky hillocks rising against the horizon, like the vertebrae of a massive sperm whale motionless below the water's surface. He squinted to let the necessary light in, and no more; any excess would devour the scene. The sky was a taut canvas, pilling at altitude beneath a few stringy clouds.

"There was this fisherman," he said. "We'd always cross paths at Pierres Blanches, making our way up the river, each on our own side. One day he stopped coming. That changed everything."

"Who was he?"

"Doesn't matter who he was."

"But why did he stop fishing?"

"He had his reasons. What's for sure is that, whenever I went fishing, after, I always had the impression he would show up. At the end, I wasn't going for the trout anymore, but to be there when he did."

Leonard's hands clenched around his cane, fingers caressing the sculpted snake.

"And he never showed," said Joseph.

"Not much chance he would, but it took me a while to accept that. At the end, I didn't even fish anymore, I'd sit on a rock, listening to the river, watching the trees. I wanted them to tell me everything they knew. I thought that for once, nature would be on my side, but it didn't give a damn about me... like always."

Leonard stopped talking, extended his cane in front of him, pointing to the trees in the distance, then resumed: "Nature does just as it pleases. You can glue yourself to a tree, but you won't turn into bark... lie down in a river, you won't turn into water either..."

"And you never saw him again?"

"He left."

"Just like that, out of nowhere?"

"Just like that."

"So people can disappear for no reason."

"Not all of them, son. Not all of them."

Leonard smiled sadly and tapped Joseph's hand with the end of his cane.

"From the look of your hands, looks like you did more than just fish."

Joseph bent and unbent his fingers crusted with red earth.

"While I was at it, I dug up some nice clay on the way down toward Saint-Paul. I know a good spot."

"When are you gonna show me?"

Joseph took a long look at the carved fox head.

"I'd be too embarrassed," he said. "Look at it. It's like the fox is alive, ready to catch a chicken."

A smile spread across Leonard's face.

"Need to carve a bit more for that," he said.

"I'll never be able to do as good."

"It's just a matter of time."

"I'm guessing it's a bit more than that."

"You should have seen me when I was starting out."

"Give me a little more time, and I'll show you."

"All right. Now go on, musn't make that clay wait. If it dries, you won't be able to do anything with it," said Leonard, grabbing the carving and setting it on Joseph's satchel.

The young man's gaze went from the fox head to Leonard.

"What are you doing?" he said.

"Maybe it will inspire you a little."

"I can't take it."

"Why not? You're gifting me these two nice trout."

"Trout are easy to catch, but this . . . it's too much."

"It's just a piece of wood, and anyhow, it makes me happy to give it to you."

Joseph stuffed the carved head in the front pocket of his satchel so it wouldn't get dirty.

"Thank you, Leo."

"No need—"

"No need to thank you, I know."

Private Victor Lary left the Aurillac garrison on August 7, 1914, with his regiment, accompanied by a still jubilant crowd of civilians, this time in the opposite direction, from the barracks to the train station. A crowd that saw its soldiers as victorious before the first shot was even fired against the enemy.

Colonel M. took command of the regiment, assisted by battalion leaders R., T., and J. First troop inspection. Colonel M. had a stormy gaze, thick eyebrows, and a cultivated mustache that rested on the shadow of a top lip. M., who imagined himself handsome and grand, with a destiny to be carved from the wood of a docile infantry. Soft meat. M. and his harangue as cultivated as his mustache, and just as shiny. M. standing rod-straight in his tailored uniform, hands behind his back, as though preparing to force each man to guess in which clenched fist he would find his destiny. An aristocratic presence, which the grunts would follow into fire without question. M., who still believed in the grandeur of sacrifice, in his own grandeur, before setting one polished boot on the front lines. M., who would obey the orders handed down by generals hunched over geological survey maps, who would never doubt their irrevocable decisions based on well-informed strategies involving lives other than their own. M., who would never falter, who would set the example, and anyone who didn't fall in line wouldn't be perfunctorily judged but shot dead. One thing was certain: the weight of a bullet didn't change from one camp to the next, and cohesion was built on fear and submission.

The full regiment reached the outskirts of Épinal two days later. Then marching drills for ten days, to prepare for attack operations. Cannon fire was heard for the first time in Varennes. The column went silent. The men looked at one another, incredulous, as if seeking some vain explanation for their presence there. And they each lowered their eyes in a singular silent prayer, for their parents, brothers, sisters, wives, children. A poignant scene. This moment when the idea of death sank in beneath the kepis, the acute awareness that the voyage hadn't yet begun, the true voyage that would cast them into the horror like lemmings programmed for suicide. One soldier blustered for a few minutes, then began to sing to try to cover the sound of bullets. Others followed suit. Their voices trembled with emotion, and the ground trembled, too. Victor couldn't join in the singing. His heart was breaking, and he imagined he heard a dog barking.

The house was quiet now that everyone had gone to bed. Joseph waited a bit longer, then grabbed his satchel and climbed out his bedroom window. He often snuck out to an abandoned cellar beneath the bread oven, which no one entered anymore for fear of collapse. But Joseph, unbeknownst to his family, had set up two stays of thick acacia wood and created a secret workshop of sorts. He was aware that this ritual would soon be threatened by the deluge of work, his new responsibilities, and the resulting fatigue.

When he reached the cellar, Joseph took out the piece of lard he hadn't eaten that morning, which he used to coat the bolt, then slid it into the peephole and opened the door, shutting it behind him. Inside, he lit a match and daubed the wick of a candle glued to a rock by streams of wax that resembled a long ball gown on a decapitated body. Shadows of various animals molded from river clay began to dance on the walls. All Joseph's carvings had been placed on two planks once intended to hold barrels of cider and coarse wine, which had long since been moved to another cellar dug beneath the main house. He walked to the back of the cellar and set Leonard's gift on one of the planks, and the fox's shadow danced indiscriminately among the rest.

With his knife blade, Joseph scraped pieces of crusted clay off a large, round log slice, then poured water over it with a porringer floating in a bucket. He then placed the lump of clay gathered that morning from the riverbank on the wet block. He stared at it for a while, meticulously thinking through the series of gestures needed to implement his design, lips moving as his hands wove through the air, like a man inventing his own language.

Once he'd gone through the motions, Joseph built a cursory structure out of wire that bent and curved like a letter from the Greek alphabet. Then he dipped his hands in the bucket and started to soften the clay, kneading it into a malleable form, which he divided into two equally sized balls. He began with one piece, adding water frequently. His tongue traveled along his lips. Squat hindquarters with a large neck materialized, and he tossed the shape onto the log. Then took a little clay from the other ball and formed a powerful leg that he added to the body. The same for the three other limbs, until the joints disappeared and contours formed. Then he molded a horselike head, which he immediately attached to the animal's neck. Before the clay could harden, he carved a delicate mane with the tip of his knife. During the operation, Joseph periodically took a step back and then forward again to perfect a detail, so the copy was as close as possible to his memory: a massive Percheron named Caesar, the companion he had always known.

Once he had decided he was done, exhausted and face dripping with sweat, he assessed the carving with a critical eye, then looked at the shadow cast and confined to the wall, to which he began to speak, as though conversing with a ghost. His voice a trickle of water flowing freely all the way to his father astride the valiant messenger. This new shadow drawn as much by memory as by his two hands. Then, when his words ran dry, he pinched the candle flame between his thumb and index finger, abandoning his mysterious world to the darkness of the cellar.

Back outside, he felt a slight breeze rustle across his face and the tension gradually leave him as nocturnal animals jabbered nearby. He noticed the lit-up sky twisted by the mountains. Joseph knew that the stars did their best dancing in August. He waited for one, knocked from its incredible pedestal, to cross the universe from one infinity to the next, ready to cast in its wake the only wish in his mind. Normally, on clear summer nights like this, the stars would perform, as if a celestial mouth were amusing itself by spitting them out one by one.

Joseph tilted his head back, the better to take in the nighttime pasture abloom with thousands of suns. But with no shooting star in sight, he randomly chose a glimmer of light suspended among the rest. Watching it change and fade was a phenomenon he had observed plenty of times, a phenomenon that surpassed his understanding, not unlike the idea of an architect god. In truth, eyes glued to the sky, he was still hoping to see the target of his wish emerge.

He waited. Nothing appeared, nothing emerged from the emptiness to spread the good word to him. He felt an intense desire to shout, to scream as loud as he could at the sky, to tell it to stop playing this cynical game, to yield and finally offer him a star, that it owed him and his family that much. This sky that had unleashed lightning on his grandfather and now threatened them all, in another manner, could give him a sign, at least. This was the moment to show itself, to seek redemption, now or never. Joseph waited. He waited a long time, but the sky maintained its silence, and so did God.

Later, lying in his bed, after a tenacious battle against sleep, Joseph closed his eyes and streaks of lightning appeared in his dream, like bullet trails in an inky sky.

In the week that followed, in Chantegril as elsewhere, everyone dove into their work in an effort to think about the war as little as possible. No one said much, and when they did it was simply to divide the labor equally and according to ability. Joseph harvested the buckwheat plot on his own, while Leonard and his mother tied the sheafs and loaded them into the mule-drawn cart. Marie, whose health had been deteriorating for several months, no longer left the farm, handling the meals, the chickens, and a little gardening, when the sun was less piercing. A routine dictated by the constraints of her body.

Leonard came to Chantegril every day. The visits did him good; they calmed him. Despite the heat, he always turned up in his black serge jacket, wearing his hat and wobbling as he walked, a consequence of forever bending over and standing back up. In the end, his bones had grown accustomed to a pain he accepted and hadn't bothered to fight for some time now. And all the while a feeling of brushing up against old age, even as a boy.

Now he was looking after this family, without authority, offering what help he could, giving what advice he had, never imposing himself. He felt useful each time he left his own farm, though he couldn't really call it that once he had sold twelve of the fourteen cows he owned, and sold the majority of his land to Joseph's father. A transaction that had earned him the enduring resentment of his nearest neighbor, Valette, a man determined to be a have and not a have-not. A violent man, snide and envious, who had offered a price much higher than what Victor could offer at the time. But nothing could have convinced Leonard to allow the owner of Grands-Bois to seize the most precious thing he owned. Valette had respect for nothing, not land and not his fellow man.

Leonard remembered the day Valette showed up to make him an offer he couldn't, presumably, refuse.

"Well? What do you say?" Valette had asked, sure of himself.

Leonard had looked at his neighbor draped in arrogance, idiocy, and self-importance. He let a long pause go by before answering: "I say that news travels quick."

"But what about my offer? What do you think?"

"I have to admit it merits being taken seriously."

"So that means you accept."

Leonard removed his hat to scratch his balding head, then repositioned it at a slight tilt.

"And what are you gonna do with my land?" he asked.

"I'll farm it. I'm even willing to buy your cows too."

"My cows?"

At the mention of his animals, a sudden shadow stretched across the old man's face.

"Two thousand francs per head. It's a good price," said Valette.

"My cows aren't for sale yet."

"As you like. We'll see about them later..."

"Your farm can already feed two families, and your brother's gone. What do you need with another one?"

Valette came closer to Leonard, looking him up and down.

"I won't bother telling someone like you everything a man on his own can do," he added.

Leonard gave Valette a fierce glare, but his neighbor didn't seem intimidated in the slightest.

"There some message I should be getting here?" the old man asked.

"No. I'm thinking about Eugene's future is all."

"Kids nowadays would rather go see what's happening in the city than stay here. You ask me, soon there'll be nothing but land for sale. Wait a bit longer and you'll have your pick."

"The other farms don't interest me."

"What's got you so interested in my land?"

"If you want more than what I'm offering, name your price and let's be done with it."

Leonard feigned a sad look.

"Problem is, you're not the first one to make me an offer."

Valette had leaned forward, struggling to contain his sudden rage.

"Victor?"

"Don't tell me you didn't know. I figured the reason you're pushing this so hard is so that he doesn't get the farm."

"How much is he giving you?"

Leonard wagged his finger at Valette, from right to left.

"None of your business."

"I know you didn't sign anything. We can come to an agreement. It's in your best interest..."

"Sounds like you know plenty, but what you clearly haven't understood is that you're wasting your time. There'll be no deal with me."

"I'm not even sure he has anything to pay you."

Leonard swept his hand through the air, anger rising inside him.

"Not your concern," he said.

"Think about it. I have plenty of time."

"Not me. I've thought plenty and I keep my word. My land won't end up in the hands of a vulture like you."

Valette took one step forward, fists clenched.

"You think you intimidate me?" the old man said without a beat.

"Too bad... You're gonna regret this."

"If ever I do, I doubt you'll be around to see it."

After their conversation, and more than once, Leonard had discovered Valette's cattle destroying young seedlings or a patch of rye ready to be harvested. A fence accidentally left open. He had let it go, not wanting to wage that war. Back then, he thought Valette's frustration would subside with time.

Helping out the family at Chantegril wasn't the only thing drawing Leonard away from his farm. There was also Lucie, his embittered, impotent wife. At least when he went to see Joseph, he still felt as if he belonged in this world for a reason other than maintaining an old farmstead, milking two sleepy cows accustomed to his presence, and enduring Lucie's icy stare. It had been a long time since he'd stopped hoping for a few kindly words that might have broken, for a spell, the silence surrounding them.

Each time he returned home, a frail gnome of a man tottering along, he wondered whether he should confront the silence, or his wife's reproaches, but invariably gave in to both. He wasn't angry at her, not really. He was well aware that he hadn't done anything to change things, couldn't even imagine what that change might have looked like, and what he should have done to make it so. They were each perched on a bluff trying to protect themselves, sludge accumulating in the middle, in everlasting and consensual isolation. And all because of a ghost, a ghost buried beneath that same sludge.

In early afternoon, the omnibus made its way around Saint-Paul cemetery, then entered the silent village beneath a lethal sun, looking more like a hearse drawn by two retired, sweat-drenched horses whose legs continued to tremble once they stopped at the marketplace, a few steps from the cattle scale and the imposing church.

The coach driver descended, and not easily, from the jump seat, and two passengers got out of the omnibus. No one else. The women were of identical height, several years apart, with shared features. They were wearing long white dresses and polished shoes made for walking on manicured sidewalks. By their finery, manners, and reticence, no need to be a soothsayer to realize they came from a city; not that it had spared them the palpable sadness casting shadows across both their faces. Standing beside the squeaky vehicle, completely disarmed, distraught eyes taking in the surrounding desolation, so far from home. Forced to come here, to get lost here, ever since husband and father had left to command squads of infantryman on the road to glory.

The driver absent-mindedly helped them unload their suitcases from the upper deck, then limped his way to an inn whose façade was overgrown with vines and around which hovered an agitated cloud of noisy insects. The door was open, and as he entered he lowered his head to avoid hitting the lintel. Silence settled over the square, absorbing the horses' snorts and grunts and the interminable orchestra of insects.

An old woman emerged from the church, a rosary dangling between her pale hands. Surprised to find two strangers smack in the middle of the town square, she adjusted her straw hat with its black ribbon, without taking her eyes off the newcomers. Helen, the mother, affably approached the woman to ask her if she could point the way to the Grands-Bois farm. The woman looked the pair up and down in turn and at length. When she finally spoke, her words were hard to understand, as though they were being scraped off the bottom of a pig trough; it took her two pained attempts to cast them over the ledge formed by her ashen, split lips.

"Not many folks live up there. You ask me, you won't find anyone to take you there at this time of day, not to mention in this heat."

"That's all right. We'll walk," said the mother, forcing a smile.

"Quite the walk."

"Meaning?"

"Little over three miles. And most of it uphill."

"Which direction do we go?"

One bony hand, struggling to lift its index finger, pointed to a sunburnt path weaving between the church and a flock of houses with closed shutters and worn-down walls.

"I think the best, for you two, would be to go that way. After, there's just a crummy path that you'll need to take all the way to Vielmur's Hamlet. Once you pass that, turn left right away, then go straight, it'll be the first farm you see..."

The woman paused, appeared to think for a moment, then resumed: "There's a shorter way, but you'd risk getting lost."

"Thank you, ma'am," replied Helen.

The old woman said nothing, dropped her hand, and wove the rosary back through her fingers.

Mother and daughter set out immediately, a suitcase in each hand. The superstitious woman watched the two strangers walk away, curious but not truly believing they existed.

They passed the final houses, then a massive black rock looming above the town, at whose summit presided an immaculate Virgin Mary. The road ended soon, and mother and daughter began to walk uphill along an overgrown path. They stopped often to rest and chase away the dust that kept returning to settle on their clothes and faces. After an hour-long ascent that felt interminable, they emerged from the forest, the sun straight ahead, its iris reduced to a cat eye at midday, to a baptism of moors and sparse meadows, leaves and pine needles unfurling in the distance like a large mismatched rug of yellow and green surrounding the mountains. They walked through a hamlet, saw a figure rush inside a shack and a door squeak shut. They didn't encounter anyone else on the way.

Once they reached Grands-Bois, exhausted and dripping, they stopped to dust off their dresses, looked at each other and then immediately away. The Valette farm was composed of a row of dark gray stone buildings with slate roofs, which included the house, the barn, and the wooden storehouse, with a shed and cellar underneath, accessible via a ramp. Helen took a deep breath and smiled sadly at her daughter, as though to apologize for the nasty turn she was dealing her. They entered the adjoining yard, skirting past a pile of sunken manure surrounded by a moat of gleaming slurry. A large, lanky dog sniffed them disdainfully before lying back down under a lean-to, at the feet of a man pounding a scythe on an anvil with a hammer.

When the man noticed them, he gave no visible reaction, merely slid the hammer handle into his belt, squinted, and waited for them to approach. He was tall and burly, somewhere in his forties. Two large veins danced along biceps constricted by his rolled-up shirtsleeves; his right hand was endowed with only a thumb and a little finger short a knucklebone.

"We weren't expecting you so soon," he said.

"Hello! We were able to catch the omnibus earlier than planned," said Helen.

She pushed her daughter forward by the shoulders, like merchandise that can't be refused.

"My daughter, Anna," she said.

As she spoke, Helen couldn't help staring at the man's atrophied hand.

"A dumb accident, a long time ago," he said, not paying any attention to the young woman.

"I didn't know."

"And how would knowing have helped?" he said cynically.

"Emile could have helped you."

"I've never needed his pity."

"He is your brother."

"Seems like he only just remembered."

Helen avoided Valette's gaze.

"For now, it's you all who need help," Valette added contemptuously.

Helen simply looked around in response. Despite the blue sky, everything was so gray—the stones, the slates, the dog, Valette's skin, and even, it felt like, her own heart. As for Anna, she was intimidated by this uncouth uncle teeming with palpable rage escaping from his mouth after a few bites.

"Thank you for hosting us," Helen said feebly.

Valette displayed a short row of rotten teeth.

"Just because I'm not learned doesn't mean I don't have a sense of family, you know."

He walked ahead toward the house, without offering to help carry their suitcases, then suddenly turned around, still walking, and lifted his atrophied hand:

"If only I could use a rifle, I'd be there, too, believe you me."

Despite the shutters kept closed to keep in the coolness, scraps of light snuck in between the slats of wood, casting a stubborn glow over the gloom before fading. A pitcher and a wire salad basket full of walnuts were sitting on a rectangular table. A clock pendulum was keeping time in this large room that seemingly produced nothing else. There was a small stove and a dresser strewn with a few knickknacks of the kind to summon memories: a photograph of a child and of a couple in their Sunday best, a neatly polished shell case, and a dried box tree branch. There was the cold weight of a fireplace with its two cast-iron andirons, framed by two singed benches. There were pieces of salted meat hanging from blackened joists sticky with grease, and dented, freshly picked tomatoes lined up along the edge of a stone sink attached to the wall, whose siphon was allowing a bit of light to trickle in. There was the omnipresent smell of smoke that seeped into meat, clothes, wood, stone, and warped objects. And there was a woman sitting, shelling beans with her thumbnail. She was wearing a midnight blue bib apron over a black cotton dress buttoned to the collar, black stockings, and brown ankle boots with worn toes, and her chestnut hair was gathered in a bun at the back of her head.

"They're here," said Valette.

The woman looked up at the new arrivals, all while continuing her task, without a word.

"Hello, Irene," said Helen.

"Hello," said Anna.

Irene nodded.

"See to them. I've still got things to do," said Valette before leaving.

Irene spread her legs beneath the table, placed her apron beneath the dish, brushed off the bean husks with the flat of her hand, then folded the apron against her chest and stood.

"I'll go fetch some cold water. You must be thirsty," she said in a lifeless voice.

With her free hand, she grabbed the pitcher and left as the other two women looked on, stunned. Pausing in the courtyard, she dumped the scraps. Hens came running, fighting to be the first at feeding time, hopping from one foot to the other, like an onslaught of tiny puppets, then aggressively pecking at the dregs. Husks flew up in the air, then back to the ground, or into a beak or down a toboggan of gleaming feathers. Irene continued to the well in front of the barn. She released the roller brake and lowered a wooden bucket at the end of a chain until it hit the water, whose level was dropping daily. Waited a few moments, then brought the full bucket back up using a whistling crank. She filled the jug with clear, cool water and poured what was left in the bucket down the well and put back the brake. She glanced at the hens quarreling over the bean remnants and returned to the house using the access ramp.

Helen and Anna hadn't budged an inch.

"You're allowed to breathe," sneered Irene as she set the jug on the table.

"We were waiting for you," said Helen, embarrassed.

"You must be awful thirsty, what with this heat."

"Yes," said mother and daughter in unison.

"The glasses are in the sideboard, right door," said Irene, looking at the girl.

"All right."

Anna hurried to the sideboard, took out two glasses, and went to fill them. Irene watched the two women drink.

"You'll share a bed, in the scullery."

"That's not a problem," said Helen, attempting a smile.

"I'd rather not give you Eugene's room, if ever he were to come home unannounced."

"I understand."

Irene looked at her sister-in-law as though she'd said something stupid.

"Have you heard from your man?" asked Irene.

"Not yet..."

"I'm guessing you'll hear before me."

"Why?"

"Someone like him must have more free time to write."

Helen didn't respond. She and Anna each drank another glass of water. Irene nodded toward a door.

"Over there, in the cupboard. All the bedding you'll need. I've got work to do, too."

A warm wind was teasing the hanging laundry, occasionally lifting up a piece of fabric. An empty basket against her hip, Mathilde realized that she had automatically left spaces around each item of clothing, spaces large enough to fit a man's garments, spaces unconsciously preserved to guarantee Victor's good luck, wherever he was in that exact moment. In truth, these empty spaces clearing the way for the whirling wind were the very embodiment of loss, albeit nothing compared with the sudden absence of a person.

After her husband left, Mathilde had cried tears of whose provenance she was unsure. In secret. Cried like somebody's wife, no more no less. She cried over his absence, over the unknown, over the possible tragedy to come, but also, just as much, over the unbending course of history. The true fearmonger. And then she stopped crying, quickly, too quickly perhaps, taking on roles she normally would have never taken on. She removed her wedding ring, not in defiance, but simply because she felt as if it was a marker of her unhappiness, whatever the task before her. A distant war had reshuffled the cards without asking her opinion, and she had no other choice but to come to terms with the new rules forced upon her.

Mathilde Capy had been wedded to Victor Lary to unite two farms and to produce offspring. Over time a sense of mutual belonging formed, without effort, like two delicate blades of grass twisted together to create a more solid string, though without any mention of love. To each their place, to each their role. The acceptable expression of happiness on a farm. Joseph came the first year after their marriage, followed by a sister one year later, who was fever-stricken from the day she was born. The unlucky creature died without ever opening her eyes. Joseph's parents had never told him about this sister's fleeting existence, both believing that there was no point, though they never conferred on the subject. There were no other children—too much torn flesh—almost as if people believed that mountain women were able to produce only a single viable egg, and that you were tempting the devil if you asked for more.

All the things Mathilde forgot about in her frenzied, labor-filled mornings inevitably, and quietly, crept back, fangs bared and ready to pierce the spot in her heart where reassuring habits nestle. Like now, as she stood motionless before the missing laundry. Victor would return, and she would fill this cursed rusty clothesline, and they would be together again. If not, she'd merely need to reduce the distance, and only later seek meaning for her act. But for now, she had to hold steady.

She placed the basket on the ground, smoothed her long hair with the palm of one trembling hand, and began to ragefully rip the clothes off the line that embodied absence and loss, in the blistering heat.

In late August, a peddler from up north stopped in the public square of Saint-Paul, where he proceeded to gather the townsfolk by ringing a tiny bell hanging from one of his wagon rails. The man was old but well-built, stocky in the way of a former wrestler, caricatural almost. People approached in curiosity. The peddler began to speak, his face cracking as if it were about to shatter into a million pieces, uttering his words at rapid-fire pace in an accent that swallowed every first syllable. His spiel, far more effective than any sermon, sounded almost like an incantation, his intonations so fervent that they could lead a person to believe that he had exactly what you needed and that he would let you have it with some reluctance, his heart heavy even.

Eventually, concluding that no one else would come gather round his horse and cart, the peddler unrolled a swathe of cloth and passed his hand over it several times, back and forth, like a knife grinder sharpening a blade on a stone, without taking his eyes off the crowd. Then he abruptly halted his hand movements and adopted a solemn air to speak of the combat raging in the Ardennes. They could no longer keep track of the dead, much less the injured, he claimed. He spoke with more ardor than before, in an exquisite torrent of words, as if recounting such unverifiable tragedy granted him a certain, superior, importance. He looked as if he was chewing mud, albeit with great relish, and two threads of saliva accumulating at the corners of his mouth transformed it into a sort of birdling's beak.

The stunned onlookers observed the cloth as if it were a punched organ card on which had been recorded news from the front, and not at all something that could become a dress or any other garment. Granted, the townsfolk had read the papers, but a single man speaking with such conviction—that was something else entirely. Someone asked where he got his information. A look of outrage darkened the peddler's face. That they considered, even for a moment, doubting his sources was its own irrevocable response. No one else dared ask the question, hoping to convince themselves that he must be exaggerating. Still, any hope of a swift victory was dashed clean that day by hearsay that all those present rushed to sweep under someone else's door, to bury as deep as possible in a corner of their minds, the one in which dark, slippery thoughts dwell. This wouldn't last. The first letters were already en route, attempts to voice the veritable horror that was to rain down in a relentless and deadly four-year-long storm.

That day, no one bought a thing from the street peddler, and no one was there when he left, cursing, pulling his wagon shafts adorned with tiny terra-cotta jugs and a variety of colorful trinkets.

Joseph was fixing the fence that separated the harvested field from Bélier Meadow, which had been almost entirely destroyed by a herd of wild boars. Creatures that, once they decided on their destination, didn't bother with detours. They raced straight ahead, heedless of obstacles. Leonard had told him that once, when he was out searching for firewood, he came across a sow with her babies. The female had charged without hesitation, lifting the cart as she ran beneath it as if she were crossing through a shrub, before continuing on her way with her placid boarlets.

Joseph raised his head and, with the back of his arm, wiped the sweat dripping down his forehead. A kestrel hovering above the stubble field dove to the ground at staggering speed. It struggled for a few seconds, short stalks of hay flying from its outstretched wings, then clumsily took off, a vole in its talons, heading toward the Bois Noir.

Joseph leaned down to grab a few nails from a box and slid them one by one between his lips.

"Hello there!"

At the sound of the voice, he turned around, sweat trickling down his face again. For an instant, he attributed the apparition before him to the veil of heat distorting his vision.

The girl was wearing an off-white linen dress that left her shoulders bare, and sandals on her feet. Her long brown hair was loose, a few locks dangling over her eyes and periodically forcing her to blink. A butterfly was flitting around the bouquet of wildflowers she had just picked.

"I'm Anna, the Valettes' niece."

He took the nails out of his mouth.

"Hello," he said.

"I assume you know them."

"We're neighbors."

Joseph tried to hold back the flood of anxiety that had taken hold of him when he saw the girl. He wiped his forehead again, then set his hammer and nails on a chopped beech tree trunk adorned with ivy and transformed into a stake. Hands now unoccupied, he immediately regretted his action and pointed to the rooftops visible in the distance.

"Joseph," he said. "I live over there, on the Chantegril farm."

Anna cupped her hand over her eyes.

"My father insisted that my mother and I go far from the front," she continued.

Silence floated like a snowflake swirling, landing, and melting. Around them, the wind picked up, whisking the clumps of wild oat prostrating themselves against the fence. An oak tree and its parade of branches resembled a slave fanning a pair of monarchs; the taut air was a musical staff upon which insects crackled and passerines cheeped. A deluge of sounds, a modest din, the delicate clamor of a world.

Joseph felt like one of the daisies the girl held in her hands—as though the rest of this August day now depended on her goodwill. He wouldn't have been able to identify the nature of her obvious beauty. He was incapable. Incapable too of thinking beyond the present moment. Anna observed him, more intrigued than embarrassed by his silence.

"Is something wrong?" she asked.

Joseph looked at her but couldn't respond. A heady smell hit him, a mix of fresh milk, red berries, and soap, with something animalistic as a binder. Of course something was wrong, but he couldn't determine exactly what. A voice never heard, a fragrance never smelled, and yet all of it already and inexplicably existing in Joseph's mind before he had ever met the girl. Everything around her was in motion, even the shadows rustling at the sound of her voice, and it had nothing to do with a simple sensorial impression. Which was precisely what was wrong. A general unease beyond mere anxiety.

"You don't feel like talking to me," she said.

"My father went off to the war, too," Joseph managed to say.

"That's what's making you sad?"

Joseph didn't answer. He wasn't truly feeling sadness in that moment, which only added to his incomprehension. His father's leaving had dried up a part of his heart, and the girl was now abruptly irrigating another, indeterminate part, without warning.

"I'm sorry, I shouldn't have..."

"No, it's fine. Probably just the heat and exhaustion, is all," he said.

Anna approached a fence post and, without dropping her bouquet, placed her hands one on top of the other as she stared at the reaped field with a look of concern. Larks rose into the air with a song, then landed a little farther on, before resuming their flight in successive waves.

"I've never seen someplace so calm," she said.

"Can't say that calm is in short supply around here," said Joseph, looking in the same direction, as if he was trying to experience the same thing she was.

"Do you have brothers or sisters?"

"No, I live with my father, my mother, and my grandmother."

"I don't have any either."

Lost in thought, she dropped her chin onto her hands.

"Do you think there are parallel worlds?" she said after a moment.

Joseph turned toward the girl, surprised.

"Parallel worlds?"

"Yes, where we would be living different lives."

"I dunno, I never thought about it. I'm sick enough of this one. Why do you ask?" he said.

"I read a book that talked about it."

"Well, I haven't read many books."

She lifted her head, taking the countryside as witness, and said: "I get the feeling that life here doesn't happen in the same world where our fathers are."

"I'm pretty sure it's the same one, sorry to say."

The girl let a few moments pass.

"I suppose the idea helps me bear his absence," she said.

"My father said the war won't last long."

A dimple formed in the corner of Anna's mouth, like a nervous tic, then her face turned impassive and impenetrable.

"Have you ever heard of a war that didn't last long?"

Joseph frowned.

"That's what he said."

"A quick and dirty war..." she said softly. "I wish I could believe it."

Joseph leaned down and began putting his tools into a wooden box.

"I need to get back to help my mother," he said.

"Did I upset you?" she said as she watched him.

"No, that's not it. I just have lots of work."

"Maybe we could see each other again."

"Who knows," said Joseph, taken off guard.

"Don't you want to?"

He grabbed the handle and lifted the box.

"No, I do," he said weakly, avoiding the girl's questioning gaze.

"When, then?"

"Couldn't say."

"Don't tell me you work on Sundays, too?"

"Sometimes I go fishing."

"Then bring me with you the next time."

"I'm not sure I'll go this Sunday," he said.

Anna made an impish face. "Please!"

"I'll try but no promises."

"All right, I'm counting on you. You know where to find me to let me know," she said with a smile.

Carrying the box with his right hand, Joseph felt heavy beside this girl, unable to measure what their encounter meant.

"Since you're going back, we can walk part of the way together," she said.

He wished she would vanish on the spot, that she would let him gather his thoughts, that she wouldn't see him move like a clumsy beanpole. He wished he could tell her to go ahead, but he was incapable.

"If you like," he said.

She began to walk and he joined her, his gait stiff, looking straight ahead. They advanced side by side in silence, occasionally disappearing into the shade of ash and rowan trees, then reappearing in the garish light of a setting sun that stretched their shadows along the path. A group of starlings passed in the clear sky in search of a roost. When they reached the fork in the road that led to Chantegril, Joseph stopped.

"This is me," he said with relief.

"Don't forget me," said Anna, dramatically furrowing her brows.

"Forget you?"

"For the fishing."

"Oh, yeah. I won't, I promise."

Anna continued down the path to Grands-Bois. Joseph watched her walk away, slender body nonchalantly floating and fading in the air vibrating with heat, before disappearing around a bend. Then he turned around, lifted his toolbox to one shoulder, and headed toward the farm, cursing himself for hoping the war would last a little while longer.

If you went by the calendar, summer was drawing to a close, yet the sun continued to bear down with all its weight, from sunrise to sunset, a good little soldier. They had fallen behind in the fields, and Anna was helping Valette turn over the harvested second crop, the better to dry it; it would then be stored indoors and used to feed the animals over the winter. Anna's mother had stayed at the farmhouse, stricken with sunstroke. After one day of rest, the new arrivals had had no choice but to get to work, dividing the labor the best they could, as Valette barked orders.

Usually, at Grands-Bois, as elsewhere, it was full-on war against the flies, doors and windows kept shut to keep the insects, maws gaping and tiny legs ridden with germs, from spoiling food or laying their eggs on, for example, a cut of drying meat that hadn't been sufficiently salted. But today, the door had been left open. Inside, the oven was roaring as in the deep of winter. Irene was chopping onions into thin slices, which she then tossed into a heavy pot on top of the cast-iron stove slab. She sniffed at regular intervals, and dried her cheeks with the back of the hand holding the knife.

Once she was feeling better, Helen joined Irene in the kitchen, observing her with surprise.

"What are you making?" she asked.

"Can't you tell? Onion soup," said Irene.

"In this heat!"

"There's no season for soup."

"Would you like some help?"

Irene scratched her nose a few times.

"It's Eugene's favorite," she said, ignoring the question.

Tears were still streaming down her face, but she didn't bother to wipe these away.

"Damn onions. Not like I haven't peeled a ton . . . 'Spose you never get used to it," she said.

"I can help, if you like," Helen offered again.

"There's some potatoes in the cellar. Fetch ten or so, and one of the cheeses drying in the larder while you're at it."

Helen made her way down to the cellar. She brought up a block of cheese and the potatoes, which she immediately started to peel. Once the onions were ready, Irene moved to the table and watched her sister-in-law insistently as she rubbed her hands to get rid of the bits of peels stuck to her skin. Then she lifted her chin with an air of superiority.

"Don't peel them so thick."

"Not that easy. These potatoes are all dried up."

"Bet you haven't peeled many."

"There are hardly any left in the cellar."

"Which is exactly why we can't waste any, not as long as there's no new ones to dig up."

Helen continued peeling, redoubling her efforts.

Irene watched her for a few more seconds, then grabbed the pitcher, went back to the stove, poured water into the pot, and began to stir without taking her eyes off the mixture.

"We don't belong to the same world, but you're better off forgetting yours," she said.

"I'm doing what I can."

"Gotta do more. Around here, what you can won't cut it."

It was Irene who spoke, and yet it sounded as though an ancient ancestral voice had uttered the words, which had caught and snagged inside her mouth before escaping. Her jaw was tensed now, revealing tiny wrinkles above her upper lip, as though she was holding back from saying anything more in order to revel in her superiority for a few more seconds.

"Emile will come get us when it's over, and then you'll be rid of us," said Helen, on the verge of tears.

"Can't imagine he'll be able to anytime soon..."

The knife blade slipped and went deep into the flesh of the potato Helen was peeling. She took a long breath.

"You must miss Eugene, too," she said, trying to break the ice.

Irene froze.

"No point talking about it," she said.

"You're right. We should keep the faith."

"Things happen, including the worst of it. That's the way it is. Least I don't lie to myself."

Helen set the potato and knife on the table. Her eyes were glistening.

"How do you do it?" she whispered.

"How do I do what?"

Helen looked at Irene for a long moment, then went back to peeling, hands trembling.

"Nothing," she said.

"You're really not gonna be much help if you start spouting nonsense on top of everything else..."

Irene abruptly turned around.

"Feel like you can handle watching the stove and stirring from time to time so it doesn't stick, or is that too much to ask?" she said.

Helen nodded. "All right."

Irene crossed the kitchen to Eugene's bedroom. She entered, closed the door behind her, slowly approached the bed, removed the sheet with one energetic, broad movement, as if she were throwing a net into water, and then paused at the window before opening the shutters and pushing them against the outer wall. Her eyes narrowed. At this hour, the sun was at full force. The buildings, trees, animals, and hills disappeared instantly in a bright tidal wave. Irene closed her eyes and spun around, and, when she opened them, tiny inky dots began to dance in front of her, suspended between two blazing embankments—a vision, a precognition of what might happen to Eugene. Everything she was holding back. The bed reappeared first, little by little, followed by every piece of furniture and every object, and, when everything had regained its place in the tiny room, Irene promised herself she would fight that fiery vision with her own weapons, determined that no one would take away her son, that no matter what, he would live. The son. By every method that came to her. The eternal son.

Mo was what his mother and little sister called him, but to everyone else, he was the Pionier boy, and to his father, Maurice. The father who had taught him the secrets of iron, how to work the metal to make it yield, the age-old movements of the blacksmith: heating the stove and operating the bellows, bouncing the hammer off the anvil to save your strength, and then the precise blow, the making of a strap hinge. A long apprenticeship of actions outweighing words, of restrained pride blowing on the embers of a living forge. To keep the flame alive. All these things patiently passed down beginning in childhood, all these things patiently acquired, would never again be of use to Mo or to Maurice. The Pionier boy had fallen. A mention of honor as heroic as it was useless. Confirmed by a letter, five sentences written on a piece of yellowing paper torn from a notebook.

The mother screamed, one September morning, and the sound of that indescribable scream echoed across the valley. A heart shattered. The moment she felt a Mauser C96 bullet pierce her body, a bullet that came from her own son, a simple bullet that continued its trajectory through the village, for the scream in itself confirmed the villagers' fears and destroyed any remaining illusions. Maurice Pionier, the first in a series of names soon to be engraved on the surface of a stone still slumbering in the hollow of a peaceful quarry bathed in birdsong, names that would on occasion reappear in an ominous stammer on monuments erected to the glory of the great culprit itself. Names engraved with that bullet, which would continue to carve out death in the war to follow. All the screams that would soon emerge from other mouths, all the tears that would spill from other eyes, and all the powerlessness that would ravage defeated souls. That first scream, which robbed hope from some, who prepared for the worst, to scream in their turn, even as others took hope, waiting for a beloved body to appear before them, even if crippled, as long as something, at least, came back.

In the Pionier home, the forge went quiet for five days, during which each member of the family felt their faith shaken by grief, each silently cursing the heavens, in their own way, though never anything beyond the heavens. But once past those five days, and five interminable nights, they went back to speaking to their cursed god, the mother first, in a whisper, so that none of it would have been in vain, and because it was the only way to imprison a chronic ache, like a parasite inside a tumor created by the body, not knowing any other way to fight it. The father prayed a different way. He relit the stove and placed irons in the embers, and the forge came back to life, only slightly out of breath.

Valette stopped moving atop Irene's inert body. He rolled onto his side with a sigh. In the darkness of the bedroom, he could feel his flaccid penis weighing pitifully on his thigh, glued to his leg hairs.

"How do you expect me to finish if you don't do your part?" he said, pulling up his drawers with his good hand. Irene drew her nightgown over her knees and pulled up the sheet.

"I'm not in the mood," she said.

"You worried they'll hear?"

"Maybe I am."

"The girl's old enough to know how it works."

"Still."

"You weren't so bothered when Eugene was right next to us."

Irene squeezed her thighs together and slid her hands between them.

"What would you know about it?" she said haughtily.

"Well, at least you never showed it. Why the change now?"

"I don't know how you do it."

"How I do what?"

"Think about that while he's out there fighting."

"And you think you'll help him by turning into a nun?"

"We're not animals . . . It's almost like you're sick for it."

"If this was the first time . . ."

Valerie turned toward his wife, trying to pierce the darkness.

"I won't stand it much longer. A man has needs," he added coldly.

"I've never stopped you from taking what you wanted, but don't ask me for more right now."

"I don't like cold meat."

"Well, I'm not warming up for you tonight, so take it as is or go to sleep."

"Goddammit, wife!"

Irene gritted her teeth to keep from responding to the provocation, impatient for the conversation to be done with. Rage roiled in Valette's gut. He sat up on the edge of the mattress, pulled on the pants draped on the bedstead, stood, and paused briefly, his back to Irene.

"Things had better change," he said.

Valette left the bedroom. As he walked by the scullery now used as a bedroom, he thought about the girl bent over in the fields, awkwardly wielding a rake to gather the cut grass, small unbound breasts swaying beneath her light dress. When his blood began to pulse harder against his temples, he'd approached her, to guide her hands and correct her movements, feeling her adolescent body tense at his touch, at his lamentable infirmity that surely disgusted her as much as it did him. "You'll have an easier time if you do it the way I'm showing you," he had said. "Thank you," she'd replied, embarrassment evident in her voice. He moved a few feet away, continuing to turn over the regrowth but still observing her, ogling her like an exquisite animal to be brought to heel.

He entered the kitchen, lit the kerosene lamp, and turned the ferrule to increase the flame. He served himself a full glass of hooch and drank it, head tilted backward with each gulp, like a bird from a puddle. Once he finished, he picked up the lamp, placed the empty glass upside down on the bottle, which he braced beneath his arm, then walked to the front door, opened it, and went outside. He sat on the highest stair step, set the lamp beside him, refilled the glass, and drank it in one shot as he looked at the sky sparkling with stars.

His head was starting to spin. He loved this moment, when the alcohol performed its gentle rites inside his surrendering body, unburdening him of the weight of his existence. The moon resembled a white porcelain dish reigning over a black tablecloth full of holes. The smell of dew-sprinkled grass floated through the air as male crickets rubbed their elytra together in concert with the quivering gleams of light. A barn owl crossed the courtyard, wings flapping like sheets in the wind. The dog emerged from the darkness and playfully ventured closer before lying down at his master's feet with a sigh.

Valette served himself another glass, which he sipped this time. He was thinking about the soldiers fighting at the front. About Eugene, who, he hoped, was fiercely defending the family's honor. A good-for-nothing who, at just past twenty, still needed a kick in the ass to fall in line and do things the way they ought to be done. It was enough to make a person think that a father never finishes training a son, unlike animals that retain the lesson once and for all. Enough to make a person think that there's always a hint of rebellion inside a man, though the more he thought about it, that rebellion didn't bother Valette when it manifested in Eugene, whom he could then beat to his heart's content.

In truth, Valette didn't really know why the war was being waged. What the papers said. Shooting down a few aristocrats in a country he'd never heard of didn't strike him as a valid reason, and was surely a pretext that someone in his position wouldn't have been able to understand. Regardless. In his mind, if man had been fighting wars since the dawn of time, then they must serve some useful purpose to the world order. Nations made men, and men had to be willing to sacrifice their lives in return and without hesitation. In his opinion, the price of a life fell well below the price of honor.

It enraged him that he couldn't be at the front to prove himself, and all because of that damn accident that had cost him three and a half fingers, and now, speaking of, his honor. Eleven years spent considering how to hold this tool or the other. Eleven years since that ten-foot-long, sixty-pound oak timber, which he had crudely propped two feet off the ground to take some measurements, had slipped. The alcohol he'd drunk at lunch had dramatically slowed Valette's reflexes. The timber was transformed into a dull guillotine blade crashing down on his hand. He hadn't screamed, merely winced. The pain only came once he looked at his crushed hand, and still, since hardly any blood was seeping from the wound, he didn't panic. Using his free arm, he grabbed a crowbar he'd been using to tear out old roof shingles, slid the flat side under the timber, and levered it upward. Terror set in only once he saw the mash of flesh that bore no resemblance to a working man's hand. Medicine didn't perform any miracles, just a few stitches, the tatters left to heal the best they could.

In the lamp's glow, his parody of a hand was creating a shadow puppet—the head of an aurochs charging into the night. What's the point?! he thought. What's the point of a man slaving away all his life if he never gets the chance to transcend himself in an act of heroism? Or something nearing it. Hadn't God himself wanted the Crusades, wanted his obedient sheep to turn into magnificent caparisoned wolves thirsting for blood? Didn't revelation lie in blood given for a noble and grand cause? For while everyone can spill blood, giving it is something else entirely, the business of men and men only. For their blood is not the same as women's. And so, peace is worth nothing to them. Peace is slumber, and then death.

In any case, Valette had never truly felt at peace. And now his own wife was refusing him the only war he was capable of waging, the one between her thighs. The rage continued to rise. He stood, tottering, and dealt a hard kick between the dog's protruding ribs. The animal yipped and jumped up, puny body trembling, and slinked into the darkness. Valette heard it slump down by the well and restrained himself from finishing it off with a stake.

Then, since he knew that nothing would be able to temper the violence growing inside of him, he buried his crippled hand in his armpit and stared angrily into the sky, attempting to widen the spaces between the stars. And he drank. He drank more still.

In the days following the girl's visit, Joseph tried to chase away her image by working furiously during the day and, at night, by sculpting strange deformed animals. Sleeping little. None of it helped. He had never met someone like her. She clearly had nothing in common with the girls in town. Joseph sensed that she wasn't one to shy away from her own beauty, or hide her hair under a headdress or bonnet and her body beneath sweeping garments, like those girls in town. The ones who simpered and always avoided eye contact with Joseph, instead casting him sidelong smiles to innocently arouse desires about which they still knew nothing, almost as if such piddling tricks were the only way to ensure that an unstoppable power of seduction was handed down from generation to generation. Anna, because that was her name, and he would never forget it, even if he never saw her again, didn't look sideways when she spoke to him. She offered her gaze as pledge, along with the sight of her body, with no ill will, for it was clear as day that she had no ill will, that her movements weren't calculated, nor her formidable smile.

Anna came to life in windowpanes, in puddles of water, in the air. It couldn't be helped; Joseph was powerless. The harder he tried to forget her, the more insistently her memory forced its way back. She was there in the morning fog, and in the evening mist, too. Her whisper entered his bloodstream like a poison, eradicating time. At any given moment, anywhere, everywhere, her face, her eyes, her skin, her graceful body continued to arouse him, the feeling an odd two-headed creature: one head for desire, the other for veneration. A paradise of open wounds. Unease turned to pain, sublime pain of the kind only a heart can create without preexisting matter.

Lost in his thoughts, Joseph sometimes found himself smiling dumbly at nothing, wondering how something that seems to make you invulnerable at certain moments can feel like your downfall at others. At school, he had been taught that the earth rotates around the sun, and for the first time he could conceive of that hitherto abstract fact, of the reality of movement beneath his feet, not as if it was a scientific truth, but rather as if that rotation had always been blocked by some obstacle, which this girl, by her grace alone, had removed.

On multiple occasions, his mother reproached him for his lack of concentration, for being elsewhere, but he didn't confess the reason for that elsewhere, determined to keep the secret for himself, and this even when he fell from the hayloft while thinking about the girl, just barely catching himself on a joist, the only mark a gray bruise on his hip, which he'd cherished since.

Seeing the girl again became an obsession. When his mother asked him to go to Saint-Paul to buy supplies, he took a detour across the Valette farm and hid, waiting to see the girl who'd emerged out of nowhere, chased by a war, the girl who haunted his days and his nights, without any say in the matter; not that he wanted one in the end. He was aware they had nothing in common, and still, she had spoken to him, Joseph, the last-born of the Larys; she had smiled at him and asked to see him again. Ever since, she had been brightening his dark, devastated life with a burning light that was slowly consuming his capacity to reason. And who cared about reason anyway, who cared if it was just a ploy. He had to see her again. He would go to Grands-Bois at the end of the week to suggest a fishing outing that Sunday, while the women were at church, in the hope of not running into Valette. Because dreaming wasn't enough for Joseph, was no longer enough. He wanted to rediscover her voice, her smell, and the shadows that enveloped her. The shadows as much as she herself. And if his desire led him to nothing more than an illusion, at least it was the most beautiful of illusions.

Joseph rushed to finish feeding the animals. He left the farm without a word to anyone and discreetly made his way to the path. As he descended, he occasionally cut through a tight bend, scrambling over piles of fallen rocks gleaming with scoria, before returning to the narrow trail pockmarked by hooves and wagon wheels. The closer he got to Grands-Bois, the heavier his legs felt.

The dog was stationed in front of the barn, barking and jumping in the vain hope of catching one of the many white-bellied swallows noisily flying in and out of the wide-open door. Valette was crossing the courtyard, a resistant roped calf in tow, to which he was making terrible threats. Joseph froze at the farm entrance, praying he wouldn't be spotted. He didn't even have time to hide behind a pillar before Valette turned slightly, as if from a sixth sense, dragging the calf around with him. The animal began to kick and Valette dealt it a sharp punch, cursing, his eyes glued on the young man. He spat straight ahead of him.

"What are you doing here?" he barked.

Joseph stepped forward, intimidated.

"I'm here to see Anna," he said.

"Anna?"

"Your niece."

"How do you know Anna?"

"We met the other day..."

"And what do you want with her?"

"Talk to her, is all."

"What makes you think she wants to talk to the likes of you?"

Joseph didn't answer, looking desperately around. Valette shortened the rope by winding it around his hand until he could feel the calf's snot-covered muzzle.

"I'll tell her you stopped by," he said coldly. His face twisted as he spoke, as though trapped in wire slowly being tightened by someone wielding pliers.

Joseph felt like running away. Normally he never would have stood up to Valette, but his desire to see Anna again was stronger than any threat.

"Maybe she's around," he insisted.

"You see her?"

"No."

"That means she's not around."

"Please."

"Did you not understand or are you deaf?"

Valette extended his fingers covered with calf snot before tightening them back around the rope. A massive blue vein swelled and wound its way up to his biceps.

"Get out of my way. I've had enough of you," he said.

"I'm gonna knock on the door to see if she's there, and then I'll leave."

Valette stepped sideways to block Joseph's way.

"You're not going anywhere," he said.

Joseph's face suddenly lit up. Anna was coming out of the house. Valette swiveled around, wrenching the calf's head in the opposite direction, spotted the girl, then turned back to Joseph and spat at his feet.

"Clear the hell out!"

"I won't be any more bother," said Joseph, skirting around Valette and the calf as Anna walked toward him, a smile on her lips.

Valette's face went crimson, flushed with blood and inordinate hatred.

"You'll pay for that," he muttered, before leading the animal to the barn, promising it a fate worse than death.

Valette entered the cowshed and closed the door panel behind him. Once inside, he went to the calf's mother and tied the rope to one of her back legs, then, using a free headstall, gave her some hay to keep her still as the calf suckled. Back in the main stable, he stood beside a loophole so he could spy on the girl and boy talking in the courtyard. Fists clenched, body pressed against the wall, he waited until Joseph left, then ran out to intercept the girl before she entered the house.

"What did he want?" he asked.

"He offered to take me fishing, tomorrow morning."

"Fishing?"

"Yes."

"We all got better things to do than fish."

"But it'll be Sunday, the Lord's day."

"The Lord doesn't keep grass from growing or animals from getting hungry on Sundays, as far as I can tell."

Anna pretended not to understand and headed back to the house.

Valette rushed after her and roughly grabbed her arm.

"Watch out for that boy," he said.

"Why?" she asked, pulling herself free.

"His family's cursed. Everyone round here knows it."

"What's that supposed to mean?"

"Lightning struck his grandfather in broad daylight. And if that ain't a sign they're not under the good Lord's protection..."

Anna rubbed her sore arm where Valette's fingers had left their mark.

"It was an accident. There's nothing anyone could have done," she said.

"Bad luck follows for generations... Once it's found pay dirt, it sticks like shit on your shoe."

Anna shifted her gaze to Valette's stump.

"So, according to you, one tragedy necessarily leads to another," she said sarcastically.

Valette stuck his mutilated hand under her nose, trying to contain his rage.

"Watch what you say, little girl, you're still too young to understand life the way I do."

"I'm listening to you, is all."

"You better," said Valette, dropping his arm.

Exhausted by its unproductive chase, the dog trotted over to them. Anna held out her hand, and the dog immediately cozied up to her in search of affection.

"We just want to have a little fun," she said, running her hand across the dog's rough coat.

"The time for fun is long gone, and it ain't coming back anytime soon. You'll do as I say, and that's the end of it."

"We're not doing anything wrong."

"End of discussion."

At that, Valette returned to the stable. Before he went in, he turned around, to add something maybe, but then changed his mind and spat at the wall. Anna watched him disappear into the dark mouth of the doorway, secretly hoping he would never come back out.

Rays of light formed a glimmering train along the river as birds flew from bank to bank, nabbing insects midflight. The Maronne was speaking in hushed tones, its whisper an eternal apology for carving the rock.

Anna pulled back suddenly on her fishing rod. A trout erupted from the river in a jet of water. The girl stumbled backward and the fish dropped to the ground, wriggling as it attempted to escape through the grass. Joseph was watching closely from the opposite bank. He doubled back a few feet and crossed the river on an uprooted tree trunk, beside which had formed a small reservoir of frothing water muddied by twigs. When he reached Anna, she was on all fours, the fishing line tangled around her arms and her hands pressed against the fish squirming with decreasing ardor.

"It can't get too far now," said Joseph, struggling to contain a laugh.

She turned sideways, only then noticing the boy's presence.

"What is it?" she asked.

"A trout."

"My first catch," she said proudly.

"It's a fine-looking fish."

Anna gripped the trout tightly and, standing up, extended it in a sacrificial gesture. Her cotton dress was covered with dew and sticking to her thighs.

"Want me to unhook it?" he asked, not looking at the fish.

"No, I ought to learn how."

"Wait, let me see," said Joseph, coming closer. He pulled on the line to check how deeply the hook went.

"The hook's not too far, you just need to push it down the throat and it should come out on its own," he said.

Anna stuck two fingers into the trout's mouth, grabbed the end of the hook, and began to wiggle it.

"I feel it," she said.

"Don't think, just do it!"

Anna gave one clean push and the trout's sharp teeth tore the skin on her fingers. She pulled them out and studied the tiny trickles of blood in surprise.

"Try again, it'll come eventually," said Joseph, miming the gesture, stopping himself from grabbing the girl's hand.

She stuck her fingers back in the trout's mouth and pushed again, heedless of cuts, then cautiously pulled out the hook. A piece of bloodied cartilage was hanging from the barb.

"Seems dead," said Anna, looking at the motionless fish in her hand.

"Not yet. Now you need to slip your thumb under its mouth and give it a hard yank."

"Do I have to?"

"If you don't break its spine, the fish will keep suffering for no reason. Plus, it'll get stiff as wood."

Anna hesitated briefly, then did as Joseph had instructed. After a few tries, the trout's spinal column finally yielded with a crack; the small, viscous body began to tremble, then stilled. The girl's hands were speckled with translucent scales that she stared at intensely, as if she'd just committed a terrible act that made her happy all the same.

"Hand it here, I'll put it in my bag," said Joseph.

She held out the fish and he immediately placed it in his satchel. Then he leaned down, ripped up a tuft of grass, and offered it to Anna.

"To dry your hands," he said.

"Thanks!"

"You learn quick. I'm still empty-handed."

She wiped her hands vigorously with the grass, then let the mucous- and blood-stained blades fall to the ground, without taking her eyes off Joseph. There was an odd gleam in her gaze, a challenge of sorts.

"My uncle didn't want me to come," she said.

"I figured. And you're not scared to disobey him?"

"He'll never know."

Joseph stared pensively at the river.

"I would hate to cause you any problems," he said.

"Don't worry about it."

"Well, I am, a little. Valette's a strange guy... From what I know about him, there's not much that can stand in his way."

Anna waited a beat, and her face hardened.

"I shouldn't have brought him up. We're not going to let him ruin everything, are we?"

"You're right. Leave him where he is for now."

She pushed back a lock of hair dangling over her forehead.

"I wanted to thank you for bringing me here."

"It's nothing..."

Face now relaxed, she approached Joseph solemnly.

"I got you a little present," she said.

"Shouldn't have."

"It's not much, but it means a lot to me."

Joseph couldn't take his eyes off the girl in her simple dress, wondering where she could have possibly hidden a present.

"Close your eyes," she said, barely enunciating the words.

He obeyed without thinking, his eyelids flickering beneath the weight of what felt like an interminable pause. He was dying to open his eyes to see what she was preparing.

"Don't cheat. I'm watching you . . ." she said.

Soap, milk, and red berries, again, like the first time. A soothing blend that chased away the smell of trout.

"What are you playing at?" he asked with a strained smile.

"Shh, not another word."

Cloth rustling, then a steady breath swept across Joseph's face. The girl's lips pressed against his. Joseph froze, abandoned by his every instinct. He succumbed once he felt Anna's hands on his cheeks, her fingers like a spider's delicate legs exploring his skin. It no longer required any effort to keep his eyes closed, and he automatically parted his lips. The girl's tongue darted into his mouth, rummaging and rolling around his own inert tongue. Set ablaze by this wet fire, Joseph felt himself harden and clumsily grabbed the girl's hips, more to keep his distance than to get closer to her. Exquisite panic flooded over him. He had never let himself go like this, a consenting toy, persuaded that he could never repay such a debt and that he would owe this girl for the rest of his God-given days.

He didn't realize when she stepped back, and felt like an idiot when he heard her speak again.

"You can open your eyes now."

He waited a few more seconds. The memory of Anna's lips was as powerful as her lips themselves. He opened his eyes. She was smiling. The corner of her mouth twisted into a pout, creating tiny waves of skin, like when you throw a pebble on the surface of still waters.

"Are you okay?" she asked.

Joseph let his body recover before answering.

"I think so," he said absently.

"You think so?"

"It's just..."

"You've never kissed a girl before?"

"Not like that."

Anna furrowed her brows.

"And?"

"And I hope that you'll catch lots more trout and that I'll be here when you do."

The house was peaceful this Sunday morning. Certain she wouldn't be disturbed, Helen locked herself in the bedroom. She took her favorite dress out of the wardrobe, slipped it on, then put on the ankle boots she'd been wearing the day she arrived and laced them tightly to better show off the form of her calves. With a sigh, she ran one finger along the wavy line left by a bramble and that went down one shin. Then took a mirror speckled with brown stains off the wall and examined herself from every angle. She realized she had lost some of her curves, which saddened her. She mustn't let herself go, for one day Emile would come back, wearing his handsome uniform.

She sat on the bed and closed her eyes to escape her rudimentary surroundings, to try to dispel the terrible energy of this tiny room, and for a few moments, she succeeded.

Before leaving their home, she had briefly considered going with Anna to her parents' vast estate outside Paris, but Emile would have never allowed it. Narrow-minded old aristocrats, both of them, who had never accepted their daughter's relationship, much less marriage, with a simple schoolteacher. They had tried everything to dissuade Helen, even threatening to disinherit her. In their eyes, Emile was a bumpkin in mud-caked boots with farm-boy manners, and would remain so, whatever he might undertake and whatever success he might have. Emile had suffered through her father's outright rejection, and the disdain of both her parents. In the end, he came to terms with it. Helen had told herself that with time, perhaps, circumstances would change for the better, but time did no such thing. She wrote her parents after her husband was conscripted, thinking that a war was the type of situation to ease bitterness. They hadn't deigned to respond.

Hold steady. That was all that mattered to Helen. When it was all over, Emile would return to his job as a school principal. Everything would go back to normal. She'd be able to resume her urbanite pastimes and never spare another thought to the grim drudgery of the farm. She nostalgically thought back to the last concert they had attended at the Grand Théâtre—she had always loved classical music—Bach's suites. She could still feel Emile's hand on hers, and see the tears of joy on his cheeks.

This life, far from the city and its charms, wasn't for her, but she had no choice but to endure it. She did what she could to help on the farm but had never exerted physical effort in her life, apart from putting away the expensive porcelain cups she didn't dare let her maid handle, or planting begonias and impatiens in the window boxes in spring and forget-me-nots in autumn. Anna, at least, seemed to be having an easier time getting used to this new life, or maybe she was simply putting on a brave face. Helen was careful not to ask her daughter if it was the former or the latter.

A knot of anxiety formed in her stomach. She furiously pulled off the boots and her pretty dress, which she threw in the wardrobe without folding it. Tears came to her eyes, fell, quickly rerouted by her cheekbones, and reached the corners of her lips to conclude their journey in her parted mouth. A taste of salt, a taste of impotence.

Helen was a foreigner to this land, to its people and things, overcome and unable to truly hide it, and not strong enough either. The green grass in the pastures was dirty, pebbles dug into the soles of her slender feet, the morning air reeked of manure, and even the blue sky struck her as a vast ex-voto in honor of the lives sacrificed to the earth. She didn't belong in this land that was too much and not enough, sprawling yet narrow, a prison made of habits and customs, and she the prisoner behind steel bars that no one had ever thought to saw through. For Helen, life here was nothing more than an unbearable provocation slowly transforming into great lassitude, though not yet despair.

They squeezed onto the church benches, as much out of superstition as true faith. Because, though no one would ever admit it, they each blamed God for allowing the slaughter of innocents but came all the same to hear the priest speak of crusades and just sacrifice. Church and State, only recently divided, seemed to be conspiring to do Satan's dirty work. And so the townsfolk listened to sermons in an attempt to uncover, at best, a glimmer of hope, and at worst, a tangible sign of their submission, say in the ray of light striking a saint in an alcove, or the confident smile on the Virgin Mary's face that they had never noticed before, or perhaps her blazing eyes, which were at times fixed on the baby Jesus in her arms, at others on the man sacrificed on the cross. And they secretly watched each other too, to make sure they weren't dreaming, then looked back at the holy man, without joining in to his increasingly frenetic sermon borrowed from whatever Gospel suited, and with an interpretation he felt justified in offering his poor sheep sick of war and misery. Anything that would soothe their minds even a little.

"...Alas! Satan respects nothing, my brethren. He is the invisible captain of an enemy army whose sole terrible goal is to fight Christ and destroy his kingdom. Satan, my brothers!

The devil who stole man's reason and then gave it back inebriated with his power. But we won't let ourselves be taken in, my brethren! In the name of freedom, of our freedom, we will stand tall, otherwise we will cease to be men and women and we will fall, lowered to the ranks of brutes without reason or hope or a future. For no one may subjugate us without according due attention to our souls, our moral and religious lives, and our eternal future. You, my brethren, you hardworking souls who so often struggle to meet the needs of the present day, sometimes unable to imagine the morrow, must without cease aid the fight against the oppression that would take away our future, our home, and our god. Our infinite god, who also put us on this earth to fight the disciples of evil. Let's fight together, my brethren! Like our brave soldiers against the cursed empire Satan is preparing for us, to replace the blessed kingdom of Jesus Christ our Lord and Savior. For if he ever triumphs, we will see his sinister legions of nonbelievers devoted to the worship of a nameless barbarism multiply. Yes, my brethren! Live up to the trust that God has placed in us, for God wills it! God wills it! God wills it! God wills it! . . ."

Everyone took up the chorus, "God wills it!" thundering like a battering ram against the doors of a fortified castle. The vicar never uttered the terms "Boche," "German," or "Teuton"; he had only Satan in his mouth. For a moment he relished the effect of his words, before raising his hands above his transfixed audience, who immediately went silent and, in the same breath, sat back down. Then, the sound of benches creaking and shoes scraping against stone, breathing and the annoyed hissing of flames extinguishing atop tall altar candles, throats cleared and jaws grinding accompanied by musty smells, the niggling sound of a drop of water dripping from the vault and crashing onto the floor after its thousand-year journey, and the friction of clammy hands around rosaries with tarnished beads.

The vicar mounted the altar. He raised the consecrated host, which he broke into pieces and chewed slowly, then drank the wine. He next grabbed a ciborium full of the small wafers and descended the altar steps, and the communicants approached docilely, almost noiselessly, starting with the first row, like beggars with bowed heads, not truly knowing if they were going to commune with the Creator or tame Satan himself. Stirring in their wake smells of smoke, sweat, and incense. Then returning to their places, seated behind a long rack on which rested missals at regular intervals, each churchgoer inventing their own prayer to save themselves from evil, beneath a sky of gray stones speckled with cherubs and streaked with cracks.

Surprised at the lingering silence, the communicants lifted their heads and saw the holy man frozen at the foot of the altar. He was looking at a dog at the end of the central aisle, a flea-ridden griffon with trembling legs. The creature barked, revealing blunted fangs black at the root and sending quivers through a meager coat of spiky fur poking out between hairless patches of mange. To the vicar, the animal's pupils resembled two punched-out nickel coins against a wall of horned faces.

Once the vicar had recovered from his surprise, he pointed at the dog, as though he wanted to challenge it to a supernatural battle, for he had no doubt that it was in fact a diabolical apparition. "Out, Satan, I banish you. This isn't your home... out!" he said, as though performing an exorcism. The animal began to growl, pitching its head from side to side toward the rows of benches. The vicar took the gauntlet: he slowly approached the dog, his alb trailing along the ground and his body appearing to float. The feeling of having been given a divine mission, buoyed by the fearful gaze of the audience imploring this warrior of God to repel the demon with exhortations of "God wills it!," a savior now fully confident, ready to rout Satan's incarnation.

The dog jumped forward in a great leap of which no one had thought it capable. It dug its fangs into the vicar's arm, and the holy man screamed and thrashed before finally flinging the creature onto the ground. It whimpered upon impact, then rose and scurried for the exit, claws sliding on the flagstones, and disappeared through the open door.

The vicar remained in the aisle for several minutes. A holy man become legend, the inscrutable and haughty face of a vanquisher wielding the banner of heaven, inwardly astonished and reassured. This man who had unhesitatingly confronted the devil in disguise and succeeded in sending him running. This man whose words would never again have their legitimacy questioned, and the same for the might and glory of his god.

Then, extending his sore arm, which was covered by the ample sleeve of his immaculate garment, he scanned the speechless churchgoers, who were now averting their eyes, their faces betraying utter incomprehension and, on occasion, pity for this man who had begun gesticulating in the aisle for no reason, screaming like a devil.

"What are you doing?"
"Looking at you."
"Stop!"
"Why?"
"Just stop already!"
"I could do this all day."
"Someone might see us."
"Don't worry."
"I can't help it."
"And anyways, we're not doing anything wrong."
"I feel like we are."
"You need to relax a little, enjoy the moment."
"You have any more jokes?"
"How do you feel?"
"I have no idea."
"If you could do anything, what would it be?"
"If we weren't here, you mean?"
"Yup."
"Something I've always dreamt about doing?"
"Go on."
"Visit the sea. That's what I would do."
"That's not such a big dream."

"Maybe not for you . . . I'd like to know what it looks like, before I die."

"I'll take you one day."

"Don't talk nonsense."

"I promise you."

"You ought to think long and hard before you promise someone something."

"I always keep my promises."

Marie was expending considerable energy to conceal the fact that her heart was misfiring, either racing like a cart hurtling along a pitted path or slowing until she could no longer feel it beating in her chest. These cardiac irregularities weren't accompanied by pain, only fear-induced fevers. Though it wasn't death she feared, despite the sensation that she was diminishing daily. She feared never seeing her son again, as well as leaving the farm to Joseph and her daughter-in-law. They still had so much to learn, so many things that she wouldn't be able to teach them, once she was six feet under. Of course, they could count on Leonard, but for how long? She had caught them staring at her, more than once, watching her struggle more than usual, but never insisting, acting as if nothing had happened, no doubt to deceive themselves, or else out of simple resignation.

Mathilde had turned out to be a pleasant surprise. Once Victor left, she had assumed his responsibilities without complaint, boldly braving adversity. Some evenings, in the kitchen, Marie would feel like talking to her, after Joseph had gone to bed, to share the absence, to ease some of the tension in their bodies. Maybe Mathilde wanted to talk too but didn't dare. Who knew? Instead they gripped utensils, any number of solid objects, which returned them to their solitude.

For women, life was made of actions and very few words. They had been taught that words were the expression of a careless mind, unless accompanied by concrete actions, such as shucking an ear of corn, kneading dough, chopping a log down the middle, or building a fire. And so words, when they came out, struck them as turgid with reason, but never lightness and even less so gaiety.

Mathilde was scouring pots in a large tin basin by the light of a lamp on a stool. Seeing her hunched over, furiously scrubbing the dented metal with a brush, Marie had the sudden desire to shatter the certainties inflicted on her by a nearly complete life. She felt the need to let her words out, like birdlings leaving the nest. Urgently. Tomorrow might already be too late.

"Let them soak overnight. You'll clean them faster in the morning," she said.

"What's done is done."

"Getting your rest is important too."

Mathilde looked up at her mother-in-law seated at the table in the gloom.

"I never would have thought I'd hear you say that one day."

"Go on, now."

Mathilde dropped the brush in the water, straightened up, pressed her wet hands against her lower back, then wiped her forehead with the back of one sleeve. She stayed like that for a few moments, staring into the basin at the thick layer of grime floating on the surface, as if she was trying to pin down an idea that had crossed her mind without stopping.

"The days aren't long enough," she said, before bending over again, grabbing the brush and a pot.

"You won't make them any longer by working yourself to death."

"I don't like having nothing to do."

"Sit down for a second. Please."

The old woman's intonation, more than the words themselves, sounded like a supplication. Mathilde observed her mother-in-law intently. She had never known her to distract someone from their work, or even to speak of idle hands. She dried hers with a rag hanging on the back of a chair, then slowly walked to the table, dubious, fearful almost, carrying the lamp, which she set down as she sat, then clasped her hands, waiting to see what the old woman was getting at.

"Good," said Marie, allowing her voice to gently splinter the silence in the room.

"You're not going to bed? You've done more than enough for today, too."

Marie appeared not to have heard. She was staring at Mathilde's hands.

"That boy's strong," she said.

"True. I haven't heard him complain once..."

"Like his father."

The old woman's face was distorted by beams of light coming from the lamp.

"Does he ever mention his father, to you?" she said without looking up.

"Never."

"Maybe he ought to."

"Well if he doesn't, it's because it suits him not to."

Marie felt tremors in her heart. She waited until they calmed, taking deep breaths in and out. Nothing serious for now.

"Surely it's not that simple," she said.

"Could it be that it's you who needs to talk about your son?" said Mathilde defensively.

"He's also your husband."

"You think I need reminding?"

"I don't mean to hurt you."

"So what then?"

Marie smiled sadly.

"You're holding up marvelously, too," she said.

"Like everyone else, I reckon."

"Well then, every day must be hard. If you're like everyone else."

"What is it you really want?"

Marie nodded her narrow chin at Mathilde's hands, staring at the white mark on her left index finger. The removed ring.

"We try so hard to get rid of the reminders, but if you ask me, it's not the best tactic... They always turn up when you least expect them."

Mathilde curled her fingers into a fist.

"This way I don't risk losing it while I work," she said like a little girl caught red-handed.

Marie's face hardened.

"I'm not judging you."

The old woman raised her left hand in the air, showing the gold ring nearly swallowed by a bulge of flesh, like a rope left around the trunk of a sapling.

"What God has joined, nothing can separate," she said solemnly.

"I don't want to cause harm to anyone."

Marie leaned over the table, commiseration in her eyes.

"So then never show your weaknesses, or give people the opportunity to exploit them."

Mathilde looked away, unclenched her fist, and her voice broke.

"Maybe I'm not strong enough to endure everything that's happening to us," she said.

"It's not a question of strength."

Marie softened and placed one hand on Mathilde's. Her daughter-in-law tensed, as though paralyzed by the touch.

"You have plenty of strength. Don't let anyone tell you differently. Ever," said Marie.

"I thought it would help."

"You know perfectly well it won't."

"Sometimes I don't know what else to do to stop from thinking. Even the work isn't enough."

"People like us aren't made not to work."

Mathilde's eyes glistened.

"So it never occurs to you that things might not end up the way we hope."

"Never!" said Marie coldly.

One of the women was lying, and the other knew it. Mathilde slid her hand back across the table, abandoning the contact she hadn't wanted but had nonetheless accepted, and rose. She paused for a moment, looking at her ring finger.

"I'll wear it," she said.

She put the dirty pots in the basin to soak, then left the room. Marie said nothing, face expressionless again, victim to the racing of her tortured heart, eyes fixed on her gold-ringed finger.

A slight breeze was ruffling the foliage. Two black-speckled pigs were eating acorns softened by the cool shade, letting nothing go to waste, and using their noses to turn over dry leaves and moss, under the supervision of a young man lost in contemplation of Puy Violent. The basalt neck farther down the mountain resembled the snout of a sleeping dragon. Joseph's gaze went from the summit to the fawn fields to the forests, then returned, in reverse order, to stare at the peak before turning to the slumbering behemoth that was Roc des Ombres. He attempted, unsuccessfully, to imagine he was seeing these mountains for the first time. They had always been here, of course, and they wouldn't move an inch, even if he were to turn his back on them.

Joseph had long believed that he could never leave this region to which he was intimately connected, simply because he was born here and had been taught that it suffices to be born somewhere to belong there, that there was no point hoping for anything more than climbing up and down these mountains indefinitely.

But now two events were disrupting everything: his father's departure and Anna's arrival. One indirectly linked to the other. He attempted to classify the events by order of importance. First, his father, of course. Joseph blamed the mountains for not being able to keep him home. They had managed to hold generations of Larys here for some unknowable destiny and yet proved incapable of keeping this last Lary in their mineral bosom. And then the girl. The girl after. No, the girl first, of course, his father's memory relegated to the background. In spite of himself. He tried to remember what his life had been like before her, and the image that came to mind was Puy Violent, an extinguished volcano on the horizon, unaware of the smoldering fire. The fire inside Joseph. Would he be able to contain it by will alone? The question rattled around his skull. A mountaineer in distress, dangling from the rocks on a fraying rope. A shadow descended, dismissing the question and also any hope of retaining his grip on the rock face. He felt as if anything of importance to him would inevitably slip away, now that Anna, the girl he couldn't get out of his mind, was looming above him like a high peak. A steep ascent he hoped to attempt without the slightest assurance of ever reaching the summit.

Joseph tried to think rationally, questioning how something that hadn't existed before could take on such importance from one day to the next. He wasn't thinking only of Anna, but of the trace she left behind like a footprint frozen in perennial snow—that kiss, which had completely frazzled his sense of geography. He couldn't find the right words to describe the insatiable feeling inside of him. In any case, he would have needed to invent new ones, and invention wasn't his forte. To start with, he didn't know all that many words, at least not the ones that could have adequately and elegantly expressed his preternatural awareness that their kiss wasn't a stone set somewhere by chance, but was part of a majestic construction rising far above the mountains. Recognize and identify the fragrances of blooming acacia and honeysuckle, birds by their song, most of the animals lurking somewhere on these mountains, every tree, yes—all that was in his power. But how quickly that encyclopedia became obsolete, respectfully edged out of the way by new truths, a foreign presence, the body in its most magistral form, a miracle incarnated.

Describing Anna wouldn't have done justice to the feeling growing in Joseph's heart, so much more than the mere desire for another kiss, powerful though that desire was. Everything about her, in her, was in motion, in perpetual harmony with nature in all its wildness and in no way betrayed. When she set her eyes on him. Capable of giving life and taking it away in the same fraction of a second, which at that point was no longer time but a tiny abstraction of the space separating two bodies. For this girl was all of space; she was the Milky Way, in which the celestial bodies bathe. Because, yes, he had tasted her lips, but he had also pressed against her chest and stroked the curves of her hips.

There had been other kisses, more confident than the first, which brought together similar desires. Anna and Joseph had agreed to meet in secret at the cowherd's cross, as often as possible. A few minutes sufficed to spend the remainder of the day on a cloud. Thieves of time driven by urgency. Urgency on their skin and in their eyes. They weren't old enough to fear the extremes of desire. The perfection of the unknown was for them the gentlest of music, a symphony in the midst of being composed.

They hid, not from shame, but so that no one would dream of robbing them of even one iota of the magic that the adults in their lives, clearly long past the point of being able to access their adolescent emotions, henceforth restrained, decimated, or perhaps unknown even, would certainly have dismissed as ridiculous. Those adults, who thought that life was more than just violins playing, wouldn't have hesitated to lecture the young and carefree lovers. And yet, Joseph and Anna desperately wished they could express their deepest emotions without a care for what others might think. They opted for restraint instead. A way of delaying the turbulence that might come out of a declaration as powerful and cloying as "I love you," words they still didn't dare utter. So they fled their fear by stretching space and time.

Even when apart, the lovers continued their advances, in their minds, reliving kisses and caresses, remembering the flame left behind by a palm on a cheek, or even by the shadow of that palm. They ventured into frightening territory replete with beauty and gentleness and the unknown, miles away in a lighter, unburdened world. Two bodies sheltered from the storm.

Leonard was scraping manure in the cowshed with the underside of his pitchfork. A prominent bump rose and fell beneath his jacket like a trapped ball with a life of its own. He gently poked a cow in the rear to get her to rise, and apologized to her by name for the disturbance. She struggled to stand, shifting her weight onto her back feet first, then the front, shook her head and whipped the air with her tail. The hunched-over farmer resumed his task, collecting manure until his pitchfork was full, tiny mounds of shit piled one atop the other, which he then dumped into a wheelbarrow in the entryway. Where Joseph had been waiting for a few moments.

"Ah, there you are," said Leonard, continuing to scrape clean the floor.

"Hi, Leo. I'm bothering you, maybe?"

"It's been a few days that you haven't bothered me."

"Well, we haven't seen much of you at Chantegril lately."

Leonard prompted a second cow up.

"Path goes both ways, you know. Even easier coming here, seeing how it's downhill," he said gently.

"Exactly. I was getting worried," said Joseph to justify himself.

"Shouldn't have. I've been awful busy lately, and anyways, I figured you and your ma could use a break, that maybe you were sick of having me around."

"You know perfectly well that's not true."

"Could be."

"Do you need some help?"

Leonard raised a corner of his mouth, making a sucking noise as if food was stuck between his teeth.

"I'm guessing you got plenty of work at home. No reason to look for more."

"And yet you always do."

"It's not the same."

Joseph turned toward the cows swinging their roped heads through the air.

"We brought ours in too."

"This winter will be tough."

"You sure about that?"

"Who can be sure about anything, but I think so. After the summer we had, chances are winter will be just as bad."

Leonard's words landed like mallet blows on a stake.

"Did you wanna ask me something, or you just stop by to say hello?" he continued.

"A little of both. Would you lend me your mule and cart? I want to collect some dead leaves before the weather gets bad."

"I won't need either anytime soon. I'll empty my wheelbarrow and yoke her for ya."

Joseph came closer and walked around the cart.

"Leave it. I'll empty it," he said.

"Won't say no to that," responded Leonard, planting his pitchfork in the hill of manure.

With one hand, the old man placed the harness over the mule, stroking her gray, silky cheek with the other. He spoke gently, as though he needed her consent. Then, with Joseph's help, he attached the wagon shafts to each side of the docile animal, adjusted the tatty leather buckles, and tightened the ties, notch after notch, up to a lighter mark of wear.

"We could put the ladders on the side, that way you can load more leaves on each trip, seeing how they don't weigh much," he suggested.

"Yeah, let's."

They went into the barn to fetch two ladders made from thick beams and several rows of battens, which they carried to the cart and slotted into metallic rings along the rails. The operation concluded, Leonard approached the mule and began stroking her back with a hand coated in grimy sebum, exploding small bouquets of brown dust in the air.

"And you better listen, you hear me," he said to the mule.

"She's starting to get used to it," said Joseph.

"True, but sometimes this girl's like me. She goes and forgets things with no warning."

Leonard gathered saliva on his tongue, and his Adam's apple rose beneath his chin, then returned to its place in the fold of his neck as he spat onto the bare ground. He looked down, seeking some meaning, perhaps, in the sticky, almost pristine patterns of his expectoration. He raised his head and returned to the mule, to check the fastenings.

"You don't want my help gathering those leaves?" he said.

"Nah, I'll be fine," said Joseph eagerly.

Leonard kept his eyes on the mule.

"You'd rather be alone, that it?" he said.

"You're busy, you said so yourself."

"I wouldn't mind. I'm done with the manure."

"Thanks for the offer but another time."

"As you like."

Leonard took off his hat, scratched his head, then put it back on.

"It's true what they say about mules, you know," he said.

"You mean about them being stubborn?"

"Yeah. And this one might be even more stubborn than the rest."

"I hadn't noticed..."

"If she starts pouting, don't rush her. Just wait for it to pass, it always does, eventually."

"I don't see any reason why she would."

"There's not always a reason with animals."

Joseph grabbed the bridle, preparing to go. The old man furrowed his brow and took a long sniff. He stroked the bridge of the mule's nose with his fingertips, then turned his head, as if he didn't want her to overhear.

"Plus, she don't like strangers much," he whispered.

Joseph felt uneasy all of a sudden.

"I'm no stranger," he said softly, giving the animal a kind glance.

The old man looked mischievously from the mule to Joseph. He smiled, each tooth distinctly separated from the next like the slats of a fence. A fan of deep wrinkles unfurled at the corner of each eye.

"Yeah, you're not," he said.

"What are you trying to say, then?"

"If ever you run into a stranger..."

"Around here? Not much chance of that..."

"Maybe just a recent acquaintance then, who knows. If it happens, do as I said, take your time with her, there's no need to rush."

Joseph reddened.

"I'll bring her back tonight," he said to end the conversation.

"All right."

Joseph pulled on the halter. The mule advanced slowly with the cart, its iron-rimmed wheels clattering over the farmyard stones. Leonard dug his hands in his pockets, waited for them to leave, his entertainment over, and got back to work.

Joseph returned the mule and wagon that evening. He helped Leonard unhitch the cart and put it away, then they led the mule to the stable, where they currycombed her, carefully attending to her saggy body with the same respect and deference as for a prizewinning steed, as she munched on alfalfa hay.

"You get done what you planned?" Leonard eventually asked.

"Yeah, all good."

Leonard paused mid-stroke, then stepped back to look at his mule.

"I bet you have no idea how old she is," he said.

Joseph's body untensed. He placed one hand on the mule's back, as if he was thinking, but mainly relieved that Leonard wasn't doubling up on that morning's warning, about a possible encounter.

"You've had her as long as I've known you," he said.

"She'll be turning thirty soon, if you can imagine."

"Doesn't look it."

"You saw, not a single wrinkle," said Leonard, winking.

"I'm sure she has plenty more years ahead of her."

"Who knows. I never had a mule before this one."

Leonard inched closer and rubbed the back of his hand under the mule's nose a few times, as if something was itching him, then stroked her between the ears, her favorite spot, a tiny valley of bones covered with velvet.

"They say mules work till their last breath..."

The old man's face abruptly clouded over, his forehead cracking like parched earth, eyebrows forming a thick ash-colored hedge.

"Not that I can think of a better end than to drop dead out of the blue, no time to suffer, or make others suffer."

"If you ask me, she's not gonna drop dead anytime soon."

"She knows better than to do me like that."

The mule swung her head up and down, as though she was agreeing.

"Looks like she has no plans to prove you wrong," said Joseph.

"By this point, we understand each other, she and I," said the old man, his mood slowly lightening.

"I bet."

"I think there's more common sense in her eyes than in the eyes of most of the people I know. Sometimes I wish she'd tell me how she sees things with those eyes of hers.

"What kinds of things?"

Leonard straightened up, staring at the mule without touching her.

"It's stupid, but I'd like to know if she's happy," he said.

"She doesn't seem unhappy, in any case..."

"But how can we really know?"

"You can tell when something's wrong with an animal."

"You're right . . . I mean, you can tell when something's wrong with a person, so why would it be any different for animals?"

Leonard gave Joseph an insistent, playful look, like a little kid who just whispered a swear word.

"By the way, you never said . . ." he added.

"Said what?"

"Whether she behaved?"

Joseph felt a prickling in his chest. He sucked air in through his nose.

"Everything went fine," he said.

"Good, good."

Leonard pulled a chunk of hard bread out of his pocket and offered it to the mule in the palm of his hand. He waited for her to finish chewing, then continued:

"Some folks put on blinders so the mules look straight ahead and never to the side, but I'm not for 'em. If I did that, how would she imagine the world around her?"

Joseph looked up at the milky sky pulling away from a horizon set ablaze by the setting sun.

"Well, I better get going before dark," he said.

"You know, there's not all that much beauty that comes within a man's reach, in a lifetime. So no point looking away from it."

Joseph felt something inside his body waver and his embarrassment transform into an almost pleasant feeling, as if Leonard's words were reminding him what truly mattered and there was no longer any reason to pretend not to understand what the old man was getting at.

"Don't you worry. I have no intention of looking away."

Leonard walked around the mule and placed one hand on Joseph's shoulder, and his touch felt as light as the flapping of a butterfly's wing.

"I'd best get home," said Joseph.

"Hold on, I have something to show you before you leave," said Leonard.

"What is it?"

"Can't you guess?"

Joseph's face lit up.

"So she had them?" he said.

"This afternoon."

Joseph followed Leonard into the barn. A large scraggy dog was lying on a patch of cool hay beside four motley puppies greedily suckling and whining. The dog lifted her head when she saw the two men, then, reassured, set it back down heavily, tongue darting in and out of her mouth like a snake.

The last dog at Chantegril had died over the summer. Joseph's father, a few days before he left, had buried it in the back of the yard, where generations of faithful servants who had belonged to the family had always been buried. This last one, like all its predecessors, had been a valiant companion, with no equal when it came to shepherding a flock, barking gently to avoid agitating the animals, sniffing out wildfowl and game, as well as scrawny wolves who, in the dying days of their species, continued to sporadically venture onto farmland, trotting from one decaying carcass to the next on their delicate feet with a lingering pride that would forever blaze in their gray eyes.

On farms, dogs were taken care of, even though they were the only animals that weren't truly productive. They were loyal, however, the frequent confessors of one's darkest torments and deepest secrets, even seemed to have been made for that too and perhaps above all, in exchange for a little supper and the occasional pat. And there was no reason to think any of that would change—things die and others are born, and those "things," transformed into truth, encompassed everything that a life could contain. And so people believed it would go on forever, that the way it was would always be, somehow, without having to ask someone to make it so, and that this was where the true miracle resided: life begat life, the cycle continued, sometimes with a little delay, and a few surprises.

"Just need to pick the one you want," said Leonard.

Joseph observed the puppies frantically tugging on their mother's inflamed nipples, prompting pained spasms from the resigned dog.

"What are you gonna do with the others?"

Leonard shrugged.

"No one else wants them?" asked Joseph.

"Not as far as I know. That's why you better pick quick, before they open their eyes... It's not so easy after that."

"I dunno. They're all cute."

"Take 'em all, then," said Leonard without the slightest irony.

"Wish I could."

Leonard shrugged again, watching the poor tired mother dog, still being rudely mistreated by her brood.

"In any case she won't have enough milk to feed them properly. She'd probably die trying, and I'd hate myself if I lost her like that."

Joseph pointed to one of the puppies.

"The black one with the yellow spot on its head," he said.

"That's my favorite too."

"Why aren't you keeping one?"

"The next litter, maybe... I wouldn't want to bring it bad luck."

Joseph kneeled and stroked the mother's head.

"You think she knows what'll happen now?"

"It's not the first time."

"Her eyes are really sad."

"All dogs look like that."

Joseph thought for a second.

"And what does that sadness come from, you think?"

"Who knows. Resignation, maybe. What you gonna name it?"

"Tom, like the others."

"It might not be a boy. It's too early to know."

"Doesn't matter."

Leonard concurred. "You're right. Tom fits just fine."

"Well, I'd better be off now."

"Does your mother know?"

"A farm without a dog ain't a farm. We need one."

"I'll tell you when it's weaned."

"I'll come see it from time to time."

"As often as you can. It'll need to get used to you."

Joseph stood, keeping his eyes on the puppies.

"The other ones will be gone."

"They won't have been long for this world."

They walked out together. As soon as Joseph was out of eyesight, Leonard returned inside the barn.

At first, Marie told herself it would pass. A sensation of sawdust collecting in her bronchial tubes, which she couldn't clear even by spitting into her large embroidered handkerchiefs, on the verge of vomiting. An old person dying, one way or the other, was in the order of things. A sick animal often merited more attention. Mathilde, monopolized by the farm and housework, didn't have time to take care of her mother-in-law. Not that Marie would have let her; she didn't want any fuss. Not rich enough to live beyond her due. In any case, nobody could find a doctor anymore; presumably they'd all been deployed, even the old ones. Out of the question to go to the hospital. To end up where everything had begun, between two moments of silence troubled only by the taut line of existence. One family's survival couldn't depend on one old lady, and, in normal circumstances, Marie would have been the last to complain.

She watched the digitate leaves of the chestnut tree turn yellow and then brown, an unchanging phenomenon that bore witness to the gradual slowing of circulating sap, which would result in the vessels drying up, before scarring. Marie had always been surprised that such subtle colors could announce death. A scheduled death that, granted, would lead to a rebirth the following spring, which she could merely imagine. She wondered when man's spring would arrive, and whether there was even a single good season in life. No! At most a few days in a row, certainly not an entire season, not on the land she was living on—too much pain to endure, too many tragedies to bear. All she could do was hope for better seasons up above, in a corner of the cursed sky, far beyond the horizonal strands of clouds illuminated by a pallid sun. In the shadow of a merciful god.

In Marie's mind, life was a nasty trick. You came into the world, barely had enough time to blink, and then you shriveled up; then it was over, or nearly. The world would continue to exist after her, but she would no longer be a part of it. She would exist elsewhere and in a few fleeting memories; who could say for how long. Even if it was impossible to capture the shape of the soul, she still believed. Because otherwise life would have no meaning, and people in these parts needed meaning to keep their fires burning, fires they would use to feed the generations to follow.

Marie hardly left her bed anymore. Back glued to a pillow stuffed with goose feathers, she explored her memories as she neared the abyss. Since it was her time to go, may as well do it on tiptoe, with the least bother possible to the others. Because she could feel she was on her way out. All that was expected of a dignified seventy-two-year-old woman. It wasn't so bad—seventy-two years spent nose to the grindstone without complaint. And if her death could work in her son's favor, in the eyes of the Lord, a discreet exchange of sorts, it'd be worth it, she told herself. Her only request was not to pass in the middle of the night.

Joseph knocked on his grandmother's door. He entered carrying a bowl of steaming broth. Every time he found her bedridden, Joseph's eyes would fill with sadness and his mouth would empty of words. Marie thanked him with a smile, then she pretended to sip some soup before setting the bowl on the bedside table, saying it was "very good" and that she would finish it later.

She held out one hand and let it drop heavily onto the bed.

"You'll find a little box in the chest, in the bottom drawer, under the sheets. Bring it to me, please," she said.

Joseph complied. He recognized the small box that his grandmother gripped tightly during every storm. He hesitated before touching the object, as if the responsibility was too much, then he placed his palms against the cold metal and carried the box to the bed. His grandmother patted the sheet.

"Set it down," she said.

The old woman's chin began to quiver.

"You're going to keep this, until your father returns."

"Isn't it fine where it is?"

Marie turned to Joseph. She smiled and her face resembled sand carved by the wind.

"Come closer."

Joseph kneeled.

"I'm becoming hard of hearing. I'm not sure I'll hear the next storm," she said.

Joseph was staring at the box.

"You can open it, you know."

Joseph didn't move, so she turned the key and opened the lid, then leaned over anxiously.

"Look," she said.

Joseph timidly peeked inside the scratched-up box's rectangular mouth.

"These are all the letters your grandfather sent me when we weren't together. And his wedding ring, which I found intact in the courtyard."

Marie caught her breath, then went on: "The other papers are the property deeds."

"All right," is all Joseph could say, giving his grandmother an incredulous look.

She placed one hand on her grandson's arm, solemnity etching away the little loose flesh remaining on her face.

"When I'm gone, I want you to put the letters and the ring with me . . . in my coffin."

Joseph swallowed.

"You're not gone yet."

Marie squeezed Joseph's arm.

"You'll do as I say?"

Silence wedged its way between them.

"I will," he finally said.

"It's not meant to make you sad."

"You're asking a lot."

"No one can stop what's meant to happen one day or the next."

Joseph took a long breath to summon as much conviction as he could.

"You're not going anytime soon. I'll take care of you."

"Don't you worry. I have no intention of dying right away."

"Good. I'll let you get some rest now..."

Marie lifted her head from the pillow with surprising vigor.

"You need to keep the deeds somewhere safe. They're the only way we can win our case if ever anyone goes moving the boundary markers."

"That would be stealing!"

"The war's turning everything upside down."

"What does that mean?"

"When your grandfather died, people took advantage of me being a woman, and confused and overwhelmed on top of it... But that didn't last long, believe you me."

Joseph clenched his fists.

"Valette," he said.

"His father."

"Well, he'd better not..."

Marie placed one hand on the box.

"It's only proof that counts in this life, and from now on, it's on you to take care of it."

Marie didn't linger.

Joseph was with her when she died. For a time, he would wonder at what precise moment she had stopped living, what had truly happened inside her body to bring about death. Had it occurred when her eyes rolled back into their sockets, or when her head dropped to one side and her grip on the sheets loosened? When? Did death drag on or was it as sudden as it seemed? Where exactly had it taken hold of his grandmother? How does a life end for good? Was there a rule on passing to the other side, the same protocol for everybody? And after that, where and how did the soul escape? What remained on the inside and on the outside? Joseph had seen animals die, plenty even, and never wondered such questions, but this was his first time seeing a human being die.

Mathilde dressed the deceased in a long black dress, found in her wardrobe, which no one had ever seen her wear. Leonard came to take measurements, and he wasn't wearing his hat. He was quick about his task, then returned home to build Marie a beautiful beech coffin. It took him two days to saw the planks, artfully level and assemble them, without a single nail, simply using mortise and tenon joints. He transported the finished coffin to Chantegril in his wagon, and this time he was wearing his hat and sporting a close shave. Joseph helped him unload the casket, which they carried to Marie's bedroom and set on two trestles. They stayed like that awhile, two silent figures, eyes downcast and carefully avoiding the body lying on the bed, attempting to summon some pleasant memory, a consolatory abstraction of the reason for their presence.

They were still reflecting when Mathilde entered, a coarse white sheet in her hands, which she swiftly placed along the bottom of the casket. Then Leonard approached the body, eyes on Joseph: "You'll have to help me put her inside... That okay?" The boy didn't respond. He hesitated, then nodded, agreeing to touch the stiff, turgid body and help Leonard lift it into the coffin. A terrible smell spread through the room's stale air. Marie's dress, hands, and waxen face blended into the light color of the wood. Overcome by emotion and disgust, Joseph rushed out, unable to bear the sight of what his grandmother had become—a reeking goatskin filled with death.

Leonard stayed in the room a few more minutes, turning his worn hat in his hands, as if he were working a valve. Mathilde stayed too. Without looking up, the old man said he would dig the hole, seeing as there was no more gravedigger. Mathilde knew perfectly well that wasn't the real reason, just the only admittable one. He added that he would come fetch the coffin and take it to the cemetery whenever she wanted. Then he left without waiting for a response.

There were a few visits and then, no one. The night before the casket was closed, Joseph hid the letters and wedding ring beneath a fold in Marie's dress, unbeknownst to anyone else, per his grandmother's wishes, as well as a miniature seated cat he had carved himself. He had read in a history book, in elementary school, that in ancient times, people used to place ritual objects in graves to ease the passage of the dead to the other world. A paltry gift for the woman who had made his life as gentle as possible. He wondered who would be proud of him now, and who would tell him as much, light shining in their eyes.

One week after his resounding victory against the canine from hell, Saint-Paul's priest left for the front to combat evil and accompany soldiers' souls. No one replaced him. The priest in Salers came to Chantegril to bless Marie's body, then left just as quickly. Once he was gone, Mathilde asked Leonard to close the casket, but the stench quickly seeped through the wood. The grave was the only relief left.

It rained nonstop for two days in a row, making it impossible to lay the body in the ground. A violent rain that saturated the earth. Every drop that fell was a voice joining the chorus, or else a tiny, ephemeral dancer gleefully leaping across a liquid stage before rejoining the corps, water streaming in a monastic whisper—a Passion, according to Marie. Once the rain finally stopped, Leonard dug the grave, then returned to the Lary farm for the casket, loaded it into his cart with Joseph's help, and transported the body to the cemetery.

Marie hadn't wanted a mass. Her final wish. Twenty-three people attended the funeral. They each threw a handful of dirt on the coffin placed on two planks set above the grave, faces contrite. Leonard, Joseph, and two other men lowered the casket into the hole using straps, which they then brought up, and the cemetery emptied.

Joseph insisted on staying to help Leonard fill the grave. A magpie landed on the tall stone cross near the cemetery wall, shaking its tail each time it chattered. A talkative creature, gesticulating in its two-toned habit and appearing to mock the gingerly efforts of the two poor sods before it, their hesitation to bury what needed to be buried.

The old man spat into his hands. He tossed in a first shovelful of dirt, which smashed onto the wood with a boom, then another. Joseph followed suit. The magpie flew away. It sounded as if it had a tiny bell in its throat, which it was vainly trying to get rid of through flight. Leonard straightened up, staring at the adjoining grave.

"I dug that hole too. For your grandfather," he said.

Joseph paused. He looked at the grave, the lopsided stone engraved with his family name, partially whittled away by bad weather and covered in lichen.

"I didn't know."

"It was important to me."

"Did you know him well?"

"Couldn't have known him any better, I reckon."

Leonard rested the shovel handle against one shoulder, rubbed his hand on his pants, and adjusted his hat.

"We were born two days apart, him first. My mother didn't have enough milk to feed me, and your great-grandmother had too much. So you could say that, from that moment on, we became almost like brothers . . . Surely milk counts as much as blood sometimes."

The old man looked amused. He lifted his head, as if he

was talking to the man buried beneath the strip of earth beside him: "We used to chase animals through these woods. Skirts, too... And we certainly got ourselves into plenty of trouble, didn't we."

Leonard paused. Joseph didn't dare break the silence.

"Once, we gathered rabbit droppings from a hutch, hard black ones, not the soft green turds. We soaked them in honey, let them dry, and then put them in little bags that we sold at the square in town, on fair day, like they were candies."

Leonard smiled and Joseph let himself be carried along by that nostalgic smile.

"Folks didn't realize they were rabbit turds?" asked the boy.

"Well, they did after they tasted them. For that matter, we never did it again," said Leonard, massaging his lower back.

"I didn't realize you were so close."

"After we met our wives, it wasn't the same anymore, but we still saw each other from time to time. Thing is, no one could take away what we lived through as babies... It was always inside of us."

Leonard's face darkened. In the distance, particles of light were going out gradually in the humid air, as if a patient ghost were blowing them out one by one.

"We think that if we keep things to ourselves, they'll be faithful to us," continued Leonard.

"And that's not the case?"

"Forcing a thing to stay on the inside isn't always for the best."

For a moment, Joseph allowed Leonard his inner musings, before impatiently adding, "Grandmother never talked about him."

"Probably too painful for her to remember. When a patch of forest burns down, the scorched trees never flower again, they just stay there like black scarecrows. But the vegetation grows back around them, hiding them even, unless someone makes a point of cutting it back so the trees remain visible . . . Your grandmother wanted to let the vegetation grow wild."

Joseph let the mental image sink in.

"I'd have liked to know him," he said.

"He'd have liked to know you too, for sure."

"What was he like?"

"Your father was his spitting image."

Thoughts raced through Joseph's mind, colliding with nowhere to land.

"It took courage, you know, when he died, for your grandmother to run that farm with a ten-year-old on her hands," said Leonard.

"I never heard her complain."

"That wasn't her style."

The boy ran his hand over the nape of his neck.

"I don't understand why she didn't want a mass," he said.

"If you ask me, she still believed in the good Lord but not so much in priests."

Joseph thought for a second, then asked, "Do you think there's something that comes after? A place where we can find each other when we're dead, I mean."

Leonard stretched out his arm, as if he was about to bow.

"'Course I do. Look around you. If this many people are taking care of their dead, there must be some truth to all of it."

"Yeah, but God hasn't exactly been kind to my family."

"You can't blame him. He has plenty to handle in the afterlife. As for this life, it's on us to figure out."

"Even so. He might not recognize me."

"Who? God?"

Joseph pointed to the grave.

"Grandfather. He might not recognize me, seeing how we never met, and I might not recognize him either."

"You've got plenty of time to figure it out. And anyways, he's been watching you since you were born, I'd bet my bottom dollar on it..."

Leonard paused, a conspiratorial gleam in his eyes.

"You've never felt like you're being observed even when there's nobody around?"

Joseph's face brightened, as though something had just clicked into place.

"I have!"

"Well, there's no mystery. That's his soul watching over you."

"So the departed watch over the living but can't interfere to keep bad things from happening to us... Is that what you're saying?"

"I reckon they're just like everyone else. Some do their jobs better than others. But you've got nothing to worry about... Go on, we need to finish before nightfall. Looks like the rain's coming back."

Leonard spat in his hands and resumed shoveling. Joseph watched him for a moment, then said, "That man who you used to see at Pierres Blanches... it was him, wasn't it?"

Leonard's face didn't betray the slightest emotion, as if he'd been expecting the question. Then he turned to Joseph and smiled. The sky looked like a gigantic expanse of mold surrounding the moon and the evening star.

"It's good you're here," he said.

"So it was him."

"You know, I don't think a man truly becomes a man until he's dug a grave."

"But I didn't dig this one."

Leonard had stopped smiling.

"I'm counting on you," he said.

Joseph bit his tongue. He gathered a few handfuls of heavy dirt, removed the impurities, then began to mold a large, compact ball. Leonard watched him but didn't ask any questions. They eventually filled in the whole grave, in silence, then flattened and smoothed its surface with the back side of the shovel. They paid their respects one final time, leaning on their shovel handles, as if that was the only thing keeping them upright. Then they left.

That night, even though his grandmother hadn't eaten with his mother and him for some time, Joseph couldn't take his eyes off the spot that had been hers for so many years, in the fraying straw chair. It was as though a gust of wind had blown her away, her life robbed of all meaning from the moment she had left the table, as though all that had remained was for her to close her eyes, relieved at last to slip into the eternal night. Joseph felt an enormous emptiness inside of him, and that void prompted him to burst into tears as his powerless mother looked on. He stood, paused for a second, then left the room; his mother didn't move.

Before going to bed, Joseph went into the small square bedroom that his mother had aired out, though the smell of death, old age, and, more faintly, dried roses and waxed wood lingered. The trestles on which the coffin had rested were still there. It was as if the walls, furniture, and floor had absorbed time, done away with, as it were, by the mystery of death.

Standing still on the disjointed slats of wood, in a room full of memories, Joseph thought about what Leonard had said about benevolent souls and began to pray fervently that his grandmother would find the path that would lead her to the man she had spent so much of her life missing. A man who, when he disappeared in a flash of lightning, had broken every clock, taking with him the secret of time. A wave of melancholy swept over Joseph. He thought about death and how it sealed man's fate, about this sacred space—a cemetery of clocks—and, in that moment, his memories rattling the broken hands. In his mind, fate was simply a matter of observing a frozen clock hand, nothing more. So he folded the two trestles and slid them into the wardrobe, thinking he would put them in the shed the next day. Then he walked out of the room, the box in his hands.

Joseph crossed the courtyard carrying a wooden pail filled with whey, bits of stale bread floating on the surface. The Saint-Paul church bell rang out through the valley, clanging against the frozen silence of the previous night. He stopped to count the eight chimes, then continued walking in line with the stable, the bucket bumping against his leg with each step. Soon he reached a small door with rickety hinges, which he opened to the sound of loud snorting. He made his way down a dark, narrow corridor, passed a recess on his right that was used to boil potatoes and sunchokes for the animals in a large pot over a wood fire. All the way in the back, there was a long, dented trough built from scrap iron and covered with a heavy wooden plank. Joseph emptied the bucket into the trough, then removed the bolt on the hog gate, which he opened to allow access to the meager meal, and slid the bolt back into a wrought-iron ring. Two hogs rushed out and began fighting for the food, splattering the sow and making the door panel shudder with their frenetic head movements. They guzzled down the whey, after which Joseph guided them back behind the gate and locked it. The trough was as clean as if it had been scrubbed with steel wool. The boy observed the pigs reclining against each other like two flea-ridden sphinxes, satiated, barely snorting now. Then he turned around and headed toward the exit, empty bucket in hand. A motionless form emerged in the weak light in the doorway. He recognized it immediately and rushed over, concerned.

"What are you doing here?" he said in a hushed voice.

"I wanted to offer my condolences," replied Anna.

"Thank you. That's very kind."

She tilted her head slightly to the side.

"I would have liked to come to the funeral," she said.

"It's fine. Let's not stay here. Follow me," he said.

Once outside, Joseph cast a worried glance at the house and set the bucket on the ground. Anna followed him to a rear courtyard where the odd patch of withered grass made the tired rutted ground even sadder. There was a pile of stones against the wall, which Joseph's father had never removed, that dated from the time he had dug the new cellar, for convenience. Beyond a wire fence from which tiny sleeping snails hung like floats on a fishing net, a frosted meadow stretched out in the distance. Farther still lay the forest spreading across the desolate summit of Puy Violent.

Anna grabbed Joseph's hands. He stiffened at her touch and glanced around. She tightened her grip.

"You're afraid your mother will see us?" she said.

"It's not that..."

"Would you rather I go?"

Anna took one step back but didn't release Joseph's hands. He clumsily pulled her back to him.

"Stay," he said.

"I don't want to put you in a difficult situation, but I couldn't wait, you see."

"Forget it. You did the right thing."

Joseph's gaze slipped past the girl's shoulders, drifting into the meadow, where a pair of wagtails were walking like mechanical little toys from dropping to dropping in search of worms.

"You miss her," she said.

"Now there's just two of us left on the farm."

"I'm so sorry..."

"I don't know when all this is gonna end," said Joseph, as if he hadn't heard Anna, then he paused, before continuing.

"She didn't have an easy life, you know."

"Your grandfather!"

Joseph looked rattled.

"I'm guessing whoever told you the story was smiling at the time," he said.

Anna said nothing. She emptied her face of all compassion, as though she'd been able to materialize the couple in a single image, and she didn't want to share that image with anyone.

"Now I'm realizing that I didn't know her as well as I thought," said Joseph.

"What makes you think that?"

"People have an easier time talking about the dead than the living, though I don't blame them. We're all doing our best, I suppose."

Joseph turned toward the back façade of the house. There was ivy climbing the wall. Its leaves resembled web-footed bird prints leading to the roof. He pointed at a window with open shutters.

"That was her bedroom. She died in her bed... I was there."

Anna stared at the window, squinting. She narrowed her field of vision to the glass opening with a slightly rounded lintel overhead, which reminded her of the top of a hopscotch board.

"It's what she wanted," she said without the slightest hesitation.

"It's what everyone wants, I reckon."

Joseph looked away from the window and back to the girl.

"Would you like to sit for a bit?" he said.

"What about your mother?"

"Don't worry about her."

Joseph led Anna to the pile of rocks. They sat, she a little higher than him. In the distance, the mountain formed a springboard that might have propelled a few thin clouds into the sky.

"Are your grandparents still around?" he asked.

"The ones from here died a long time ago. I don't even know when."

"I meant the other side of the family."

Anna picked up a pebble and trapped it in her hand.

"They don't get along with my parents," she said.

"And with you?"

"I don't see them anymore."

"That's idiotic," said Joseph, offended.

Anna sighed, dropped the pebble, and rubbed her palm.

"They're blinded by prejudice," she said.

"Prejudice?"

"They never accepted that my mother married my father, given his background. They believe they belong to a superior class."

"Well, that's not your fault."

"To them, I'm the product of an illegitimate union," she said sadly.

"If they knew you, they'd change their minds, that's for sure."

"Well, they certainly don't want to."

"I'm sure it'll get better with time."

"I don't think so, but it's fine."

Anna blew at a lock of hair, which flew off her forehead, momentarily suspended by the swell of air, then landed in the same spot.

"I didn't come so we could talk about me," she said.

"Yeah, well, I like it when you do..."

Mathilde suddenly appeared at the corner of the house. When she saw the two adolescents, she froze, stick-straight, staring hard at Joseph and ignoring the girl. He stood immediately, giving his mother a panicked look. Mathilde's mouth slumped into a disdainful pout.

"Leonard will be here soon with his cart to gather the sunchokes, and you haven't even cut off the leaves yet, like I asked you," she said coldly.

"I'll go right now."

"You should be there already."

"It's fine."

"Remember to take the baskets."

Anna stood next and walked over to Mathilde.

"Hello, ma'am," she said in a friendly voice.

Mathilde looked the girl over from head to toe, as if she had only just noticed the presence of an unknown weed amid the rest. Her eyes resembled two small pieces of lava ready to spurt out of sockets hollowed by fatigue. Then she turned around and walked away.

"Don't pay her any mind," said Joseph once his mother was gone.

Anna forced a smile.

"No harm done."

"She has a lot on her plate."

"I understand. I won't delay you. We'll see each other later."

"All right."

"Tomorrow, same place as usual?"

"I'll figure out a way."

As she crossed the courtyard, Anna felt a gaze weighing on her shoulders and she turned back toward the house. A figure was observing her from the window, making no effort to hide.

Joseph didn't take the risk of lying down, for fear of falling asleep. Seated on his bed, he waited for the lights in the house to go out. His mother hadn't made the slightest allusion to the girl as they picked sunchokes, nor while they ate supper. They had made a concerted effort to avoid eye contact.

He hadn't sculpted anything in several weeks. With the house calm again, he felt an irrepressible need to, even after an exhausting day of work. He crept out his window and made his way to the unused cellar, the dry earth he'd gathered at the cemetery in his pocket.

The clay animals set on planks were giving a performance, their shadows etching dark shapes onto the light gray stones. A centipede was perched atop a pantry hung from a ceiling beam; it was fearful but curious, half its body suspended in the air, between the light and the darkness, wiggling the long translucent feet that gave it a resemblance to one of the little combs Joseph's grandmother had sometimes used to tame the hair behind his ears. The insect hesitated a few more seconds, palpating the air with its slender antennae, then retreated to the shadows, feet rippling in fluid succession like a row of falling dominos.

Joseph thought back to his very first carving. A simple snail shell. An exercise devoid of complexity, he had thought at the time. But the attempt had confronted him with the vast space that lay between the seeming simplicity of what he saw and the complexity of capturing it faithfully with his hands. Try as he did, he found no solution. He hadn't spent enough time observing and studying his subject, and so the shell ended up looking like a crooked mountain encircled by a winding path, and not much like the marvel of architecture that had been his model. All the same, the experience had served, as would, in his mind, every other. He had retained the lesson. And the shell remained in his workshop to remind him that facility was always an illusion, and that it took a great deal of work to obtain a result of which you weren't ashamed.

This evening, Joseph's initial plan was to pay homage to his grandmother using the cemetery clay he had collected. He thought he could. He twisted some wire strands into the approximate shape of a cross. Extremely focused, he began kneading the clay, in total control of his fingers, seeking the perfect inspiration. But then instinct took over, guiding his movements with startling precision to build something whose proportions had nothing to do with those of an old woman worn down by life's ordeals, but with glimpsed, elusive, or imagined forms, which he faithfully re-created.

Hours passed. The candle flame flickered on a mound of waxy droppings. Joseph, a fever burning inside him, continued to sculpt in the waning light. Nothing mattered more than the final form, the all-consuming representation of the desire clinging to his hands and soul.

Even when the flame was reduced to a thin scrap of cloth teased by a draft, before it drowned in liquid wax, Joseph continued to mold the curves of the statue in the dark, like a blind man guided by an obsessional memory, and, without the slightest effort, he passed from homage to grace.

"Keep your voice down."

"Is this okay?"

"Shh."

"I think you're handsome."

"Don't be silly . . ."

"I wish I could kiss you."

"We can't here. You know that."

"Don't you want to?"

"I just told you. We can't."

"That's not what I asked."

"Yes."

"Say it again."

"Yes, I want to."

"Follow me. I know a spot."

"I don't know . . ."

"There's no point fighting it."

"All right, but . . ."

"And then I won't ask again. Promise."

"Never?"

"Never."

"Don't sound like you."

"You can't go against what's meant to be."

That week, the torrential rain returned. In the kitchen, at a corner of the table, Anna was immersed in a large book. Occasionally, she would look up and mentally recite what she had just read, before continuing to read. Irene was standing at the other end of the table, peeling vegetables for lunch, discreetly observing the girl. Once she'd completed her task, she set her knife on the well-worn surface, dried her hands on a fold of her dress, and walked over to Anna, planting herself in front of the girl, shaking her head like someone who feels sorry for a person, not for some tragic event endured, but more so to spare them a pointless and avoidable fate.

"What's that?" said Irene, scornfully nodding at the book.

"A history book," replied Anna without looking up.

"You bring a lot of books in your suitcases, huh?"

"I need to continue my education."

"Ask me, you loaded yourself up for nothing."

Anna tore her eyes away from the book, staring at Irene's stained hands and dress, and stopping there.

"I don't want to fall too far behind, for later. One's studies are important."

"Later," Irene repeated pensively.

She paused, wrapped her hands over the back of a chair, then continued:

"If I can give you one piece of advice, it's to think about the after once it's here... The present is all that matters now."

"You still need to prepare for the future."

Irene stiffened so hard her limbs became one with the burnished chair frame. For a moment, her lips trembled, then she managed to speak.

"The future, you say... Thinking 'bout it just means you're preparing for things that might never happen."

"I have plans."

"I suppose it's not my job to give you an education, but if it was, I'd tell you that you'll learn everything you need to know for living round here by watching and by listening. You'll find nothing in your books that'll serve you. Read, write, and count. That's what's important. The rest just clutters your head for nothing."

"Mother says that learning elevates us."

Irene snickered.

"I don't think she and I are talking about the same learning."

A door opened. Helen walked into the room, her gait sensual, floating almost, an envelope in her hand. Irene returned to the other end of the table without a word. Helen reflexively kissed her daughter on the forehead, not paying much attention to what she was doing. She looked out the window at the rain falling on the other side, then sighed and slid the letter into her pocket. She sat down across from Anna, picked up the book, and skimmed it distractedly. Something darted through her weary eyes, as though, from the moment she entered the room, she had been unsuccessfully trying to shake loose some unpleasant vision, or chase away a shadow. She set the book back down in front of her daughter and placed her hands on the table with a resigned air.

"Very good, darling," she said.

Irene hadn't missed a beat, her annoyance betrayed by her agitated movements.

"You'll need to go feed the chickens. I don't have time, you know," she said.

"It's raining," responded Helen in a neutral voice.

"Animals still eat."

Anna shut her book.

"I'll go," she said.

Helen smiled sadly. In her eyes, something like rain streaming somewhere inside of her.

"Keep doing your reading. That's more important," she said.

"I just finished, actually."

"Leave it. I'll go."

Then Helen went out into the rain without bothering to grab a jacket.

Irene's movements became fluid again. After a while, she said to the girl, "Go tell your uncle it's time to eat."

"Why didn't you ask my mother to before she went out?"

A snide smile spread across Irene's face.

"It wasn't ready yet," she said.

"Where is he?"

"Not here, that's for sure... And be quick about it. You'll need to set the table too."

Anna put the book away in her room, then threw on a coat and went looking for Valette. Outside, the dark sky descended to the trees. Rain was falling on the roof tiles and whistling as it flowed to the ground. The girl checked the shed, no one there, then headed to the barn. The top panel of the door was ajar. She stuck her head inside, her hair dripping onto the smooth stones. Once her eyes adjusted to the darkness, she made out Valette sitting on a pile of hay, petting the dog with his mutilated hand, a bottle in the other. She could see his lips moving but couldn't hear what he was saying, or even tell if he was truly speaking, against the deafening roar of the storm. She loudly pulled back the door panel to announce her presence. Valette swiveled toward the entrance as he violently kicked away the dog. The animal ran to the barn entrance, prompting his owner to spit at him, and placed his paws on the door, ears flattened against his thin, bony head, and began to lick Anna's hands with his brown-spotted tongue, shuddering with contentment.

"What do you want," yelled Valette.

"Irene sent me to fetch you to come eat."

"No one taught you to knock before you walk in?"

"It's the rain..."

"Ha! Or maybe you were spying on me?"

"I wasn't, I swear."

Eager to leave, Anna opened the door to let the dog out, then closed it. Before she could walk away, Valette leapt up and rushed toward her, tottering.

"Wait!" he shouted.

Anna turned around as if electrocuted. Valette was now standing less than a foot away from her, bottle in hand, and his eyes gleamed with all the alcohol he'd consumed.

"What?" she asked weakly.

Valette looked down at his crushed hand.

"I disgust you, don't I?" he said.

The girl tensed, hesitant to respond. Rain was streaming down her face, but she didn't feel it.

"No," she said after a few seconds.

"I'd feel the same, if I were you."

Anna said nothing and he flung his hand up. "Go on, clear off, now."

The girl obeyed immediately. She'd taken a few steps when she heard the bottle shatter against the door and Valette's voice crash into a curtain of rain.

The rain had stopped. Water was dripping from the rooftops in scattered chimes, like an orchestra tuning instruments.

Valette, unable to sleep, had risen at dawn and gone to the barn to feed the animals. The calf didn't appear to want to suckle its mother. She was a young female, around two months old, and kept lifting and dropping her head, shaking the string that formed a slipknot around her neck. Valette watched her for a moment, then leaned over, grabbed the cow's teat with one fist, and squirted thick milk onto the soiled straw.

"What exactly is the problem?"

Valette tugged on the rope and pressed the calf's muzzle into the swollen udder. The cow lifted a back hoof and dropped it back to the ground with a clatter. "Plenty of nice fresh milk in there. What more do you need?" Strangled by the rope, the calf balked, keeping her mouth closed. She managed a violent head thrust, which almost knocked Valette backward.

"Oh, so you wanna play smart, you little shit . . . Well, you ain't gonna win!" said Valette, further tightening the slipknot. The calf bellowed in pain, shaking her head to try to gain some slack. Valette straightened up, untied the rope end attached to the mother's chain, and pulled on it to make the animal move, but she froze, legs locked. Valette cursed. He walked around the animal, placed himself behind her, still holding the rope, grabbed her tail, and twisted, as if he wanted to break it. The calf's legs loosened like springs. She reared, trotted to the back of the barn like a small wild stallion, skidding on the slippery stones, and took refuge in a narrow, filthy stall. The animal now trapped, Valette lifted one knee and placed it on the calf's rump to immobilize her, then grabbed a plank leaning against the wall and slid it into the notches. The recalcitrant animal was now blocked from the knees up, unable to advance or retreat.

Valette made his way to the door and discreetly glanced outside. Satisfied, he locked it from the inside, then returned to the restrained calf. She thrashed around, seeing Valette out of a single eye, brown iris growing and then shrinking against the white, as if the calf wanted to make a run for it. If there had been a stray nail sticking out of the partition, good chance she would have tried to enucleate herself just to escape the sight of the man.

Towering over the animal's silky back, Valette relished her panic for a moment, then placed a rope muzzle on her mouth and began to vigorously scratch her around the tail, which she instinctively raised, like a geyser, revealing a pale vulva and a crust-covered anus. Valette moved to the side as the calf begin to piss and shit a puddle of yellow mud. As the animal finished expelling urine that gleamed in the meager light coming from the arrow slits on the walls, Valette glanced at the cows lying down, peacefully ruminating and paying no mind to him or anything other than the slow reflux of mushed grass, honing their digestion.

"That's it... Let's see if you prefer another kind of suckling, eh," he said, moving to the back of the stall again. Without hesitation, he undid his belt and his zipper and wriggled his pants and trunks down to his ankles. "Don't move. Now you'll understand who's master here!"

In the morning, Joseph went to the river to pull out the ten lines he had placed in the water the previous night, before it got too cold. He pulled out the first one—no luck—removed the scraps of worm, grabbed a cork from his pocket, stuck the hook into it, rolled the fishing line around it, then stuffed the whole thing in his jacket. As he was pulling up the third line, he felt gentle resistance and assumed he'd caught a root. Then he saw a large eel thrashing as it approached the surface, though the creature was so exhausted from struggling all night that it didn't have the strength to fight long. Once it was on the bank, Joseph stunned it with a branch before removing the hook. A precaution he'd taken ever since his father had told him the story of a fisherman found suffocated to death along the river, an eel tail hanging out of his mouth and whipping the ground like a long black demonic tongue. The unlucky fisherman had had poor vision, and as he leaned closer to spot the hook, the fish went into his mouth, probably hoping to find an escape route. The man undoubtedly tried to pull the creature out, but everyone knows there's nothing more slippery than an eel. Panic surely did the rest.

Joseph cut down a willow tree branch, making sure there was an offshoot at one end, and sharpened the other with his knife. He pierced the eel around the gills and slid down the limp, slithery body as far as it would go. Later that morning, he caught a second eel, which joined the first on the gaff.

After he had removed all his lines, he returned home. He opened the front door, slipped inside, and walked through the gloom to the fireplace, where his mother was on her knees in front of a waning fire. He raised the branch with the dangling eels and proudly said, "Look!"

Mathilde was sorting vegetable seeds into small metal boxes lined up on the floor. She placed her hands on her thighs as if to rise, but didn't.

"I'll take care of them," she said, ignoring her son's enthusiasm.

"No, don't stop. I'll do the eels."

"Fine," she said, leaning forward.

"What are you doing?"

"Making an inventory of the seeds that your grandmother collected over the years."

With his free hand, Joseph grabbed a chopping block hanging from a strap nailed into a beam, then set it on the table and placed the eels on top.

"We'll have to take care of the garden, come spring," said Mathilde in a lifeless voice.

"I helped Grandmother lots of times."

"She'd always pay attention to the moon, I think."

"Leonard must know about that kind of stuff."

"Well, we'll learn too."

Joseph looked over at his mother, who grabbed another box. He recognized his grandmother's pretty handwriting on the label, remembering how she used to store fruits after the harvest and let them dry so she could collect the seeds.

Mathilde opened the small packet in the box. She flicked out the seeds, then looked inside dubiously.

"What did that girl want with you?" she asked.

Joseph knew the question was coming sooner or later but hadn't been expecting it just then.

"She's Valette's niece," he said, as though defending himself for doing something wrong.

"I know who she is."

"She wanted to give me her condolences for Grandmother."

"Didn't look like that's all she wanted."

Joseph took his knife out of his pocket. He sliced off the eel's head, then cut the flesh down to the tip of the tail.

"What are you trying to say?" he asked through clenched jaws.

"You don't give your condolences to just anyone . . . and you don't sneak around to do it."

"She wasn't sneaking around."

Mathilde flung the packet into the box.

"Don't lie to me, please," she said.

"I knew you wouldn't take kindly to me seeing her."

"We don't have time for fun and games."

Joseph sliced the carved eel into pieces that resembled tiny beef roasts, then placed the knife on the block, looking defiantly at his mother.

"What exactly are you reproaching me for?"

"No need to raise your voice. I'm not reproaching you for anything. I'm just saying to watch out."

"Watch out for what?"

"Valette hates us."

"I couldn't care less about your ancient history. Anna doesn't even know."

"Well, she will soon enough . . . Let me remind you that that 'ancient history,' as you call it, concerns you too."

Joseph grabbed the knife handle.

"What do you want me to do?"

"I already told you . . ."

"I should stop seeing her, is that it?"

"It's for your own good."

"I'm not a kid anymore."

"You still have plenty to learn. If Valette finds out you two are seeing each other, I doubt he'll approve."

"Let me handle Valette."

Mathilde's face reddened. "Don't give me that nonsense!"

"It's not nonsense. Let him come at me . . ."

"Valette is a mad dog. I think the man was born with rage inside of him . . . never satisfied with what he has," she snapped.

"Okay, but we're not talking about a piece of land here."

"I'm not sure he makes the distinction."

"Why can't you just tell me honestly that it's you who's bothered?"

Mathilde tilted backward, as though she'd been shoved by an invisible mass. She sighed and regained her balance.

"She's not from around here," she said.

"So that's what it is . . ."

"One day, she'll leave."

Joseph gave his mother a fierce stare. Her words, which sounded more like a desire than a prediction, nonetheless reminded him how temporary and futile his actions were, a reminder completely at odds with the unshakable feeling in his gut.

"I'll let you finish up," he said coldly.

"You've never spoken to me like this before."

"Shouldn't have pushed me."

"If your father was here..."

Joseph swiftly pulled the knife out of the block, dried it on his pants, folded it, and placed it in his pocket.

"Well, he's not here, so don't go making him say something he can't," he retorted.

Then Joseph left the room without giving his mother a chance to find a way to continue the conversation, abandoning her to a silence she didn't know what to do with, amid the gleaming boxes.

Joseph was angry at his mother. He understood that she'd spoken up to protect him, but he didn't need protecting. All he wanted was to be left alone and, more than that, to be spared lectures intended to stifle his sentimental impulses.

That night, he dreamt of his father. One of the rare and exceedingly precious moments spent in his company, during which Joseph had felt as if he had temporarily left boyhood behind.

On that June morning, his mother had still been asleep when his father woke him at dawn. He spread cottage cheese on a slice of rye bread and handed it to his son, telling him to eat all of it, that he'd need his strength.

"Where are we going?" asked the boy, who was all of eight.

"You'll see. Now eat!" replied his father, placing two fists on the table and dramatically furrowing his brows.

They made their way to the shed, the son close behind the father. Victor tossed several rags into an old grain sack, grabbed a small axe, and handed everything to his son without explanation. Then he brought down a ladder attached to the wall with two pitons and wove one arm between the middle rungs to balance the weight on his shoulder. He bounced the ladder a few times to find the best position as Joseph watched, swallowing his burning questions.

Outside, swifts whirled through the sky like kites whose trajectories were interrupted by sudden gusts of wind, and their plaintive cries rang out like nails against glass. The smell of rotting humus and mushrooms announced the forest. A springtime blend of fertile promises. As he walked, Victor cast frequent amused glances at his son to ensure the mystery was still in effect.

They crossed a wet patch that had been planted with poplars three years earlier in an attempt to dry it out and was the only spot where the vegetation grew in straight lines. Joseph had helped with the planting, holding the scion upright as his father poured dirt over the roots. He remembered that they'd often find trapped toads and Rennet apples in the three predug holes, and, once, four young polecats that the boy had thought were adorable. That was the only tree they hadn't planted that day. Victor returned later to deal with the occupants in his own way, unbeknownst to his son. He hadn't buried the polecats alive but had taken them out one by one by sliding a slipknot around their necks and hung them from the low branch of an oak tree. It took a long time for them to stop wriggling, which was when Victor tossed their small, limp bodies into the hole and planted the tree. The poplars had more than doubled in height since.

"Please tell me what we're doing..." Joseph begged again.

His father stopped and solemnly leaned over his son. The spaces between the ladder rungs looked to the boy like a series of framed photographs. Frozen visions of nature.

"We're going bird hunting," he said, as if he was confiding the greatest of secrets to his son.

"Did you say 'bird'?"

Victor continued walking. Joseph hurried to catch up with him, looking up and no longer watching where he put his feet.

"Which birds?" he asked.

"Starlings."

Joseph stumbled and caught himself on a dried stump.

"With a ladder and an axe?"

"And rags," said Victor, forcing himself to appear serious.

"Don't you think you ought to have brought your rifle?"

"There's things that work better than a rifle," he said, tapping one of the ladder rails.

They advanced deeper into the forest. Victor slowed down, weaving around tree boles and inspecting the ground like a dog tracking a scent.

"What are you looking for?"

Victor placed one finger over his lips.

"Stop making noise. This is serious business we're on," he said.

After a moment, Victor stopped at a stretch of dirt measuring roughly three square feet and blanketed with fresh guano. He looked up, following the trunk of a dying oak tree almost entirely stripped of bark and leaves. He placed the ladder beneath a soup can–sized hole, then kneeled before his son.

"They must be in there. Pass me the axe and a rag," he said quietly. "And watch what I'm doing carefully."

Victor climbed the rungs up to the hole, pressed his ear against the trunk, then looked down with a wink at Joseph. Next, he plugged the hole with the rag and began to gently tap on the trunk below, using the axe handle to find the part that sounded the hollowest. He switched to the blade, chipping away wood with small, precise movements. A few times, a pair of starlings flitted around Victor, then flew away in silence. When he deemed the opening sufficiently large, Victor hung the axe from one of the rungs and slipped his hand inside. From below, Victor heard panicked chirrups. His father already had his hand out, holding a small, thrashing bird. He briskly slammed its head against a ladder railing and dropped it to the ground at his son's feet. Victor pulled out five more baby starlings, killing them the same way. He meticulously felt inside the opening one last time to make sure there were no more nestlings, then leaned over to shout: "What are you waiting for? Put them in the bag!"

Joseph looked at the small, limp bodies lying at the bottom of the ladder, noting their featherless necks, but they didn't strike him as hapless victims. On the contrary, the child gazed with unwavering admiration at the father who had just shared this precious secret with him.

Victor grabbed the rag, let it fall. He descended the rungs with the edge of the axe resting on his forearm. Once on solid ground, he leaned against the ladder and pointed to the bag with the axe handle.

"One more week and they'd have already left the nest. It would have been a mighty shame, seeing how plump they are. When they're young like this, serve 'em with potatoes and they're as good as thrush or blackbirds."

They ransacked three other nests. For the last one, Victor prepped the operation, plugged the hole he'd chipped out, then told Joseph it was his turn, that he had observed enough. He descended the ladder and had his son climb up, standing behind to reassure him. Once Joseph reached the top, Victor pulled lightly on the rag dangling like a tongue outside a mouth.

"Go on!" he said before completely removing the rag.

The boy, frightened, nonetheless slipped one hand inside the hole and immediately withdrew it when he felt balls of warm feathers quivering beneath his fingers. Victor grabbed his wrist and guided his hand back into the opening, without letting go.

"They're not gonna eat you," he said.

Stifling his fear and, more importantly, eager to earn his father's pride, Joseph closed his hand around one swallow and brought it into the light. The bird wriggled, making shrill peeps with its tiny yellow-ringed beak.

"Hold it tight so it doesn't get away!" said Victor, who was watching closely, still holding his son's wrist. In one brusque motion, he helped him knock the bird out against the blood-stained railing. After two or three blows, the swallow went quiet, and its muscles slumped in death. Joseph dropped it without watching it fall.

"Go on, do the rest. You're on your own now," said Victor.

Joseph woke up the instant his father said those words: "You're on your own now..." and couldn't fall back asleep.

Leonard, hoary with age, hunching over to climb the ravine to the path, was a pitiful sight in his pants that were too big and his jacket that was too long. Clothing mended by Lucie countless times, which he wouldn't have gotten rid of for anything in the world. Their smell evoked wool grease and cold tobacco, or rather their remnants in his olfactory memory, now more accustomed to another odor: a blend of damp wood and dried meat. Old bark.

His silhouette was framed by the light, except for the upper half of his face, which was so neatly excluded as to give the impression of a hat floating in the air or, more precisely, above the shadow that ran from ear to ear, skipping over the deep wrinkles in his forehead, a match to the folds of his jacket. Elbows bent because he was carrying an offering in a basket he'd woven himself from spring willow branches. Making his way along the path lined with large brambles laden with blackberries that resembled small bloodied craws, his gait unsteady, his walking stick with the carved pommel stuck in his belt for the way back, lifting the back of his jacket like a musketeer's rapier. Focused and proud to deliver this gift, not victuals or incense or precious stones, simply a weaned puppy, autonomous enough to be given away.

The season of dandelions disintegrating into cottony fibers carried by a mountain wind reduced to a delicate breeze, carried by the silence. The season of campion flowers wilting into minuscule, sickly goiters. Leonard emerged from the path and paused, looking at the buildings before him, struck by a perfectly identifiable feeling. The violent return of a past that he was able to escape only after having met someone new. He placed his hand on the puppy's head, which he could have crushed like a walnut if he'd wanted.

"You'll be well treated here," he said.

He approached the house and walked inside without knocking, as naturally as someone coming home.

Mathilde was alone. Leonard set the basket on the table, lifted the puppy with one hand, and set it on the ground. The animal trembled, as if it needed to relearn how to walk in this unknown, and for now hostile, environment, henceforth deprived of its mother's help. Mathilde kneeled down in front of the dog.

"He's handsome," she said coldly.

"Joseph picked him."

"I hope he's ready to work."

"He'll do what you tell him, I reckon."

The puppy buried its head in the folds of Mathilde's dress, making a suckling noise, and she began to pet it.

"I'll take good care of it," she said.

"I have no doubt about that. Joseph will too."

Mathilde's hand paused on the dog's coat, eyes adrift.

"He'll have to find time for it," she said.

"And you don't think he will?"

"He has plenty on his mind at the moment."

Leonard hesitated. "Boy isn't short on work, that's for sure."

"That's not what I meant."

"Ah!"

Mathilde gave Leonard a wearied look.

"You know, don't you?" she asked.

"Know what?"

"The girl."

Leonard placed his hand on the basket handle, swallowed a sigh the best he could, and waited a moment.

"She doesn't seem to make him unhappy," he said.

"Sounds like you know exactly what I'm talking about, then."

"'Bout your son."

Mathilde rose, leaving the puppy on the ground. She pressed her hands onto the table, staring at Leonard. Small bones protruded above her chest like crossties.

"If it was only about him!"

"What bothers you exactly?"

"I don't want him to go through any more pain than he already has . . . and me neither, for that matter."

"That the only reason?"

"I like you, Leo, and I'm grateful for everything you've done, but this is my son we're talking about, and I plan to raise him as I see fit."

Leonard nodded.

"I wasn't trying to suggest otherwise," he said.

"What then?"

"I'm not the best-placed person when it comes to talking about these things, I know that, but at some point, you need to remember the things we discovered when we were young, without anyone teaching us," said Leonard calmly.

"So your advice is to let it happen... is that what I'm meant to understand?"

"I'm not giving you any advice. I think that deep down you know perfectly well that nobody can do nothing to stop how that boy's feeling, and that's not an easy thing for you to accept."

Mathilde glanced at the puppy, who had crawled over to her leg, sniffing around, then back at Leonard, hoping he would hand her a key he didn't have, a key that would be in her sole possession, a key to open a door that would force her to not become the worst kind of mother for a son. She closed her eyes, and for a second, her face looked completely bare, then she leaned down and took the dog in her arms, as if she were rocking a small child.

"We'll take good care of you," she said.

Leonard smiled as he watched the puppy already falling asleep and no longer trembling.

"He'll keep drinking milk for a while, no doubt, but now that he's got some little teeth, he can try other things," he said.

Leonard picked up the basket and left. Mathilde went to the doorstep without rousing the dog sleeping in her arms and watched the old man. He paused in the courtyard, slid his walking stick through the basket handle, and placed it over his shoulders, his charge now hanging down his back. Forearms over the stick, he walked away like a crucified man free to kick up dust.

Summer turned to winter, the two seasons separated by the sparsest of autumns, a hyphen tinged ocher and red. The cold set in, snow began to fall in early November, and everyone huddled inside their homes, for that was all there was left to do—submit and wait for it to pass.

Fragile humans.

Who endured the snow ridden with tracks, like a large map drawn in invisible ink.

Endured the milder spells, like lies they had stopped believing.

Endured the storms and the frost.

Endured the pale light and the additional cost of every effort, far greater than in summer.

Endured the hordes of northern winds, taking shelter around large wood fires, patiently waiting for the angry sky to calm and the days to finally grow longer.

Endured, like the first humans deep in their cave, creating words in their heads and writing their history with extinguished embers, gazing at one another in search of a good reason to be here, seeking an answer to the only questions that matter: Why do I exist in this world, and who could have allowed such folly?

Endured the silence and solitude of winter's prison.

Endured the wisdom of the world, hoping for the lakes and ponds to thaw.

Endured a shared fate, molded by resignation.

Fragile humans, who endured the way they'd always endured.

Endured the war, too, through letters stained with mud and in the long silences stretching out in the church they entered unwillingly but unfailingly.

Fragile humans. Who endured.

Standing in the shaky glow of a storm lantern, they observed the slick newborn calf, a bewildered diver emerging from maternal waters, lost within this huge universe slowly being revealed.

"Thanks for the help," said Leonard.

"Don't mention it," responded Joseph.

"You can get going if you want. I'll handle the rest."

Joseph turned toward Leonard.

"I have something I want to ask you."

"I'm listening."

"The other day, Mother and I were wondering how we ought to take the moon into account, for the garden."

Leonard raised one hand, eyes still on the calf, as if he were requesting quiet from an audience.

"It's not complicated. If you want nice vegetables, you need to sow when the moon's waning, and plant when it's full."

"That's it?"

"That's it."

"So the moon's that powerful, in your opinion?"

The old man pretended to take offense. "I read in the almanac that the moon can make an ocean flow one way and then the other, so I suppose it likes to amuse itself by playing with anything that holds water. Like us, for that matter."

Joseph thought for a few seconds. The calf tried to get up on its feet only to collapse pitifully, prompting the mother to come to its aid, pushing it with her muzzle.

"So how come it doesn't affect ponds?" he said.

"It only looks after natural things, and a pond ain't natural... Take your hair, for example. Don't get the crazy idea of cutting it during a new moon, unless you want it to grow back twice as fast."

"Noted."

Leonard took off his hat and massaged his head, on which a handful of soft white hairs were dueling.

"Though I stopped worrying about that myself some time ago," he said with a smile.

"And you'll help us with that too?"

"'Course I'll help you."

Silence set in, interrupted only by the distinct sound of animals breathing and their heavy movements.

"Thank God we have you," said Joseph.

"I thought you were going to thank me again," said Leonard with a wink.

"You see, I learned my lesson... Anyways, I'm off."

"As you should be. Meanwhile, I'm gonna help this youngin eat his first meal."

When he entered the house, Joseph was surprised to find his mother sitting at the table, lost in thought.

"Are you all right?" he asked.

Mathilde pointed to an unsealed envelope on the kitchen table, as though it was something completely ordinary, as though she was forcing herself to present it as such.

"Your father wrote us," she said.

Joseph stared at the envelope for a moment, then sat at the table beside his mother. He touched the paper and immediately withdrew his hand.

"You don't want to read it?" she said.

He had read all the previous ones, but this one paralyzed him more than the others. Reading the words wasn't what scared him. What was troubling him the most in this instant was the thought of finding his father's shadow cast onto the yellowing paper and then watching it disappear before his eyes.

"That's not it," he said.

She pushed the envelope in his direction without looking at it, eyes on him.

"Everything's fine," she said.

"Then I'd rather you tell me what it says."

"You sure?'

"Yes."

Mathilde drew back the letter.

"There's advice on how to take care of the farm, the best way to sow the lowlands come spring. He says not to keep more animals than we can feed next winter, and to sell the others to make a bit of money."

"If he's already thinking about next winter, it means he doesn't intend to come back anytime soon."

"It's not up to him."

"You already know the letter by heart...Sounds like there's nothing but advice?"

Mathilde paused before answering. She pushed her chair back and stood. Her arms, which hadn't stopped fidgeting the whole time she'd been talking, returned to her sides, her hands dangling like two fins out of water.

"He's thinking about us, too," she said.

"Did you write him about Grandmother?"

"I don't think adding to his pain will help anything."

"You'll have to someday."

"Yes, someday..."

She remained standing, forcing herself to weigh each word, starching them with a feigned assurance that didn't fool Joseph. Since the beginning of the conversation, he hadn't taken his eyes off the envelope with its sloping handwriting of print capital letters that wove around the words like fence wire. Everything written in his father's hand, beneath the French army stamp with the sower woman tossing handfuls of invisible seeds onto the faded paper. So his father was alive.

"Does he say anything about himself in the letter?" he asked.

"He says winter there is no worse than here."

"If he says so."

Mathilde's mouth widened, more grimace than smile, as if she was trying to let something slip through her teeth as slowly as possible.

"No reason to doubt him," she said.

Joseph turned his head to the side and looked up at his mother, a shape of indiscriminately connected cloth and flesh.

"Maybe he doesn't want us to worry," he said.

Stretched upright as if tied to a post, Mathilde began to sway imperceptibly, like a frail tree shoot trifled by a draft of air, then placed one hand on the back of the chair.

"We'll do everything your father says," she added in a firm voice.

Joseph stood as well and cast a final glance at the letter.

"I'm gonna go fetch some wood."

"There's enough for now. You just got back."

Joseph pretended not to hear. He walked to the door, opened it, turned around, eyes downcast, hesitated on the threshold, as though he no longer intended to confront the cold and the night, then left.

Mathilde ran her hands down her wool jacket to dry her palms, facing the door that had just opened and closed, alone now with Victor's letter on the table, with his words, with his voice in the words, with all of him, or rather an image of him writing the words.

Joseph had gone up to bed. Mathilde wrapped a clean cloth around the leaven she'd just prepared and placed it in a wicker basket. She fed the fire for the night, then removed the small bits of dough stuck between her fingers, which she tossed into the dancing flames illuminating her face from below, continuously changing her expression. A majestic, tragic vision: a figure lost in contemplation of the fire and, beyond it, the tortured forms skipping along the cast-iron fireback as the dry wood whistled and cracked like a joint being subjected to great physical exertion.

Wind rushed down the chimney stack, dispersing the orange flames and flinging a few embers onto the floor, like fireworks at the end of their performance. Mathilde took a step back and let the glowing coal particles go out in a dramatic, smoky sizzle.

A wave of emotion swelled inside her. She briefly tried to restrain it, then gave in. She knew Victor wouldn't be coming back soon. The thoughts that then entered her mind would have certainly earned her, in a different era, a public burning in the town square by the Holy Inquisition. The price of her painful freedom as a woman was a war, and at the same time, this new freedom felt like the expression of a survival instinct, a private way of bearing the responsibilities that had fallen upon her. Nothing more, for catering to her mind was a luxury she couldn't allow herself.

It wasn't a matter of erasing Victor from her life to protect herself from the worst, but simply to replace him for a time, to muffle as best she could the faint guilt of no longer being in thrall to a man. She was a draft horse now, toiling all day in the fields to then, come evening, retreat to the farm to toil some more: a mother-mare and no longer a wife. This transformation had begun the moment she authoritatively sat at the head of the table, beside the bread drawer from which she had taken a rye loaf that she clumsily cut into thick slices, which she distributed without a word from anyone. And this with the certainty that everything she undertook from then on would circumvent the destiny her father had planted between her mother's thighs.

Of course, despondency sometimes accompanied fatigue, but the urgency of mornings on the farm always prevailed, temporarily sweeping away her doubts before the wild expanse of a day to be lived, for that was just it—living without yielding to the desires of a man, or to his silences rotten with selfishness. She had two distinct bodies: the woman and the queen. A union she wasn't yet ready to celebrate.

Of course, the absence and uncertainty were unbearable. Of course, tears would continue to burst from her eyes without warning. But for now, she was facing this enormous challenge head-on, and nothing would ever be the same again, whether Victor came back or not.

They met in the hay barn. Anna climbed the haystack first, mounting the first few rungs of the wooden ladder as Joseph watched without moving. She stopped halfway, then leaned over to ask what he was waiting for in a hushed voice, with a smile that showed exactly how well she knew him. He climbed up next, head down.

Crouched in the hay face-to-face, ears pricked for noises, they looked at each other with great solemnity, the kind you might see in the eyes of someone apologizing for something they haven't done yet but which they know they will sooner or later, unable to control themselves. Nor really wanting to. Using only two fingers, Anna pulled back her hair in a way Joseph had never seen any another girl do. It wasn't a gesture meant to fill the time, but an instinctive and graceful movement, with something primitive about it. A movement made in absolute silence, which felt like torture to the boy. A silence he had to fill to keep from drowning in it.

"Do you remember the first time we went fishing?" he asked in a shaky voice.

"Of course I remember."

"You gave me a present that day."

She said nothing and released her hair, which fell back onto her forehead, then tilted her head slightly in a question.

"It's your turn to close your eyes," he said, and as he spoke it sounded as if tiny creatures were skipping along his vocal cords.

Anna placed her hands on her thighs, then closed her eyes. In her blindness, she detected the rustling of cloth and, beneath that, Joseph's labored breathing. Then he took her hand, turned it over very gently, palm in the air, and placed an object in it. Still holding her hand.

"You can open your eyes now," he said.

She didn't, instead running her fingers over the smooth, misshapen object to guess what it was.

"Thank you."

"You haven't seen it yet."

Anna opened her eyes. A small clay squirrel was sitting in the hollow of her hand, its delicate, totemic body adorned with a bushy tail. The girl's gaze went from the statue to Joseph, then back again.

"It's beautiful."

"I made it for you."

Joseph had remembered a walk they'd taken together through the woods, and Anna's amazement at seeing two squirrels, one ginger, the other brown, chasing each other from tree to tree. Entranced by the sight of two creatures wholly adapted to their aerial environment, she had said that she had never seen something so majestic in her whole life. Even when one of the squirrels lost its balance, a branch would appear as if by magic in its path. Anna had grabbed Joseph's hand, with the same hand in which the statue was now sitting. They had stayed like that, in harmony with nature, too, until the squirrels disappeared in a flurry of tiny barks, and then all that remained was a ballet of shadows and lights conducted by the wind swirling through the leaves.

"What must it be like up there?" she had said, head tilted toward the treetops.

That day, Joseph had promised himself he would sculpt one of the forest creatures, secretly hoping that his gift would capture the squirrels' dizzying falls and acrobatic maneuvers, but also the feel of their joined hands.

She ran another finger over the statue, studying it from every angle, and soon noticed Joseph's initials engraved under the back feet.

"Leo thinks you should leave a mark on something you've made," said Joseph, almost in apology.

"You showed this to Leonard?"

"Of course not."

"This isn't the first thing you've sculpted?"

"No. I haven't had much time lately, but I needed to make this."

"You're very talented, Joseph."

"You don't have to say that."

"I know I don't have to, but it's true. You must have an artist's soul."

"No one taught me, except for Leo, who gives me advice sometimes. I don't know where it comes from. Once I get started, nothing else matters. It's like I'm building a memory that I don't want to lose, so I can keep every emotion I felt in a certain moment inside of me."

Anna placed her hand on Joseph's cheek.

"Do you remember?" he asked.

"You've sculpted the most beautiful memory there is."

Joseph let the silence sit, then pressed Anna's hands together, as though he wanted to teach her the perfect way to pray.

"It'll never be as good as the memory you created for me," he said.

"Are there other things you'd like to sculpt... things you haven't created a memory for yet?"

It seemed to Joseph that the space between what Anna was saying aloud, and everything she wasn't, was shrinking, down to him and her.

"Plenty," he said, looking up at her.

They kissed, shyly at first, then passionately, kissing more than just lips, venturing into the hazy depths of the mysteries of the body, their breathing absorbed by the pockets of silence around them, which also assuaged their fears.

Anna broke the kiss. She leaned backward, trying to make eye contact, and then, because Joseph was skirting her gaze, ran her hands across his face. They remained in that position for a moment, then kneeled, like two penitents exhausted by a long walk, or preparing for one. Joseph didn't know what to do next, a bud protected by a layer of ice. But Anna knew.

"Look at me," she said.

Joseph lifted his head, gaze averted at first, as though asking for forgiveness. Soon she was the only thing he could see. Not just see, but feel, in his blood even. In her eyes, the unmistakable wild determination of a woman, any trace of childhood gone.

"Talk to me," she said.

"I can't," he whispered.

She pulled her dress off over her head. Golden stalks went flying, a few landing in her hair. The smell of milk clung to the air. Joseph noticed the soft hairs under her arms. She lay down. Until that moment, Anna's body, to Joseph, had been a distant planet observed through the eye of a telescope, and here, on this bed of hay, she was asking him to travel through space, across light and sound, to discover her eggshell-colored breasts with their hard brown nipples, her taut stomach, and the cotton border upon which his conquering and troubled gaze was now lingering.

"Come here," she said.

"You're so beautiful."

"I want to feel your skin against mine."

He took off his sweater, then lay down on his back beside her. They were connected at the hip and shoulder, like conjoined twins.

"Help me," he begged.

She rolled onto her side, then kept rolling. Her hair swept over Joseph's face as she straddled him. They were no longer linked by a patch or two of skin, but joined in the flesh, a spell cast, their desires come to life.

"Look at me," she said again.

Joseph's face was still hidden behind a curtain of hair, and his mind was a horse racing around a track beneath a big top.

"I can't do anything but look at you," he said.

"Do you want to?"

Joseph wished he could tell her that he felt as if he'd been waiting for this moment his whole life without knowing it, but all he could utter was a paltry "Yes." She kissed him then, before he could close his eyes. She guided him and he followed, obeying his desires, surprised to find he already knew this part of her, in a way, and of himself.

They made love for the first time in the trampled hay, between the tall stone walls, beneath the dusty spiderwebs and the warped beams, lulled by the music of chains, hooves, and animal breaths coming from the stable. They made love in the kind of peace that frees a person's soul, as if to seal one secret in another, as if to become the secret itself and not merely its bearers.

Mathilde was staring intently at Joseph.

"Are you even listening?" she asked.

He lifted his head, nodding, more puppet than boy.

"What?"

"That's what I thought. You didn't hear a word I said."

"Did too."

"Is something wrong?"

"Everything's fine."

"Doesn't look like it."

Joseph grabbed a slice of bread, which he tore into small pieces and tossed in his soup.

Mathilde watched him, taken aback.

"There wasn't enough for you?" she said.

"There was," Joseph answered mechanically.

"So why are you adding more on top of what I put in?"

"I'm not."

"You don't even realize what you're doing... You know you can talk to me, if something's worrying you?"

Joseph picked up his spoon emphatically.

"I'm not worried, I told you," he said, barely concealing the annoyance in his voice.

“It sure looks like you’re thinking about something that’s keeping you from thinking about anything else . . .” she said snidely.

“Nonsense.”

Mathilde slid her arms onto the table, on either side of her plate, until her elbows reached the edge.

“I didn’t see you this afternoon. Where were you?”

“I . . . at Leonard’s.”

“You were there awhile.”

“I cleared the snow from his yard.”

“Ah, so that’s it. Now I understand why you’re so tired.”

Mathilde watched her son silently, then began to eat, looking down each time she filled her spoon, then back at him as she swallowed, not like a mother looking at her child, but more as if she were sitting across from a stranger who’d gotten lost and found himself at her table, letting his soup get cold. The kind of stranger about whom she’d have liked to know everything without having to ask.

“You’ll do what I said?” she said.

“I always do what you say.”

“I need it tomorrow morning, all right?”

“Tomorrow.”

“So . . . where will you go, tomorrow?” Mathilde asked wearily.

Joseph was using the back of his spoon to push down bits of bread floating on the surface of his soup, which then disappeared before resurfacing like tiny soiled sponges.

“Exactly what I was saying! You’re not listening. I need you to get flour, salt, sugar, and coffee from the shop. You gonna remember this time?”

“Don’t worry.”

"That's not what has me worried."

"I'm fine, promise."

"Sure you are."

Joseph placed his spoon against the rim of his bowl.

"I think I'll go up to bed now," he said.

"You barely ate."

"It's fine, I'll have more of an appetite tomorrow. I must have caught cold."

Joseph rose, smiling sadly. Mathilde gave him a hard look, no longer as if she were dealing with a stranger, but with her own son again, hoping he would admit something she already knew, the kind of thing that could keep a man from eating. That terrible disease capable of distracting a person from more useful thoughts.

"By the way, Leonard stopped by this afternoon, looking for you!"

Outside, snow was dispersing the moonlight whose rays crept into the house through cracks in the shutters, freezing everything within a thick halo. Joseph lay on his bed, recalling every touch, every caress that had led him and Anna to that final embrace. Opening or closing his eyes changed nothing; muddled as they were, the memories remained. He felt older, thanks to this girl encountered at a bend in the road, when he'd been expecting nothing. Expected nothing, simply wanted to continue to decipher the mystery, a changed person now, with still more to discover. A vast realm, and the kind of overwhelming joy that is so rarely satisfied. That moment when he would have given anything to read her thoughts, know what she desired, the moment he discovered her body, knowing nothing more than what his meager instinct dictated to him, an instinct he had previously suppressed, however poorly, to restrain his clumsy body. This time, he had let it lead him.

When she takes his hand to guide it, tame it in a way, as he watches her, desperately searching for some imperfection to which to cling. The certainty of never having witnessed such perfect beauty, even though he doesn't have the slightest basis for comparison, apart from his mother's body. But that's his mother. He wonders how two female bodies can be so similar and yet so different. Feels lost before Anna's beauty, in no way worthy, inhibited by his body, by his desire, unable to connect the two in a redeeming form of adoration.

When she reassures him, then goes quiet, her body at work. Her muffled cries rising, wavering between surprise and pain. Him, attentive to the girl's moans, to the tensions in her body that stir his blood. Him, keeping the pain at bay, asking if she wants him to stop. Her, begging him to continue, excluding him from the pain, as illicit pleasure swells within his belly, him, unable to fully enjoy it, wanting to ease the pain he's causing, to take it back, and her, wishing for nothing more than the blood to finally flow, to bring the great liberating endeavor to a close.

When the blood comes, Anna abruptly relaxes, her head flung back like a dead woman's, which isn't far from the truth—the death of something as tenuous as the link between night and day, the time necessary to waken a body with a single powerful cry.

Joseph withdraws, relieves her of his body's weight. Terror fills his eyes when he sees blood mixed with his sperm on her pale thighs. Anna sits up, then takes Joseph's tortured face in her hands, tells him it's nothing, it's normal, he's the first, the only one. The blood is normal. Joseph isn't listening. Simply responds that he's sorry, that he didn't mean to. She leans closer to Joseph's distraught face, blows on his lips as she tells him it didn't hurt, the opposite, she's a woman now, thanks to him. Then she kisses him, and in that long kiss, there is the purest of feelings, there is an offer of sincerity and gratitude. Another word to invent. Their lips still intertwined, she begins to cry. Joseph feels her tears trickle down his skin. Anna stops him from ending the kiss, she holds back her tears, which are the only answer she can provide to all the questions he's dying to ask.

For a long time, they lie in the hay, in its sweet, smoky smell, holding hands, silent and still like two stones oblivious to the world's onward march. Fall asleep in a gleam of light.

As he walked, Joseph wondered which of his ancestors had had the mad idea of settling on this mountain, if they had truly considered the efforts it would entail, if it had been a choice and, if so, to what degree that choice had once been tolerable.

He adjusted his heavy wool scarf and lowered his cap visor to defend himself from the snowflakes that all seemed to be converging on his eyes. He had a burlap bag tucked under one arm, his hands deep in his pockets to better protect them from the cold.

The snow had blanketed the ground so thoroughly that it was impossible to tell whether a path still existed. The surrounding trees were listless, as if the snow had buried not only the vegetation but also the very soul of the forest. A crow emerged cawing, excommunicated by the mist, then landed on a branch, shook its wings, and went silent, casting a baleful look at the figure slowly making its way below.

Joseph thought about his father, who had sent a letter in which he said not to worry, that he was holding up, that he would hold up. If his mother believed those reassuring words, why shouldn't he believe them too? What reason did he have not to? And then there was Anna, with whom he was conquering new territories, their weapons caresses and blessed words. Anna, who brought him grace and the coup de grace at the same time, on a bed of new hay, Anna, who had brought him to the farthest reaches, where nothing remains but also where all hope lies.

When he reached town, Joseph noticed that the main path had recently been cleared. Piles of snow sat in muddy puddles, sacrificed in vain. At the same moment, the mail coach was departing, drawn with great difficulty by an emaciated horse with glazed eyes, visibly not far from death's door. Joseph moved aside to let the wagon pass, nodded to the driver bundled up in a blanket, and received a weary glance in return.

Joseph watched the mail coach drive away, its wheels squelching across the melted snow, spitting out droplets in their wake like the sour saliva of chewing tobacco. He spared a thought to the poor mailman, pondering his responsibility—to ferry news in both directions—and whether his fate was more or less enviable than being sent to the front. Wondered if the man even questioned that responsibility, or if, to him, it was the same as transporting and delivering sacks of grain, and loading new ones, wherever he stopped. Once the noise faded, and the back of the wagon was reduced to a matchbox wobbling along the road, Joseph turned away from the coach and the questions it raised and crossed the abandoned marketplace to the grocer's shop.

He tapped his boots on the swept doorstep and brushed the snow off his coat and cap. Then he entered, prompting a tiny bell above the door to ring.

Inside, the grocer was arranging canned goods on sparsely furnished shelves. She jotted something in a notebook, turned around with a mumbled hello. Abandoned her task with a sigh, walked over to the counter and then behind it by lifting a plank on two noisy hinges. Seeing her so frail in body but her motions so heavy, Joseph told himself that perhaps one of the letters carried by the mail coach had been for her, that maybe she had already read it, or that she was waiting.

"Awful weather," she said.

"And it doesn't look like it'll be easing up anytime soon."

"Been falling for four days, if I'm not mistaken."

"Who's counting anymore..."

"Brave of you to venture out."

Joseph set his bag on the counter.

"Had to."

"How are you all doing up there?"

"We're holding up."

The grocer cast a worried glance over Joseph's shoulder, as though someone or something unexpected had appeared in her field of vision, then she made the sign of a cross.

"Well, it's the least we can do for those boys fighting for our country... hold up, I mean," she said, as if she was talking to the apparition.

"I suppose," said Joseph, looking at his bag.

"Still, who knows what'll become of us, if prices keep rising. Soon no one'll have the means to buy what I'm selling, and I won't be able to stock up. It's hard already."

"There'll always be enough to survive on, round here."

The grocer shrugged.

"Survive, huh."

"Not easy for everyone, from what you're telling me."

She continued, paying no mind to Joseph's remark. "I heard that in the city, there's lines in front of the shops and bakeries, that they've even had to hand out ration cards so everyone has something to eat."

"Really?!"

The grocer stared at her customer. Joseph could make out tiny veins around the ash gray irises of her eyes, ready to burst, like rootlets engorged with blood.

"What would you like?" she said, as if waking from a bad dream.

"Three pounds of sugar, four of salt, and ten of flour . . . and some coffee too, if you still have any."

"Over there, on the shelf. Help yourself, I'll get the rest."

Joseph grabbed four packets of coffee and set them on the counter. The grocer weighed the sugar, salt, and flour on a Roberval scale, then bagged the ingredients separately. When she was done, Joseph placed the items in his bag while she calculated the price out loud. Joseph paid, and the grocer quickly placed the money in a drawer, counted out his change, still out loud, then pulled out the corresponding coins arranged by value in small compartments, holding them in one hand and placing the other on his bag.

"I heard something else that you and your mother ought to know," she said in a serious tone.

"What?" asked Joseph, intrigued.

"Apparently they'll be going by the farms to commandeer animals, seeing how the soldiers don't have enough to eat."

She'd said "they" as though referring to evil spirits ready to cast their spells.

"How do you know?" asked Joseph.

"The fellow driving the mail coach told me."

"And he was sure?"

"He seemed well informed."

The grocer opened her hand and handed him the change. Joseph verified the calculation in his head, placed the coins in his pocket, and grabbed the bag.

"You hear anything, on your end?" she said.

"No," said Joseph impulsively.

"Letters take longer to arrive in the winter," she said distractedly.

"Must do."

The grocer flipped back the plank and resumed what she'd been doing.

"Tell your mother hello for me," she said, rereading what she'd written in her notebook.

"Sure will."

It was even colder when Joseph came out of the grocer's. The sky appeared to have added another layer of frozen misery atop the silent houses. The snowfall had slowed, but the flakes were larger, swirling like immaculate ashes ripped from a distant blaze.

Joseph left town, returned to the snow-covered path that coiled through the forest, periodically shifting his bag from shoulder to shoulder. He stopped halfway to catch his breath but the chill was so biting that he immediately set off again. A wren accompanied him for a bit, crossing the path one way then another, landing on twigs swept free of snow by the wind, puffing up its ruffled plumes and shaking its short tail, as though it wanted to brighten Joseph's tiring walk, or, more simply, make him understand, in its shrill tongue, that they were no different, and that surviving, as it happened, was everyone's lot.

Seated in a chair, Mathilde folded the grain bag she'd just mended, then placed it on the floor on a pile of ones she'd already patched, and which resembled buckwheat pancakes prepared in advance for a large wake.

Joseph entered. He placed the provisions on the table, took off his frost-stiffened jacket and cap, and hung them on the back of a chair that he brought closer to the fire. He removed his soaked shoes, which he tipped sideways, mouths toward the hearth, and approached the flames, whose warmth was already nibbling at his feet, his hands, and the skin on his face. When the bites grew too strong, he took a step back, grimacing, and then approached again to acclimate his body to the fire.

"Was there coffee?" asked Mathilde without looking up.

"I got four packets, like you asked."

"I'll make some. You're frozen stiff."

Mathilde stood to unpack the supplies, putting the flour in the flour bin and the salt, sugar, and coffee in the cupboard. Joseph turned toward his mother, hands hovering over the fire.

"The grocer said they're gonna come round to the farms looking for animals to feed the soldiers," he said.

Mathilde paused before the open cupboard doors, then shut them, both hands glued to the wood.

"Every farm?"

"I dunno. Can't imagine they'll be making exceptions."

"Just what we needed," she said, shaking her head.

"But do they have the right?"

Mathilde walked slowly back to the table, holding a packet of coffee. She carefully opened it, selected a bean, placed it in the palm of her hand, and rolled it around with one finger.

"*The best interests of the nation*... that's what it said in your father's military book. It won't be up to us..."

"As long as it keeps snowing, they won't risk coming all the way up here."

"It won't snow forever."

Joseph closed his eyes to gather his thoughts.

"I could lead the heifers up to the shepherd's hut, hide them there, and bring them back down once the army's gone... What do you think?"

A slanted wrinkle formed and deepened between Mathilde's eyes.

"Those boys do need to eat," she said coldly.

Joseph cast a quick glance at his mother engulfed by the pale light, body hunched over the coffee packet, unmoving apart from the periodic blinking of her eyelids irritated by the whiffs of smoke coming from the chimney.

"'Course they do, but there'll still be the old cows... We need to survive, too," he said.

"And what will the animals eat up there?"

"I'll bring 'em hay with Leonard's mule.'

"We don't know when they'll come."

Mathilde walked to the chimney and grabbed the mill from the shelf on the lintel, beside an assortment of empty boxes.

"So . . . what you do you think?"

She brushed past him.

"Boys need to eat," she repeated quietly.

She filled the mill with coffee beans, sat down, set it between her thighs, and began to jerkily turn the crank as though an inexperienced puppeteer was operating her arm with invisible strings.

It was December twenty-fourth, and certainly the saddest day of the year. That night, there was no midnight mass in Saint-Paul, nor on Christmas Day. On all the farms, by then transformed into archipelagos surrounded by treacherous snow, people prayed for the coming of resuscitated Christ while begging the Father not to forget his other children scattered across hostile lands, and to protect those here from all manner of evil.

There were few words in the evenings. Mathilde listed the tasks for the following day, never beyond. Joseph found her stronger with each passing day, harder too, never complaining, able to make firm decisions, to compensate the best she could for Victor's absence, ever cautious not to leave any traces he might not recognize upon his return.

Mathilde filled two bowls with a bottomless bread and onion soup. She pushed one bowl down the table, in front of her son, as she'd been doing for every meal since his grandmother's death. She blew three times on the steaming liquid.

"You still seeing that girl?" she asked gently.

Joseph contemplated the soup for a few moments, the greasy droplets clinging to the bread.

"I don't feel like talking about it," he finally said.

"So that means you're still seeing her."

Joseph grabbed his spoon and pressed the handle into the table as if he wanted to cut through the solid wood.

"I shouldn't leave the farm anymore, is that it?"

Mathilde remained calm. She blew again on her steaming soup, and her mouth widened into a smile.

"You remind me of your father. He could never give up on something once he'd gotten it into his head."

"What exactly are you trying to say?" asked Joseph, losing patience.

The smile faded.

"You grew up but I didn't want to see it."

She paused to swallow. "In my eyes, you'll always be the boy you used to be, but you're not really him anymore..."

"And?"

"I better get used to it."

Joseph set his spoon back on the table, observing his mother with visible surprise in his eyes.

"I don't want to hurt anyone," he said.

"I know. But if I can figure it out, so can other people. You need to understand that too."

"Other people?"

She gripped the edge of her bowl and brought it to her lips, pausing.

"Watch out for Valette," she said, then took a sip.

"I will, promise."

They dined in silence. After they finished their soup, they rubbed cloves of garlic on crusts of bread, which they then caked in lard and ate, still in silence.

Later, Mathilde placed her elbows on the table, placed her face in her hands, closed her eyes, and dozed off. Joseph, who didn't dare move for fear of waking her, listened to her steady breathing, hypnotized by the sight of this hardworking woman transformed back into a mother, long hair hanging down, into which disappeared the tips of her fingers thickened by labor and covered with callouses. Long black hair that she continued to brush each morning after washing up, leaning to one side and then the other, pulling on a tortoiseshell comb to painfully get rid of any knots. He found her beautiful as she slept, in a cloak of silence and exhaustion. He would always find her beautiful, he thought. In a moment like this, he wished he could command the wooden floor to hush, the clock pendulum to halt its haunting to-and-fro, the logs in the fireplace to burn in silence, and his father to finally reappear in the doorway, to find them peaceful and confident. Waiting for her to wake up. The father and the son, waiting together.

Joseph traveled back to his childhood, when his mother used to lie beside him in the fetal position to help him fall asleep, one arm wrapped around his frail body, as though she wanted to tuck him back inside her belly. He would fight sleep. Felt protected and invincible. Feared she would pull away from him, that he would see her hazy figure tiptoe out of the bedroom, without turning around. The child would find himself in near-total darkness, pushing away baleful shadows and imaginary presences. One night, on the eve of his fifth birthday, Joseph had given a name to one particular shadow, which would envelop him sooner or later and steal him from the world of the living, a shadow out of all proportion that even now, some nights, he found himself fighting. Despite the whispers of an owl on the windowsill, reassuring the child that a mother's body was also made to protect her son from forces of evil.

He stretched one hand across the table to slap away the enemy shadow beginning to swell in the room. Mathilde woke without a start. She rubbed her eyes and observed her son leaning over the scratched oak surface.

"You're not in bed yet?" she said.

"I didn't want to wake you."

"You shouldn't have let me fall asleep."

"You needed it . . ."

"Off with you, now!"

Joseph placed his glass and utensils in his bowl.

"I'll help you," he said.

"Off with you, I said. Won't take me long."

He stood and set his bowl in a tin basin.

"Mother?"

"Yes," she said in a tired voice.

"Thank you."

Mathilde ran her hand through her hair, holding it against the back of her neck, as if she wanted to hide something, or rather, prevent that thing from escaping.

"If ever your father's not back by spring, we'll have to do as he said and most likely ask for some help with the heavy labor."

"We'll get it done. Plus there's Leonard."

"Leonard's old."

"I'll work hard as a man, and even two if I have to."

"I don't doubt it."

This was the first time Joseph had heard his mother talk of the future in such a way, and it filled him with infinite sadness, though he didn't seek to understand why.

"I love it when you cup my face with your hands."
"You're not afraid anymore?"
"I can't stop thinking about you."
"And that's a good thing?"
"Nothing better. But we still have to be careful."
"Don't worry. No one will come looking for us here."
"Wait, what are you doing?"
"Follow my lead . . ."
"Easier said than done."
"I want to feel your skin against mine."
"I don't know if I'm ready."
"Trust me."
"That's not it."
"Nothing else matters. Come on."
"All right."
"That's good."
"So help me."

It was the second day of February.

Valette was in the shed. He grabbed a string and, with his good hand and his teeth, made a loop into which he slid his right thumb and squeezed as hard as he could. Then he placed his thumb and the palm of his bad hand against the handle of a ten-pound mallet on the table. Irene watched him, restraining a rise of pity betrayed by tiny jolts in her arm muscles.

"You want some help?"

Valette gave her a dirty look.

"Far as I can tell, I still got two arms."

He tied the string to the mallet, then around his hand a few times, and finally made a double knot. He let the mallet hang from the end of his arm, shaking to make sure it held, before looking back at his wife with all the contempt his eyes could hold.

"Go fetch the girl," he said.

"This ain't her job..."

"Don't argue and do as I say! You'll be of more use here getting everything ready. And besides, her mother for sure doesn't have the guts."

Irene hesitated, gaze fierce and suspicious, now stripped of any pity, set on this man it would have been so much easier to hate.

"You still here?" he said.

Irene opened the door and an icy wind swept into the room. She left, leaving the door open. Valette watched her walk away and a smile stretched across his face, like a large notch in dry wood.

Several minutes later, the three women entered, one after the other. A sad procession. Valette was waiting on the other side of the table, which obscured his ballasted hand; only the top of the mallet handle was visible, a splint of sorts on his wrist. He gave Anna a hard look, then, with his chin, pointed at an enamel basin and a knife with a thin blade on the table.

"Grab that and follow me," he said.

Seeing that Irene didn't move, Helen automatically stepped forward.

"Not you."

Valette didn't give Helen time to reply, curling his lips into a sinister sneer:

"Don't fret, she'll be fine. I'll make sure of it."

Helen's weary gaze went from Valette to her daughter.

"No more time to waste," he said.

Valette nudged the basin forward. The knife blade squealed against the enamel. The girl had no idea what was expected of her, but she grabbed the basin with one hand, the knife with the other, and followed Valette outside.

They walked past the farm buildings, their feet sinking into the snow with each step, with a sound like fabric ripping. Once they reached the north gable, they stopped at a door made of mismatched planks of wood. Slurry was seeping from the gnawed-away bottom, behind which could be heard the hoarse grunting of a satiated animal. The snow was just beginning to coat a large wooden board on two wheels parked in front of the door, a sort of wheelbarrow without handles and equipped with an axle tree, which Valette had rolled all the way there. At the front of the board, he had set up a mechanism consisting of a double grid of ropes that ended in two hooks, and which could be stretched or narrowed using a set of pulleys activated by a metal crank. He used his foot to tilt the board back like a guillotine platform prepared to receive the guilty.

Valette unbolted the door, lifted the handle, and turned to Anna.

"Close behind me and when I tell you to come in, you enter straightaway with all that."

Anna looked at Valette blankly.

"Not too complicated for you? You got it?"

"Yes."

"Good. I'm gonna go teach him a lesson."

Valette entered the pigsty and Anna immediately closed the door. The hog began sniffing Valette's pant legs, twitching the ears set close to its forehead like a ludicrous visor, its glistening snout covered with crud and battle scars. Valette grabbed an armful of fresh hay from a crate set on a beam hanging over the trough and spread it in one corner. He then guided the animal to the fresh litter, talking to it like an old friend. Valette slowly raised the mallet above the hog's head, waited for it to stop moving, then dealt a single blow to the forehead. The animal's front legs gave way; it tried to get back up, sliding for a moment, before a second blow knocked it definitively to the ground.

"Open!" yelled Valette.

Anna obeyed immediately. She saw the hog lying in the straw, still twitching, attempting to scream but not succeeding, head covered with bits of brain mixed with broken bone and blood. Valette stepped in front of the animal and extended his arm with the hanging mallet.

"Cut the string!"

Anna hesitated. She extended the knife, but paused, unsure how to proceed without hurting Valette.

"Hurry up, for Christ's sake!"

She carefully positioned the tip of the blade under the string, and Valette pulled back his arm in one swift motion. The string uncoiled and the mallet fell, bouncing onto the slimy ground with a thud and revealing Valette's pale stump. He immediately grabbed the knife out of Anna's hands and kneeled beside the dying pig.

"Come closer with the basin."

Anna kneeled as well. Valette pushed the pig's head to the side with his thigh and wedged the bowl against its neck.

"Hold tight with both hands so it doesn't spill... and keep yourself steady," he said without looking up.

Anna didn't respond.

"You're not scared, right? 'Cause now's not the time."

Anna set her gaze on a nail in one of the ceiling beams, where an insect was writhing in a dusty web. A fat spider was waiting in the shadows, observing its prey as it disentangled each leg, as though whetting them before feeding time.

Valette jammed the knife blade into the pig's throat. He made a wide gash at the base of its neck and up to the lower jaw, severing the artery in the process. Blood gushed into the basin. Anna jerked back at the sight of the warm liquid splattering onto her hands. She closed her eyes. The smell of cold metal entered her nostrils. Valette kept a sideways glance on her, his alcohol-reddened eyes like worn-down rubber washers.

"Steady now," he repeated.

Valette tossed the knife onto the hay. Knees splayed, he positioned himself behind the girl, chest against her back, then placed his bloody hands on her forearms and slid them down to her hands. He leaned forward to whisper in her ear in a gentle, chilling voice as blood continued to drip from the hog's throat like water overflowing from a spring.

"There, that's good. Mustn't lose a drop, long as it's still flowing," he said.

Valette's breath was seeping into Anna's hair. His mouth stunk of garlic and alcohol, and his body, rot. Trapped in his arms, she wished she could run away and find relief in the snow and cold. The sight of blood was nothing compared to this hellish proximity.

The stream finally went dry. Valette, fingers lingering on Anna's blood-smeared wrists, let go and stood with a long sigh of satisfaction.

"I have to say, you're pretty brave for a city girl. Take that back to Irene and your mother for the blood sausage, and careful not to trip on the way. Blood's precious, you know."

Anna rose, trembling. Valette opened the door and she walked out, immediately met with a gust of snow. She advanced with timid steps, arms outstretched so she could see where she was walking, following the footsteps she'd left on the way there, her hands coated in dried blood. She clenched her jaws to keep from bursting into tears, begging her tensed body to relax as thick black liquid swished inside the basin.

Valette grabbed the knife. He stepped outside to clean the soiled blade with a handful of snow before setting it on the makeshift hoist. Fine hail whipped his face, forcing him to blink. He unwound the rope, pulling the hooks, and went back into the pigsty. He sliced the hog's legs between the tendons, well above its nails, and inserted the hooks, then lifted the animal with the crank. Once the pig was in place, he lit a wisp of straw, which he ran along its hide, using the cleaned knife to scrape off burnt bristles, as he waited for the women to arrive.

Once they joined him, the women helped Valette drag the hoist-wagon to the shed. They hung the pig, head up, from a reddish beam equipped with two rusty rings, pulling on the motionless body in intervals, like bell ringers under Valette's command. Once hung and fastened, the carcass briefly swung back and forth. Valette left and quickly returned pushing a wheelbarrow, which he placed beneath the carcass. He then inserted the blade of his knife into the animal's gaping throat and disemboweled it down to its corkscrew-shaped penis. Purple, foul-smelling entrails dripped from the incision, like large infected boils. Valette guided them into the wheelbarrow, pulling the intestines swollen with bird droppings at various stages of formation toward him, always cutting with great precision. When he was done, he steered the wheelbarrow in the direction of the pile of manure in the yard, accompanied by the starving dog jumping around the steaming viscera like a baby goat.

On his way back, Valette stopped at the house. He entered and served himself two generous glasses of hooch before returning to the shed. He wiped his hands on a rag and rolled himself a cigarette, which he smoked while sharpening knives of various sizes and a machete with a steel. As he watched Irene remove the remaining bristles from the pig's hide with a scraper and boiling water, which she periodically asked Helen to pour in a haughty voice, Valette frowned, letting clouds of smoke escape from the corner of his mouth. His tiny eyes, aggravated by the smoke, looked away from the two women and toward Anna, who was frozen before the hairless, unmoving carcass, now split down the middle.

For three days straight, the occupants of Grands-Bois worked diligently to salvage every last bit of the hog, transforming it into pâté, blood sausage, hams, lard, and different cuts of pork. The whole time, Anna, still disgusted and terrified by the memory of Valette's hands on her skin and foul breath on her neck, made sure to stay close to her mother.

Irene started awake, breathless. Sat up in the bed, stretched out one hand, and touched Valette, who stopped snoring long enough to roll onto his side. The contact revived her, bringing her back to her husband in the darkness of the bedroom. But the true darkness lay in the dream from which she'd just awoken after a night assailed by terrible, merciless visions whose every detail she remembered, as though the pig guts had revealed the future to her. Irene had seen Eugene lying in the mud. A strange, wingless angel leaning over his dying body was holding his hand and appeared to be speaking to him. Her child would not come back from the war.

Irene had learned to read signs as a young girl, filling her malleable mind with undisputed truths, all of which maintained that everything happens for a reason, and that God determines everything in the end. Here more than elsewhere, the good Lord didn't give people the choice not to believe in Him and, indeed, made no decisions lightly, liberating upon confession any souls of devilish ilk. It was understood that from birth, the Almighty laid a path for every human being and ensured that path was followed. Therein lay the supreme devotion—navigate a corrupted world in order to join, sooner or later, the highly coveted kingdom of heaven. After her dream of death, Irene knew what He expected her to do to achieve her destiny, whatever it might cost her.

She closed her eyes. She could no longer hear Valette's snoring, aware only of her own breathing, of the inordinate effort she was exerting to bring a little air into her lungs, whereas expelling it inexplicably seemed to require none at all. She wouldn't fight her fate, she would remain in her place, with the weapons at her disposal, and the good Lord would help her succeed.

Leaning forward, hands on her thighs, in this bed in which she had brought Eugene into the world, almost dying in the process, in this room whose walls and wood were permeated with his cries, she knew she hadn't suffered in vain, that no one suffered in vain, and that he too wouldn't suffer for nothing. He would die, over there, looked after by a strange figure without a face.

She wasn't the kind of woman to bring God to account. Holding men accountable instead suited her fine, though always in silence, the better to avoid uttering blasphemy. Men too, like women, came squealing from their mothers' bellies, and yet there they were thinking themselves larger than other men the second they sprouted a few muscles to brandish against the weakest, and so powerful when they rubbed their erect members between a woman's thighs to plant their eternal glory—revelation in a simple spurt of cum traveling against the current of the indelible female mystery. Men who needed to drink between two ruts to escape their own heaviness and bolster their courage. Men who weighed so heavy, even in their sleep. Men who had never carried children, never would.

Irene rose without waking her husband. She was done with the night, with that night's dream. Felt almost relieved, walking through the kitchen, draped in a long nightshirt glued to her skin by the sweat dripping between her gaunt breasts and down her spine. She plucked the coarse fabric between two fingers, but it stuck back to her skin as soon as she let go.

On the other side of the shuttered window, the moon had returned, full and fat, and its light was entering through the cracks, revealing the world to which Irene belonged, with its austere furniture and sedimented layers of utensils. Then—the crucial moment—she stood before that light, turning her back on the material world, hands clasped above her head, and she kneeled, wept, and prayed.

Irene made her way through the deserted church, between the wooden pews, in the cold light. She stopped before the altar, under the highest vault, stiff as a tree, then leaned her head back. She saw plump cherubs floating upside down on the stones, one with a leg gnawed away by humidity. The angels were smiling at each other.

Then Irene tilted her head forward, kneeled before the altar, opened her hands, and placed them on her stomach, trying to quell the unease growing in her since her dream. Like a saint before Christ's tomb, hesitant to open it at the risk of finding the speared son, but also hesitant to leave the door closed on the great mystery of faith. She was hesitant, yes, but still willing to perform every sacrament, make every sacrifice, willing to forget the eternal suffering frozen on a waxen face, to forget the enamel depictions of the Passion according to Saint John and also the careless flames burning down altar candles on a bed of nails. So she bargained her soul to God, so that he would once again come to her aid, convinced that he was answering her when a shadow crossed the nave, then disappeared through a stained-glass window. She, who had always spoken more to the son than the father, who had unreservedly accepted the latter without truly understanding how you could sacrifice a son to save all the rest, was seized by a wild desire. She said a long prayer, practiced the night before on the cold kitchen floor and invented from start to finish, which she delivered in all the splendor of her burgeoning hope. A woman smiling at the sole master of the house, hands now clasped, like two sacred doors keeping in hope. He wouldn't abandon her. She could already feel something quivering in the deepest reaches of her body, could feel him quivering. He wouldn't abandon her; he would never abandon her.

Then she turned around, lowering and lifting her hobnailed shoes along the flagstones worn down by countless Eucharists, a mournful figure relieved of one kind of pain, at least. Made her way down the road and along the trails, weighed down by the body of a child who would never leave her again, a child that nobody could take from her.

Helen and Anna had gone to bed. Valette was smoking, watching curls of smoke rise toward the ceiling like budding mycelia as his wife bustled around the kitchen, not looking at him, and taking methodical drags on his cigarette as he thought about the daughter of a brother who no longer meant anything to him.

Irene paused to cast a quick glance at her husband. Now he was chewing on the extinguished cigarette butt, moving it from the corner of his mouth to the center with his tongue. She poured half a bucket of water into a basin.

"Don't come to bed straightaway," she said coldly.

He didn't respond, merely spat the cigarette butt onto the floor, then spat again, brown saliva this time. Irene shook her head bitterly. She carried the basin to the bedroom and set it on the floor before lighting the lamp. Then she opened the two wardrobe doors, took out a clean washcloth and towel, and disrobed. Bending over naked to hang the towel on the back of a nearby chair, she glimpsed her crude reflection on the tin basin. Stood up, slid her hand inside the washcloth, and squatted over the basin to meticulously wash her genitals as she stared straight ahead at the wall covered with cracks, her knees bent, scrubbing the thick hair covering her reddened sex. Her intimate ablutions concluded, she grabbed the towel and dried herself carefully before folding it in two equal halves, hanging it back over the chair, and placing the wet washcloth on it. She pulled on a nightgown and, returning to the wardrobe, opened a drawer from which she took out a short boxwood branch, blessed on a Palm Sunday, tied with a golden string, and kissed it murmuring words so rapidly that they were inaudible, *Hail Mary full of grace blessed art thou among women and blessed is Jesus the fruit of your womb,* then put the branch back, shut the drawer, and closed the wardrobe doors, as if it was a reliquary.

She briefly listened to the noises of the house. Then she threw back the covers, climbed onto the bed, one knee after the other, and lay on her back, waiting.

The lamp was still burning when Valette entered the bedroom, surprised to find his wife in bed, eyes wide open, as still as a plaque on a tombstone.

"Are you ill?"

"No," she said without moving.

"It's not like you to go to bed so early."

"And yet."

"Well, you don't seem yourself."

She looked at him then, large eyes devoid of all expression.

"Put out the light and come to bed."

He undressed, keeping on his drawers and undershirt, extinguished the lamp, and stretched out with his back to his wife, one arm under his head. Irene let the silence spread, then hoarsely said: "Take me!"

"What?"

"Take me!" she repeated, clearly this time.

He rolled onto his back.

"You want me to . . ."

"Right now, that's what I said."

"What's gotten into you?"

"Stop asking questions and get on top of me for Christ's sake. I'll do what's needed."

Valette didn't move.

"You've been refusing me for weeks and tonight you start talking like you're suddenly on fire."

"What's the problem?" she said, annoyed.

She lifted her nightgown to her waist, bending and then spreading her legs without breaking eye contact.

"Make up your mind or I'll go back to sleep."

Valette was hard in spite of himself. He took off his drawers, got on all fours, then moved between his wife's thighs and spat in his hand to coat her vagina with saliva. He tried to push her nightgown up to expose her breasts, but she pushed away his hand, grabbed his erect penis, and guided it between her dry labia. When he abruptly entered her, she bit her lips so hard they bled, forcing herself not to scream. He continued with broad thrusts. "Don't stop, that's good," she said, "that's good."

Valette came with a gasp a few seconds later and immediately collapsed on top of his wife, as if she were an old mattress. The brief service concluded, Irene pushed off her husband's inert body with a large sigh. Then she squeezed her thighs as hard as she could to keep the semen from trickling out, pulled down her nightgown, placed her hands on her stomach, and closed her eyes in the black night.

She would let him do it as many times as necessary. She was no longer in the prime of her youth, but still, she wasn't yet forty. What her womb had been able to produce once surely could come out a second time. She would return to the church to pray that it happened, would also go see someone who could help her stack the odds in her favor. Nothing else would matter more than this promise she'd made to herself. She realized, of course, that she couldn't replace Eugene, but by superimposing a new life on a vanished one, she hoped to erase him a little and, in that way, perhaps, survive his absence. She thought of the Virgin Mary in a corner of the church, of the child Jesus in her arms, and she spoke to her in her head, as if to a sister.

On one side of the fireplace was a chest that also served as a bench; on the other, nothing. Lucie was sitting on the bench, knitting. Leonard dropped an armful of wood onto the large gray slab in front of the hearth, tossed two logs onto the fire, then rubbed his coat sleeves to shake off bits of bark and dry moss.

At seventy, Lucie left the house only on rare occasions, relying on two canes Leonard had made her due to her arthritis-ravaged hips, but also to her corpulence. Sagging from her body's weight, she resembled an enormous toad waiting for an insect to fly within reach, or some other possibility to emerge from the ether. Her thick lips trembled slightly, her tiny, keen eyes following a trail of stitches as she kept precise count in her head.

"Someone's here to see you," he said after a moment.

The old woman didn't react. Her needles moved faster. Leonard leaned against the chimney mantel and stuffed a pipe as he watched the wood burn.

"I can tell 'em to leave, if you like," he said.

"Who?" she asked, not looking up from her knitting.

"Valette's wife."

The old woman set her needles down in a cross on her legs, glanced at the door, then gave Leonard a defiant stare.

"I'm going," he said.

Leonard took a drag from his pipe and walked out. A gust of air swept the smoke inside, where it hung like a foul-smelling fog once the door closed. Lucie struggled to rise, lifted the lid to the trunk, and grabbed a ball of wool. When she sat back down, Irene had already walked in. She went no farther than the corner of the table, visibly ill at ease.

"Hello," she said, looking at the floor.

The old woman didn't respond. She cast a hard glance at Leonard, who was standing back like a decrepit butler waiting for orders.

"Leave us."

The door slammed shut again. Lucie nodded at a chair. Irene sat down quickly, forearms resting on her thighs. The old woman resumed knitting as if she was alone, then, a few seconds later, abruptly paused, extending one needle in Irene's direction.

"Why do you want another one?"

Irene's head jerked back. "Another one?"

"A child. That's why you're here, isn't it?"

Irene froze, her large eyes taking up her whole pallid face.

"How…" is all she could say.

The old woman smiled, visibly not dissatisfied with the effect caused by her prediction. Her lower lip seemed to pull away from the rest of her mouth as she leaned toward the fire.

"I ask the questions, my dear, not you."

The words hissed as they came out of her toothless mouth. Too much air. The hearth was now clearly illuminating her face. Her chin was dotted with long, gleaming twisted white hairs, and her large, gelatinous cheeks quivered as she spoke. Even after she spoke, they continued to tremble.

Irene leaned forward in her chair.

"Can you help me or not?" she said.

"I already told you it's me who asks the questions. If you still don't get that, off with you."

Lucie waited a moment to make sure the other woman had understood.

"Why don't you let nature decide?" she said.

"Nature hasn't exactly been on my side, up till now."

"Valette know you're here?"

Irene hesitated before responding. "No."

"I'm betting he doesn't even know what you're planning on doing, am I right?"

"That's my business."

"You're in my house now, so it's my business too."

"I'm not saying otherwise."

"Just as well."

Irene looked at the old lady contritely. "Well?"

"If I remember correctly, you almost didn't make it when Eugene was born."

"That's the past."

"Past can always come back, and your age don't help matters."

"I'm willing to take the risk."

"You know that if it goes badly, it'll come back on me. Valette's a hard man."

"He'll never know."

Lucie paused. She gave a deadened glance at the flames silently dancing.

"Everyone knows everything round here, in the end."

"I can sign something, if that'll save you some trouble."

A sneer erupted on the woman's face, as though she'd just been slapped.

"You wanna sign some damned piece of paper? Ask anybody and they'd swear on their life it was fake. They all think I'm some kind of witch doctor."

"I made sure no one saw me, I promise."

"You're not hard to read... A real open book, you are."

"You don't have to worry about him—"

"Quiet!"

Irene leaned forward and unclasped her hands.

"You're right. He doesn't know that I want another child."

"Fine, but the two of you will need to do what needs doing."

"Easy enough with a man. They don't go digging for reasons, and mine isn't the kind to ask questions when there's no need."

The old woman nodded as she took up her needles again.

"Been a long time since anyone asked me for something like this," she said.

"Please," said Irene, voice thick with saliva.

Lucie paused again, then gestured to one wall.

"You see that shelf, above the sideboard?"

Irene pivoted in that direction.

"I see it," she said.

"Pass me the second notebook from the left."

Irene stood, grabbed a notebook with a frayed cover, and handed it to Lucie. The old woman began to leaf through it, wetting her index finger with her tongue before turning the page. Once she had found what she was looking for, she traced each line with the tip of her finger. Then she looked up at Irene and, in a solemn voice, said:

"You willing to do everything I tell you to?"

"That's all I want."

"It's no guarantee, but it's worked on more than one woman."

"I'm listening," said Irene impatiently.

The old woman read out a recipe with various ingredients. Then she repeated it, slower.

"You don't want to write this down? You gonna remember?"

"Believe me, no chance I'll forget..."

"The *clandestina* root is essential."

"I know where to find it."

Lucie closed the notebook. She placed an open hand on the cover, like a beggar seeking alms, then added, "First thing is to find out whether you're even fertile anymore."

"I know I am," said Irene, as though she'd just been stung by a wasp.

"Only one way to know, my dear."

"Go on."

"You need to peel a clove of garlic and stick it you know where before you go to bed. If you can taste it in your mouth when you wake up, means you're ready."

"I'll do it."

"And I'll have some things to say once it's taken."

"Whatever you like..."

The old woman raised one hand in the air to silence Irene.

"If you want it to work, you can't hide anything from me."

"I'm not hiding anything," said Irene, a slight tremble in her voice.

"You sure?" said Lucie, making a fist and bringing it to her bosom.

"Yes, I'm sure."

Lucie observed Irene, as though she was expecting something that didn't come.

"Maybe you know something I don't," added Irene, visibly bothered by the silence.

"Enough! Off with you."

Irene didn't move.

"How much?" she said.

"Ask me again once you get pregnant, if you do that is."

"Thank you."

"Put this back," said Lucie, holding out the notebook.

Irene hunched over, pressed her hands against her thighs, and stood up. She put the notebook back on the shelf and walked out without a word.

Lucie didn't look up from her knitting needles. She heard the door slam. Shook her head back and forth, muttering to herself, then picked up the needles, which resumed their clinking in rhythm with the crackling fire in the hearth.

Lucie was still crossing her swords with their ribbons of beige wool. The gleam cast by the tall flames in the fireplace painted her face, her hands, and the needles in her hands in warm tones, and the quasi-entirety of her body appeared at rest, as though all the energy she was capable of summoning was being applied to the twirling extremities that were her fingers. A shawl she didn't know what to do with.

Leonard sat at one side of the table, not the end as was his custom, the fireplace to his right. He placed his hat upside down on the wood surface and leaned his head forward. His hands, partially folded, looked like tree stumps chopped at the spot they met his black cloth sleeves. He slid his feet along the ground, and his heels caught in the empty space between two slabs, with the sound of a latch hitting a strike, then he lifted his head, undid the top button of his coat, and ran the flat of his hand across his face, top to bottom. Took a breath.

"Not often we see a Valette round here," he said.

Lucie let the silence drag, then, without turning her head: "It don't mean anything."

"You think?"

“She wasn’t here as a Valette.”

“And yet she is one.”

“You can’t hold her responsible for her man.”

“Lives with him.”

The old woman looked up from her knitting. She contemplated the fire.

“You wouldn’t have let her in, I bet,” she said.

“I’d have done what I needed to . . .”

“Good ol’ Leo wouldn’t have saved a suffering soul. My, the world’s gone topsy-turvy,” she mocked.

“Her suffering’s the least of my worries . . . I don’t forget.”

Lucie turned swiftly toward her husband, staring at him as if he’d said something completely senseless.

“Do we ever really know the people we live with?” she asked.

“If you pay ’em a little attention.”

“Well, if you ask me, you’re off your rocker.”

Leonard nodded at an empty chair.

“What’d she want?”

Lucie didn’t answer.

“Someone sick?”

“You know perfectly well that I won’t tell you anything.”

“Even so, can’t believe you agreed.”

“How would you know whether I agreed or not?” Lucie snapped.

Leonard stood and walked over to the shelf that held the notebooks, then pushed in the spine of the second one from the left.

“I like things to be put back exactly where they were,” he said, lingering by the shelf.

Lucie accelerated her fingers guiding the needles and yarn. Leonard sat back in the same spot, face vacant, hands folded on top of each other, entangled in a slow, rocky kneading.

"We're exactly where we started, aren't we?" he said.

"Just who are you talking to?"

"The end's coming for both of us."

Leonard ran one finger along the rim of his hat.

"Don't you remember . . . what we used to say at the beginning?"

"The beginning of what?"

"Don't pretend."

The needles stopped mid-battle.

"Didn't last long," she said.

Leonard gave the hat a hard shove and it slid across the table, out of his reach.

"We were in such a hurry to get back to our lives . . . after."

"Enough already!"

He abruptly lifted his head, neck stiff, eyes glued to the sideboard and a box holding two baby teeth.

"Both of us were in a rush to get to the end," he said.

"Stop, I said. I don't want to hear anymore . . ."

"Whether you want to or not, changes nothing."

"It was the best we could do. To be done with it as quickly as possible. You know perfectly well that promises don't carry much weight in this house."

"So we couldn't have gotten through it any other way, that what you're trying to tell me?"

"No, we couldn't have."

"Maybe we didn't try everything."

Unable to concentrate, Lucie placed her knitting on her lap and cast a scornful look at her husband.

"It's too late now. There's no point regretting things," she said.

"'Cause you decided all on your own," said Leonard, raising his voice.

"Well at least I'm not trying to bring back something that no longer exists."

"Oh go on, spit out whatever you have to say, and get it over with!"

"You think I'm blind?! Everything you think you're doing for the Larys, you're actually doing for yourself."

Leonard's mouth twisted into a scowl, but nothing came out.

"You think you're better than me, I suppose," he finally said.

"Better, surely not, but at least I don't lie to myself or to anyone else."

"I'm not hurting anyone, far as I can tell."

"You sure about that?"

Leonard unfolded his hands, as if he wanted to compare them, or rather convince himself of their utility, then folded them again, clearing his throat.

"I don't think about it," he said in a weak voice.

"Maybe you ought to."

"What for?"

Lucie didn't take her smoldering eyes off her husband.

"Walk outside and look around you. There's nothing to hold on to and no one to hold on to it."

Leonard squeezed his hands hard enough to shatter bone, and a wave of tiny brown cracks erupted across his knuckles.

"But the land... our land... that'll stay," he said.

"The land is where we all end up, old man, full stop."

"There'll be others who'll work it after us, they'll take care of it, like we have."

"Others..."

Lucie paused. Her gaze changed abruptly, still fixed on her husband, but she no longer saw him, instead saw a void through him.

"Not the ones we'd like, whether you sell your land or give it away... not the ones we'd like."

Face buried in shadow, the woman was shucking an ear of corn across from Joseph. She was sitting with her legs spread to create a taut swathe of dress in which to catch the kernels, which she flicked off with her thumb, golden drops raining down in her lap, before tossing the worthless cob on the ground.

Joseph couldn't remember who the woman was, where the scene had taken place, or at what specific moment in his childhood. Simply remembered the burning tension that had radiated through his body when his mesmerized gaze slid beneath the swathe of fabric, between the woman's thighs, revealing to him an obscure corridor, a fantasized image that would feed him on occasion, alone in his bed, beneath a quilt heavy as a body.

The vision of a woman shucking corn, face perpetually in darkness, and an emotion he would never forget. A woman whom he had for a time suspected of being his own mother, and who was much more than that.

But then the vision faded, ceding to another—Anna, who used her charms like a butterfly emerging from its cocoon flies away to paint the sky. Joseph still couldn't believe it. When they were together, they never talked about life at

Chantegril or Grands-Bois, or the different pressures they faced. They had no time to lose. A shared impatience, and appetite, to receive beauty.

Simply gazing at each other would have sufficed, allowing their faces to reflect their joy. They could have done that for eternity, and Joseph would have been happy with that eternity. But Anna always extended her hand to liberate their hungers in an act of sublime blasphemy, revealing her desire to a young man who still needed to be convinced of his good fortune. Together, they became the inhabitants of a world that was theirs alone, an insolent world that they explored as they created it.

"I feel good when I'm with you."

"I feel good, too . . ."

"Do you know any prayers?"

"I know a few."

"A beautiful prayer, I mean."

"Why do you ask?"

"It'd be nice if you could say one to me."

"Later . . ."

"Fine. Then tell me again!"

"Tell you what?"

"That you love me. We'll call it the most beautiful prayer of all."

"I love you."

"Don't stop."

"I love you . . ."

"Never stop."

She walked across the dense snow, arms extended for balance, at times tilting to the right, at others the left, in the frosted mist, as her breath carved a pathway ahead of her, seemingly melting the air. The strands of hair peeking out from her cap had frozen on her forehead and resembled tiny, tangled crests on the verge of shattering. She periodically pressed one nostril, then the other, to expulse jets of clear snot onto the snow before they turned into stalactites, squinting as well to expose the least terrain possible to the icy particles that swirled through the air at the slightest gust of wind, light as pollen. Panting, laboriously pulling one foot and then the other from the snowy ground, she looked for landmarks to bolster her courage, a reminder that her efforts weren't in vain, nor was her assigned mission to deliver as speedily as she could the news contained in her leather satchel, however unimportant compared to the sage patience of a sleeping world.

Jeanne had taken up the torch in December when her husband was drafted, off to join their three sons at the front. Today, the last letter on her round was for the Valettes. At best, reaching Grands-Bois from the village was a two-hour walk, but that was without stopping. By bike, it took thirty minutes to ascend, and less than half that to come down. At one point, she had tried the Bélier trail to save time but sank to her thighs after a few steps, and doubled back in search of a more stable path.

Once she finally reached the Valette farm, Jeanne adjusted the strap on her satchel, like a soldier checking his uniform before a military review. A six-foot-wide swathe of the courtyard had been cleared, snowcapped stones stacked up to the doorway. Transparent crystals shimmered on the ground, like a thin, narrow ice floe, and tall snowdrifts rose thigh-high along the path. Jeanne cautiously made her way to the house, taking care not to slip.

She knocked on the door, which Irene opened almost immediately. The two women exchanged perfunctory hellos. Irene looked the postwoman up and down, as though she wanted to unceremoniously send this short messenger bundled in clothes drenched to the waist back where she'd come from. Jeanne lifted the flap of her satchel and pulled out a letter she held out to Irene, who looked at her for a moment, unmoving, and said:

"Could have waited for better weather before you came all the way up here."

"I'm used to it, and anyways, don't look like it'll improve anytime soon."

"You wanna come in and warm up a little?"

"No, I just wanna get home. Another time, for sure."

"As you like."

Jeanne, impatient, shook the letter in her hand. "Here, it's for you."

Irene looked at the letter, then grabbed it. She stayed on the threshold, in the cold, watching the postwoman walk away, and it seemed to her, as Jeanne receded in the distance, that the snowbanks were closing in around her as punishment.

Standing on one step, Irene read then reread the address written on the envelope in a stranger's handwriting. Deep in her bones, she knew what the letter said; she had prepared for it. Thought she was prepared. But as she felt blood coursing through her veins in violent waves, she understood that no one can truly prepare themselves for tragedy and that even, on the contrary, in attempting to do so, you're simply keeping false hope alive, and that killing hope is in fact the worst thing a person can face, far worse than death itself. She cast a final glance at the empty courtyard, then entered the house and closed the door behind her.

Slowly, and calmly, she walked to the sideboard and took a knife from the drawer. Opened the envelope. There was a yellow piece of paper inside. She unfolded it, and read.

> Dearest parents,
> I hope your both in good health and that all is well
> on the farm, that the birthing season went well,
> and everything else too. There's not much to say
> about where I am except the food here has nothing
> on Grands-Bois. I won't come back with any extra
> pounds on me that's for shure. What's been bothering
> me lately though is that I lost a button on my jacket
> which might not seem like a big deal to you all but it
> bothers me when the cold comes in through the hole.
> Mother, could you send me one or two buttons, the
> big metal kind, with some strong thread and a needle?
> There's plenty of boys who don't need their buttons

any more but that's no reason to take them, now is it! I don't know when I'll get my first leave. They told us we'll be allowed soon and maybe I'll already be on my way by the time you get this letter and you can sow my button for me.

All my love
Eugene.

Irene turned the letter over and continued reading.

Dear Madam, Dear Sir,
I have the honor to inform you that your son, Eugene, died gloriously on the field of battle, struck by a bullet to the abdomen after displaying exemplary bravery. Please accept my most sincere condolences.

Respectfully yours,
Lieutenant Cayrol

Irene folded the letter, slipped it into an apron pocket, and threw the envelope in the fire.

Irene lifted the stove slab and roughly prodded the logs with a poker to fan the fire. Ashes and thick smoke escaped, momentarily cloaking a large pan in which a piece of lard was sizzling. She swept away the scattered ashes with a hen's wing whisk, slid the cast-iron slab back in place using a metallic rod curved at one end, and moved the pan on top. Valette kept his eyes on her. He grabbed his tobacco pouch from his pocket and set it on the table, unopened, one hand on either side, like parentheses.

"That was the postwoman I saw, earlier?"

Irene lifted one shoulder slightly before she spoke:

"If you say so."

"So she had mail for us, then?"

"Yes."

"Eugene?"

"Yes."

Valette's cheeks hollowed. He scooted his chair back and brought his hands toward the edge of the table.

"And you said nothing."

"I was gonna."

"Well, what were you waiting for exactly?"

"I got busy and it slipped my mind."

Valette's face flushed, his eyes like thick gobs of spit.

"Show it to me," he said, clearly enunciating each word without unclenching his jaw.

Irene immediately reached into her pocket for the letter, which she unfolded and set on the table in front of her husband. The dim glow in her eyes betrayed grim purposefulness, which went far beyond the determination of that simple gesture.

"It slipped your mind but you kept it on you," he said, looking at the words neatly corralled along each line. Wide wrinkles appeared on his forehead and along the ridge of his nose. His surviving thumb was marked with grime-filled grooves, the dented nail like a pond's bogged shore. He cast a brief glance at his wife, then pushed away the letter with the back of his hand.

"You know I can't read."

Irene grabbed the letter without looking at it and stuffed it back in her pocket.

"You're the one who asked to see it."

"What does he say?"

"That he's fine. That he can't write as often as he'd like, but we don't need to worry about him . . . He just wants me to send him some buttons for his coat."

"I'm not worried."

Valette untensed, opened his tobacco pouch using the pinkie of his bad hand, and with the other hand pulled out a sheet of rolling paper and set it on the cracked flap. Then he slid a little bit of tobacco onto the paper and, with a single back-and-forth movement, created a narrow row, before sealing the cigarette with a lick. He pulled out the sprigs extending from the ends, which he dropped onto the table, gathered one by one, and placed back in the pouch. Then he took a lighter out of his pants pocket and lit the cigarette. He took a long drag, exhaling smoke out his nose, gaze still on his wife. He looked like a mythological creature emerging victorious from battle.

"Maybe he's not so clumsy after all," he said.

Irene walked around the table to get out of Valette's field of vision. Wasted effort.

"Still, it ain't fair," he continued.

"What ain't fair?" she spat out as though she'd just been insulted.

"That I'm not there. He say how many Krauts he's killed?"

"No . . ."

"Maybe he's shot down so many that he lost count. Though I'd be surprised to hear it, that boy couldn't even butcher a chicken properly."

Irene said nothing, her body a limp object no longer under her control. Valette stood, grabbed his tobacco pouch, and shoved it into his jacket pocket. He set the cigarette on the edge of the table, and ashes fell to the floor. He walked to the cupboard, opened a tall door, and grabbed an opened bottle of brandy and a glass that he wedged beneath his armpit. Sat back at the table. Fist clenched around the bottle neck, he loosened the cork with his thumb, flipped it off, and poured himself a generous serving. Gulped it back. Bluntly set down the glass and served himself twice more. Picked up his extinguished cigarette, stood, and spat into the fire. He lit his cigarette again, then slid his hands in his pants pockets as he made his way to the window. In the courtyard, the dog was shaking his head, using his muzzle to lift the powdery snow before swallowing it. A game that didn't seem all that enjoyable and yet the dog continued, as if in a trance.

"The poultry bin needs thawing," said Valette.

"I have my hands full at the moment."

"Where are they?" he asked, still looking out the window.

"No idea."

"Well, tell them to take care of it."

"Why don't you tell them yourself."

Valette spun around. His eyes now two black dots buried in their sockets, like those of a blind man vainly trying to decipher the darkness based on sounds alone.

"What was that you said?" he asked, curling his fingers.

She shook her head bitterly, returned to the range, and moved the lard around the pan with a wooden spatula. She heard the glass being filled and emptied again, then her husband's loud footsteps, and the door open and close.

She walked to the sideboard and took out a sewing box. She chose two identical buttons—large metal circles—and a needle and thread, then wrapped them in a sheet of thick paper, which she tied with a string, before writing her son's address on the front. She placed the package on the sideboard and walked back to the stove. The spatula had slipped into the melted fat. She burned herself salvaging it.

They came up the path one late afternoon, in the first days of the thaw. Three men in caps, bundled in long brown greatcoats that went down to their spats and sporting heavy, muddied boots, dragging along a sad procession of five roped cows. Mathilde watched them enter the farmyard and waited for them to come to her, stiffening with each step they took.

One of the men spoke immediately, dispensing with pleasantries, without even an introduction, as though his uniform allowed him anything and everything. Mathilde didn't argue. She resolutely led them to the stable, her face grave and rigid.

The soldiers requisitioned the three nicest heifers, the ones she would have made the most money from at the end of spring. They wanted to come in for a bit to drink something and enjoy the company of this farm woman who still had her looks, but she said she had work to do and in any case she had nothing to drink that would interest them. They didn't insist. One soldier signed a receipt on the back of an impassive cow. Mathilde watched him, arms glued to her chest.

Then Joseph entered the farmyard with the mule and cart. He walked past the men, greeted them with a timid nod, and continued on his way without a word, hand tight on the halter. They watched him inquisitively, steam emerging from their mouths like fumaroles from the underbrush of their beards. The apparent leader handed the crumpled paper to Mathilde, keeping his eyes on Joseph.

"Hold up!" he shouted.

Joseph continued leading the mule.

"Hold up, I said!"

Joseph stopped short and turned toward his mother. The same panic on both their faces. The soldier neared. He circled the mule like a horse dealer fastidious about his trade.

"That's a nice animal you got there."

"She's old," said Joseph.

"She can still drag a cart, far as I can tell."

"Can hardly call this a cart, and even then, she has trouble."

"Maybe that's 'cause you're not giving her a chance to do more."

Joseph relaxed his grip on the halter, then squeezed it even harder, turning to leave.

"I didn't say you could go," said the leader.

"She's not ours," said Joseph.

The soldier placed one hand on Joseph's arm and snidely called over his companions.

"Hey, fellows, wouldn't you agree that everyone needs to pitch in if we wanna win this war?"

"Of course," they said conspiratorially.

"I'm guessing one mule or less won't make the difference, whereas for us . . ."

"Not my problem. I have my orders," the leader curtly interrupted.

Mathilde hurried over, her arms unfolded, which was meant to say far more than her meager words.

"Take anything else you want, but not that mule," she said.

"We already took what we needed... except, as it happens, for this mule."

"Please!" she begged.

"Guess she's not that old, after all."

With a sweeping gesture, the leader rounded up his comrades.

"Help the boy unhitch the cart. We've dawdled enough. It'll be dark soon..."

The mule danced from one leg to the other in palpable agitation, as though she wanted to be free of her body's weight and her inability to do so was driving her mad. Her long ears swung back and forth like the levers of a machine operated by the wind.

The soldiers helped Joseph remove the harness, then placed the cart handles on the muddy ground. Joseph wrapped one arm around the mule's neck, and she turned her big eyes around in their sockets to keep him in her sights.

Before removing the bit, he said, "It's not right what you're doing."

"I don't think I heard correctly. Why don't you say it again, to see?" threatened the leader, approaching Joseph.

"At least let me take the cart back to its owner, so he can say goodbye to his mule. He's attached, you know."

An unsettling smile spread across the soldier's face, causing his thick mustache to rise ominously.

"You strike me as strong enough to pull that wagon on your own, and talkative enough to tell its owner what happened," he said.

One of the men uncoiled a rope, which he tied around the mule's neck before pushing Joseph back roughly with one hand to his chest. The animal bucked, and the leader gave her a violent punch to the stomach, at which she bent her hind legs with a cry of pain. Her head was now swinging up and down, as if, unable to understand the circumstances, she was praying, in turn, to the heavens, the earth, or some animal god to come to her aid, though surely not to Joseph.

"Let's go," said the leader impatiently.

"You're not gonna sign a receipt for the mule?" asked Mathilde.

His smile returned.

"What for? Seeing how she's not yours."

The soldiers left by the same path that had spat them out. The mule followed the resigned cows, her jittery legs stiffened by fear.

Joseph and Mathilde watched them leave, then glanced at each other. But finding nothing in the other's gaze that might ease their powerlessness, they looked back at the sad convoy, waiting for it to disappear in the twilight mist.

Leonard took the news in silence, bobbing his head. He kneeled down to replace the grate on the gutter he'd been cleaning when Joseph arrived. Then he stood back up with the help of a ring attached to the wall and dried his hands on his pants as he looked at the stable door behind which his mule could no longer be found.

"You know what I liked most about her?"

Joseph lowered his head.

"I'm sorry, Leo..."

"This colored spot she had under her neck."

Leo paused to scratch the underneath of his chin with one finger, as though he was squeezing a trigger over and over.

"Right here. I bet you never noticed. It was hardly bigger than a coin," he continued.

"I'm really sorry, Leo!"

"Stop being sorry. It ain't your fault."

Joseph stared at the grate, which in that moment resembled a jail cell window with rusty bars and that looked into hell.

"I should have been more careful."

"No point thinking about what you could have done."

"You have no idea how much I blame myself..."

"You tell them she was mine?"

"I said she wasn't ours, is all."

Leonard thought for a moment.

"You came as soon as they left?" he asked.

"Yes, right after."

"They say where they were going?"

"No."

"They can't have gotten far with the animals slowing them down. Pretty soon, they'll have to stop to eat and sleep. I can only think of one place they can do that round here."

"Maybe they went directly to Salers, or down to Fontanges."

"How many animals did they have?"

"Eight, counting ours... plus your mule."

Leonard adjusted the hat on his head a few times.

"In that case, I'd be surprised if they've already gone round all the farms."

"I don't understand why you care where they're going."

Leonard's face lit up. He held out one hand and slapped the back of it against Joseph's chest a few times.

"The inn in Saint-Paul, in the town square. Next to the marketplace, where you can leave your animals. They'll spend the night there, for sure."

"What does that change?"

"You still haven't guessed?"

"You're not actually considering..."

Leonard scowled.

"Did they give you a piece of paper that proves they requisitioned my mule?" he asked in a peremptory tone.

"No, I'd have given it to you."

"Well, then, I call that theft."

"They were soldiers."

"Wearing a uniform doesn't justify everything," said the old man, raising his voice.

Joseph swallowed.

"Mother says otherwise, that they're allowed anything."

"And do you agree with that, deep down?"

"Nobody asked my opinion."

"Well, I'm asking it."

"Whether I agree or not doesn't change anything."

Leonard tipped his hat higher on his forehead.

"Are you gonna help me get back my mule tonight?"

"You're not serious!"

"I don't think I've ever been more serious."

"You're asking for too much," said Joseph, distraught.

Leonard leaned forward to catch the boy's fleeing gaze.

"Earlier, you were complaining about what you should have done, and now that I'm giving you a chance to right a wrong, you're hesitating!"

Leonard grabbed the handle of the draining spade he'd used to scrape out the gutter and placed it on one shoulder. He paused for a moment, as if he wanted to add something, then changed his mind, visibly miffed, and walked toward the outhouse.

"Leo, wait!"

Leonard turned around, a weathercock spun by a gust of wind.

"What?" he said.

"Fine. I want to help you."

"Be here at eleven-thirty tonight... and don't be late."

The moon was waiting impatiently behind a row of gossamer clouds, bathing the night with its intense, iridescent light. Leonard was leading the way, a lantern in hand. Joseph followed silently, attentive to the sounds coming from the moor, and then the forest.

When they were a cable's length from Saint-Paul, they heard one cow lowing, then a second. The old man stopped. The light floated in front of his face, revealing a wide smile.

"I was right... You ready?" he asked.

"Think so."

"You're not scared at least?"

Leonard brought the lantern closer to Joseph.

"I'll be fine," said the boy.

"Don't worry, if ever things go sour, you run quick enough not to get caught... Don't wait for me, I'll figure something out."

"That's not exactly reassuring..."

"It's best to think of everything. But it won't happen."

"I'm not gonna leave you."

Leonard lifted the lantern higher and swung it in front of Joseph's face.

"You'll do just what I tell you."

"You said it wouldn't happen."

"Exactly."

They set out again and soon reached the black rock. Leonard blew out the flame and placed the lantern on the ground, at the edge of the path. They made their way down the main alley lined with silent houses and skirted the imposing church. Once on the other side, they spotted the inn, which was still lit up inside. Crouching behind a low wall, they could hear animals moving and breathing noisily in the marketplace, less than sixty feet away. They waited for the lights to go out, and then waited several more minutes before approaching the cloistered animals. Despite the darkness, Leonard confidently made his way to the pen where people tied up their cattle on market days. He clicked his tongue in contentment when he noticed his mule's head sticking out between two planks of the railing, as if the air was purer on the other side. When she saw him, she let out a little squeal, and he hurried over to calm her, stroking her back and speaking in a soft voice. Joseph, a few steps back, kept his eyes on the inn windows, behind which nothing moved. Without delay, Leonard guided the mule down the corral to the gate and lifted the latch.

"Walk round and go into the pen. Then get this smart crowd to the exit, nice and easy," he whispered.

"I thought you just wanted to get your mule back."

"That is what I want, but it wouldn't have taken them long to make the connection with you, whereas this way, they'll think they didn't shut the gate right... Go on, and be quick about it!"

"You really did think of everything."

"There's no time to waste."

Joseph made his way around the corral and climbed the railing. With the flat of his hand, he tapped one of his own cows on the back, and then she pushed the others toward the open gate, placidly swaying her head in rhythm with her plodding steps and heavy breathing.

The cows, now free, appeared to briefly evaluate the situation, before setting out after Leonard and the mule. Joseph waited to make sure no one had heard them, then hurried after the procession, catching up at the edge of the village.

"Should I scatter them?" he asked.

"Not yet," said Leonard.

"If the cows follow us, the soldiers will come looking for them real quick."

"Exactly, which is why we'll do it once we reach the forest. That way it'll take the soldiers a while to gather up the cows, and they won't even think about some sad old mule."

They passed the black rock, and the old man grabbed the lantern and lit it. After walking almost a quarter mile beneath the tall trees, he asked Joseph to disperse the herd. By the time they left the forest, the moon had elbowed her way through and was illuminating the moor and the rocky path unwinding before the trio like a dry stream.

"Leo!" said Joseph.

"What?"

"That was the fair thing to do . . . wasn't it?"

Leonard kept walking, just barely slowing down.

"Nothing fairer than getting back something someone stole from you. And anyways, my mule wouldn't have done them much good. She can't stand strangers, remember?" he said, smiling into the night.

They marched on either side of the mule, sinking into darkness softened by the astral light welcoming them like heroes, childish grins on their faces, the feeling of a duty accomplished unbeknownst to a world off its axis. They walked in silence, at the mule's pace, filled with blazing compassion for this docile creature wrenched from the sound and the fury of man.

It was a few weeks after she'd received the letter announcing Eugene's death. Irene was in the shed ladling curdled milk into ceramic molds, to make cheese. A first blow to her gut, then a second, then others. Not mere stomach cramps. No, it was him, the child was moving. Revealing himself, as minuscule as he was. She was sure of it. Had prepared her stomach to endure but also to welcome. For that's what a woman was—a receptacle for good and bad alike. Endure the death of a son and welcome the arrival of another. Because it would be a son. Twins nourished by the same flesh. Two scars etched deep inside her, Eugene's on the shaded slope, the son in embryo on the sunny side. The dead brother, who would live on in fossilized memories, would teach his double everything that life and death had taught him.

The ladle fell to the floor. The waiting dog rushed to lick it. Irene pressed her hands squarely on the table, concentrating on her breathing as burning drops of sweat crashed onto the surface and her hands, like nails. Her beaming face was trumpeting a new reality she would never again doubt. *Bless me, Lord, and I will be blessed among women . . .* Her life would henceforth be built around this reality that she would keep to herself as long as possible, but that would one day become that of everyone at Grands-Bois. She used to believe that her existence was a slow, desperate descent, but now a child was violently growing inside her belly, shattering that former certitude. Her body was reclaiming maternal suffering; it had become both a sacred temple and a dark tomb at the bottom of which a small, voracious being was feasting, though Irene couldn't imagine what such a painful banquet might resemble.

She was already thinking about which precautions she would take to ensure the fetus made it to term. Valette would no longer be allowed to touch her. For that matter, to make sure he didn't, he would be the only one she told. She would close ranks around her treasure, willing to do anything to protect him. She would go to church tomorrow, to give thanks to God, and then bring the old medicine woman a chicken.

Irene slowly recovered. When the spasms had faded, she lifted her dress, straddled the bucket of whey, spread the folds of her split underwear, and began to urinate standing up, humming a lullaby in a childlike voice.

Regardless of the season, and despite the light that seeped in through two loopholes and the open door that extended along a slight slope, the stable was always buried in shadow. The floor, littered with straw and dry leaves, was composed of small polished stones sealed by filth and excrement, and lay roughly five feet beneath ground level.

Irene stood hunched over at the stable entrance for a few moments to accustom her eyes to the gloom. Valette's outline, cut off at the chest by the gradation, resembled an incomplete ghost, as though the faint light had bounced off his body, not wanting to cling to it, and the darkness was his sole worthy companion. Irene found some reassurance in not being able to see him clearly, and also from the fact that he was below her, for what she had to say. She went through the doorway, stopped mid-slope, and placed one hand on her leg for support. Valette was washing the troughs clean of hay and dirt. She cleared her throat loudly to announce her presence. Valette kept cleaning as though he hadn't heard.

"I need to tell you something," she said firmly.

Valette finished scraping out the trough in front of him, then leaned to the side to better make out his wife.

"Tell me what?"

Irene took a deep breath.

"I'm with child."

Valette leaned over even farther, pelvis twisting in a grotesque pose. His mouth was gaping like a gargoyle's.

"What are you on about?"

"We made a child."

He stared at his wife's silhouette etched against the outside light, as though he'd never seen her before.

"You sure about that?" he said, perfectly still.

"Yes."

"I thought it wasn't possible anymore."

"Turns out there are no hard truths in this world," she said coldly, as though she'd just been attacked.

"You're not lying, now, are you . . ."

"Why would I lie?"

"Hell if I know."

"We need to be careful now!"

"Careful about what?"

Irene looked at her husband, the greatest of fools in her eyes.

"Not to lose him."

Valette stood up and wearily tilted his head back.

"Not much I can do," he said.

She instinctively placed both hands on her stomach and took one step forward, allowing new shadows to eat away at her face.

"You won't touch me anymore," she said sternly.

"Can't be much risk, if I take you."

Irene pointed one arm at Valette. There was hatred in her eyes, though it was hard for him to make out, and something else too, something verging on madness.

"You won't touch me anymore," she repeated, extending the hatred in her gaze to her voice.

Valette approached a stall, and the calf moved behind the planks.

"We'll see about that," he said smiling.

"I think not."

Irene turned around and walked out, holding her breath.

Valette remained motionless on his feet, rotten hay dripping down his hand. The news had struck him hard, though he hadn't wanted to let it show, and now a herd of thoughts was racing through his mind like animals let out at springtime.

Irene had just revealed her plan the way she would have announced the weather. But how was it possible? He hadn't forgotten that she had nearly died when she was carrying Eugene, and not just the once. At the time, the doctor had sworn that she couldn't have another child, and added that it was a miracle that both mother and infant had survived, that he still didn't understand how she had carried the pregnancy to term. Twenty years had gone by since. Why now? And how? Valette repeated to himself.

Plus she would have less mental energy to give this time around, not to mention strength. A baby was the last thing they needed right now. Unless, he considered briefly, it was a twisted attempt on her part to avoid her wifely duties. But he knew her well enough to know she wouldn't do such a thing. She was too frank with everyone, and incapable of lying, for fear of being denied entry to the gates of heaven. If she claimed she was pregnant, there was no doubt she was sure. No point imagining otherwise. So he dismissed his questions, and pride suddenly swaggered in. He placed one hand on his belt, thinking about the hidings the kid would need when he was old enough to learn the gospel according to Valette. He was itching for it. He'd already tamed one son, and he wouldn't mind teaching another the same, in fact he'd enjoy it.

Then he smacked the back of his hand against his forehead, cursing. What an idiot he was! That damn woman had spread her thighs just to get knocked up, and was now closing them over her cursed clit. Where was the logic? Moreover, Irene wouldn't let him take her any other way, never wanted to try even, claiming it wasn't Christian. He'd taken his shot one night when he'd had too much to drink, but she fought back like an untamed mule and he hadn't been able to slip his penis so much as a centimeter into her asshole. Maybe he ought to try again. He'd consider it the next time he felt the need to release his load. Rage would do the rest. The opportunity would come soon enough, he figured.

Not that the sight of Irene's rear end did much to excite him anymore. He usually imagined another rear, much younger. He ran his fingers down his fly and leaned over to look at the mound that had formed in his crotch.

"Good girl, I wouldn't have thought you capable," he said, chuckling.

In this period of rebirth, it wasn't men who leaned down to the earth—it was the earth that leaned in, grabbing firm hold of them, for all that they refused to admit it. The global, primordial earth endlessly amused by these temporary vessels, by their naive obstinacy in wanting to endure beyond their lifetimes by passing down, at best, a few arid acres spat out by the bedrock.

Mother Earth didn't create obstacles for man to overcome them and, in so doing, approach the heavens. She created them for no reason, simply because the fancy struck her. She lied, too, with aplomb and majesty, however unintentionally, for she was in cahoots with the seasons, ever careful not to mislead the roots and bodies in the ground, the plant life and the animals. The earth didn't love, didn't hate, she harbored no ill will, nor good. Didn't think. The men on her surface, miserable settlers bathed in sweat, with their need to give everything a name, to assign some artificial meaning. Men, with their need to find explanations for that which demanded none, when what was needed was to listen, to watch the earth lean in, drawing all life forms to her, including the slightest mineral particle, and even the birds always landed in the end, and the dust always fell. Mother to all, without the slightest concern for her innumerable brood intent on some imagined conquest. The earth, and the vast sky above, silent as well, but which man still questioned, still made to say whatever he wanted to hear.

Life resumed as the earth warmed again, as the greenery set its sights on every horizon.

Leonard was waiting at the edge of the field, attentively observing Joseph, who had a firm grip on the handles of an ox-drawn plow bouncing up and down, the middle bridle around his neck, uttering a word emerging from deep inside a centuries-old throat at the end of each furrow, a word his own father used to say to make the draft animals advance. As was often the case, the walking stick was resting on the old man's shoulders, held there by his dangling arms, limp counterweights seemingly nailed in place.

Once he'd reassured himself that Joseph was managing just fine, Leonard, tottering slightly, began to make his way across the fallow ground. He stopped periodically to jab his stick into the plowed earth, moving around the tip before bending down to grab a clump of dirt and crumble it in the palm of his hand; he then brought the pieces to his nostrils, before letting them slide through his fingers with a long sigh of contentment. He felt an overpowering surge of emotion each time he touched the ground, and smelled it, a feeling that nothing, not even if the morsels were to contain gold, could surpass. It was as if the earth was speaking to him whenever the whistling plow blade loosened thick slices of dirt. An underbelly revealed by the stubborn movements of a pair of oxen joined by a walnut-wood front yoke, their auburn coats blending with the ground, as though this breed and no other had been created to perform this illustrious task.

The field Joseph was plowing used to belong to Leonard and in essence would always belong to him, a protean, reassuring truth. To own, or be owned, was a distinction no man could assume continuously, especially not Leonard. He had given too much not to feel forever linked to this sparse stretch of land, this earth into which he'd sunk to his shoulders to dig his own child's grave. And when the land spoke to him, he also heard the voice of his son, who died crossing the fragile icy surface of a fishing hole scarcely larger than a pond. Neither Leonard nor his wife had heard him cry out when he sank into the frozen water, never to reemerge. Or perhaps he hadn't had time to cry out. The ice had already begun to reform when his parents found him, a tiny, stunned shape floating beneath a frosted magnifying glass, and now buried in silty clay, but also in the depleted memories of an old man and an old woman. Ever since, the earth had clung to Leonard's soles, like his son's body, everywhere he went.

Each time he looked at Joseph, Leonard couldn't help but think of his son whose name he hadn't dared utter since the accident, a son who would have worked his plot of land better than anyone else. He was no longer angry. Too much time had passed for anything to remain apart from great sadness, intimate devotion, and infinite respect for the Mother Earth now carrying their child, eternally parturient. Too many nights had gone by for there to remain anything much to curse. Leonard had come to accept the power of fate, the way you watch the clouds slip away, knowing others will come sooner or later. His son had simply gotten a head start.

Lucie was wrong. Yes, Leonard loved Joseph like a grandson of sorts, with only slightly more distance, but certainly not like a son, for that would have been far too easy a way of lightening the cross he was duty bound to bear until the very end.

He was too old to think that life might offer second chances, but watching Joseph steer the ox and carve grooves into the earth, he began to believe that perhaps hardships were never entirely in vain, that they were the rocks that sometimes diverted the plow from a straight furrow, which you then tried to make up for on the next pass. Once a plot of land had been turned over, what remained of the accidents, of the slip of the plow blade, if not a uniformly swollen surface ready for the harrow's teeth and belated frosts? What remained, if not those very stones removed by hand and piled up to mark a boundary? All those lives spent digging, spent erecting lunar walls to feel themselves masters of the unmoving world. Those lives built from reassembled screes, from pieces put back together the best you can to nourish wild dreams. And when there was a good harvest of rye, and sometimes barley, the hardships and the boundaries were slowly forgotten. They were forgotten because man is made to compensate for the slipping of the plow; more, he spends his whole life at it. So, yes, Leonard had put himself back together after their son's death, in secret, without a word, and Lucie hated him for that, also in secret, without a word either.

Leonard made his way to the north edge of the plot, where he had buried a bottle of cider to keep it cool beneath the freshly turned ground. He unearthed the bottle, raised it in the air, and called Joseph over.

When he reached the end of his row, the boy stopped the ox, lifted the strap over his head and wrapped it around the coulter, then edged around the plowed sections to join Leonard. They drank, Joseph first. They drank as they contemplated, in turn, the brown earth and the clear sky, in silence.

Irene appeared rejuvenated. Slipping away from the others to stroke her belly through the fabric of her dress, a blissful smile on her face. Everything was progressing as it should, the son continuing to grow without obstacle. She never spoke of the pregnancy to Valette, nor did he ask how it was proceeding. The only thing that mattered to Irene was to see the next second arrive, and the next, and so on. Anything that brought her closer to her son's rebirth.

As she'd promised herself she would, she snuck Lucie a chicken, along with two bottles of cider. The old woman welcomed her with a suspicious look and paid little attention to the gifts. After saying that the hardest was yet to come, she sent Irene on her way with a brisk nod. Irene wasn't bothered by the woman's reaction; she knew her past.

Once a week, Irene dragged her fertile soul to the house of the Lord, since he'd played his part as well. She would pray at length, abandoning the Apocalypse for the Gospels, swelling in return with undreamt-of joy, which she would have happily showered upon her narrow universe in shameless provocation if ever her self-interest hadn't stopped her.

One drunken night, Valette entered the bedroom first, stumbling. Collapsed onto the bed without bothering to undress. Irene waited in the kitchen, hoping he would fall asleep quickly, then went to bed herself. The lamp was still burning when she entered the room, trying to muffle her steps the best she could. Valette's eyes were closed, his face split in two by a terrible smile. Irene hurriedly slipped on her nightgown, blew out the lamp, then climbed over Valette's shins and lay down, face a few centimeters from the wall.

"Took ya long enough," he slurred.

Irene stiffened, as though her vertebrae had instantaneously closed ranks and her blood had turned to mercury.

"You're not asleep?"

"I was waiting for you."

"You're drunk... go to sleep!"

Valette abruptly pivoted toward Irene and found the pale nape of her neck and her loose flaxen hair floating before his eyes.

"And you got a problem with that?" he said.

"There's work to be done tomorrow."

"Exactly. So you ought to help me find my motivation."

Irene appeared to weigh her words.

"We already talked about this," she said.

Valette released a long sigh.

"You talked about it. I never said I agreed."

"I won't change my mind."

Valette pressed against Irene, cornering her against the wall.

"Don't you move. You'll see, it'll be smooth as butter, just let me do it," he cackled.

Irene squirmed away, rolled over her alcohol-dazed husband, and leapt to the bottom of the bed.

“Not that way, and not any other either,” she said in an icy, almost disembodied voice.

Valette tried to make her out in the darkness, gathering his wits in the process. A long silence stretched across the room, like a blanket they were each tugging to their side, the only sound their breathing. Irene succumbed first to the words filling her mouth like pebbles with sharp edges.

“You can take me by force, that’s for sure. You’re a man. But if you do, I swear to you I will make you regret it.”

At those words, Valette immediately sobered up. He could barely distinguish the figure huddled beside the wardrobe. He suddenly remembered a female rat he’d flushed from her hiding spot in the barn, who hadn’t hesitated for even a second before jumping at his dog to protect her litter. The rodent had stood no chance of surviving, but she’d attacked anyway, from pure survival instinct. Ready to die. Valette swallowed a long gob of spit, which he felt descend and then disappear down his throat.

“That’s the last time you threaten me, you hear me? The last time!” he said in a voice that was surely not as calm as he’d have liked.

Valette waited for her to respond, to apologize, but she said nothing. He thought about the dog whimpering, its throat bloody, and the rat’s body between its paws. A rat that had transformed absolute certainty into a new fear.

Anna entered the henhouse holding a basket full of freshly picked dandelions. With her free hand, she closed the wire-mesh door behind her to keep in the dozen young hens that rushed up to her, circling and clamoring. Anna nudged them away with her foot, then opened the grate to one of the hutches and tossed part of her harvest inside. Three rabbits sitting in one corner began to nibble eagerly on the tender leaves, ears folded back against fur glistening with sebum, tapping the thick layer of manure with their back feet. She watched them for a moment, lulled by the chickens' clucking, then pulled out the small squirrel sculpted by Joseph, which never left her pocket. Lost in her daydreaming, she didn't hear the door open.

"They like that as much as clover," said Valette.

Anna dropped her basket as she spun around, squeezing the statue in her other hand. Valette observed her closely, as if he was trying to gauge the price of an animal down to the penny. Then, with his good hand, he gestured toward the dandelions scattered across the ground covered with droppings.

"It'd be a shame to let them go to waste. Let me help you," he said.

Anna desperately wished she could leave the henhouse, but Valette's imposing frame was blocking the door and there was no other way out.

"No, don't bother," she said, struggling to mask her unease.

She tucked the statue into her pocket as discreetly as possible, crouched down, and began to pick up the dandelions amid the hens pecking at vegetable peelings. Valette kept a close eye on the rabbits, hands in his pants pockets, conspicuously touching his penis through the cloth.

"Those critters have a nice life, don't they? All they think about is eating and fucking."

After salvaging what she could, Anna rose, opened a hutch door, and began to toss in the dandelions, standing in such a way that she didn't have to turn her back on Valette, thinking that once her basket was empty, he would let her leave.

"Doesn't get much better than that..." he said, coming closer, pointedly scraping his shoes along the ground.

Anna stepped aside to open another hutch.

"'Cause if you ask me, instinct is the only thing that's real. Shouldn't ignore it, when it turns up, right?"

Valette took his hands out of his pockets and leaned forward.

"Nothing to say?"

"Nothing to say."

Valette stopped to stare at Anna, a serious look transforming his face, as if he'd just grasped an unshakable truth and the importance of translating it into equally unshakable words.

"Must be plenty of boys after you... In the city, I mean, must be plenty after a pretty thing like you. Can't imagine there's the same ilk here."

Anna said nothing.

"Unless you do manage to turn some heads, round here."

Anna dumped the remainder of her basket into the last hutch. She backed toward the door, trying to get away from Valette, but he was quicker and stepped sideways to block her.

"Don't run off so quickly. Don't you like being with me..."

"I have things to do."

"Around here, it's me who decides what things you have to do."

"Let me by."

Valette, eyes gleaming, looked like a devil who'd fallen to earth, a little surprised at his luck.

"You think I didn't see you before."

"See me what?"

"Hide something in your pocket."

"I'm not hiding anything."

"Show me, or I'll grab it myself."

Anna hesitated briefly, but the idea of physical contact with Valette was more than she could bear. Trembling, she took out the statue, which Valette grabbed, curious, quickly noticing the engraved initials.

"I see," he said, making a stern face.

"It's none of your business..."

"I reckon I know who gave you this present."

"Give it back."

"Sounds like you're awful attached to it."

Anna was on the verge of tears.

"Give it back, please," she begged.

"That's better, but not quite enough, for now. I'll think about it."

Feigned compassion swept Valette's face.

"You know, if your father doesn't make it back, you could stay here, kind of like our daughter," he said.

"My mother would never allow it," Anna spat out.

"I don't think your mother is in any condition to look after you properly."

Valette had spoken in a very calm voice, which, for Anna, was worse than if he had shouted. Blood was rising in the rims of his eyes, and the two wide wrinkles cleaving his cheeks stretched like drawn bowstrings.

"You sleep in my house and you eat my bread, so don't try your high and mighty act on me, it won't work."

"What do you actually want?" she said.

"Nothing, for now. I know you're a good girl, nice and obedient, and that's how it'll stay, right?"

Anna's voice shook.

"Please let me by," she said.

"'Course I will, but first, I want you to promise me something."

Valette took a long pause.

"You're gonna stop seeing him."

Anna felt an enormous ache in the pit of her stomach. She wanted to say something, but found herself momentarily incapable of speech.

"Nothing gets by me... Get that into your head, once and for all," he added.

"We're not doing anything wrong..."

"You're not to see that Joseph boy again, got it?! I warned him too."

"What?"

"You heard me."

"What did you do to him?" she snapped.

Valette merely smiled.

"You have no right," she said.

"Round here, my dear, I have every right."

Valette brought his face so close to Anna's that she could smell the alcohol and cold tobacco on his breath. He was about to stroke her cheek when she slipped beneath his arm and ran out of the henhouse. Blood was rushing through her whole body, like an animal caught in a trap. Over the sound of her footsteps and the pear tree branches whipping her, she heard Valette laughing like a lunatic.

"No kiss for your old uncle?" he shouted after her.

Perched on the stony pedestal of the cowherd's cross, hands gripping the lichen-strewn rock, Joseph looked as far up the path as his eyes could see. A stubborn wind was flattening the grass in the surrounding fields, revealing tiny rises in the ground and a few vulnerable insects scattering to better shelter. Worried that he hadn't seen Anna yet, Joseph descended from his perch, then rubbed his hands together, releasing a blueish powder. He was about to backtrack down the road to search for the girl when he finally spotted her around the last bend.

She stopped when she saw him coming, as though she needed to gather her strength, her face expressionless and veiled by an unhabitual mist. When he reached her, Joseph didn't ask why she was late, too impatient to take her into his arms. He kissed her passionately in search of warmth but found nothing of the kind on her cold, trembling lips. Surprised, he leaned back, holding her by the waist, and stared at her. She turned away, avoiding his gaze. An ember jostled in Joseph's stomach, then rose and got stuck in his throat.

"You didn't want to see me?" he said.

Before responding, Anna closed her eyes, trying to rid her mind of the poisonous thoughts rushing in, and when she opened them, her gaze struck Joseph as bitterly cold as her lips.

"I'm here," she said.

"Look, you're trembling . . . I can tell something's wrong."

A grimace lifted one corner of Anna's mouth.

"Did my uncle come to see you?" she asked.

"No, why?"

"No reason."

"If you're asking, there must be a reason . . ."

"Hold me tight. Please."

He wrapped his arms around her. Her breathing was rapid, small warm clouds rising in the chilly air, and she kept her two clenched fists against Joseph's chest. All she wanted in that moment was the noise of the wind and the faint sound of cowbells coming from the cattle grazing in the distance.

"You feel better now?" he said.

"Yes, a little."

Joseph clasped Anna's hands in his.

"Come on, tell me what's going on!"

"I don't know . . ."

He let go of her hands.

"Guess I should get going, then," he said coldly.

Anna grabbed back his hands and tried to speak but couldn't find a sufficiently stable anchor in her body. She tried again.

"Valette," she said, as though vomiting up a poisonous word.

"What about Valette? All you've done since you got here is bring him up," he said.

"He disgusts me."

"Yeah, he disgusts me too."

Anna took a long swallow.

"I'm . . . I'm afraid, Joseph."

The boy's face twisted in panic.

"Did he do something?"

Anna had no response. Simply began to sob, furiously rubbing her cheeks with the back of her hands to wipe away the flowing tears.

"He touched you, didn't he?!" yelled Joseph, distraught.

Rage flooded his dry eyes.

"I want to know what he really did to you."

Anna focused on her breathing, her sobs ceased, then she looked up at Joseph, her eyes glistening.

"It's not what you think . . ."

"You don't wanna tell me?"

"Of course I'm going to tell you."

"That piece of shit! Whatever he did, he went too far!"

"He's capable of anything . . ." she said, almost as though she was talking to herself.

"Did you tell your mother?"

She stiffened.

"My mother," she said in a cynical voice.

"Yes, your mother."

"She's in no condition to hear me."

Joseph, fighting to contain a surge of hatred, thought hard.

"You can't stay there," he said.

"Where do you expect me to go?"

"My house."

"You know perfectly well that's out of the question."

"Why?"

"Your mother would never agree, and then there's mine too. I could never leave her alone with them."

"What if you both come? I'll find a way to convince my mother... You said yourself that you don't know what Valette is capable of."

The girl invited a burst of air into her lungs, then said, "I'm sure he'll stop."

"Why would he?"

Anna looked toward the horizon, at the tatters of steam escaping from Puy Violent and rising into the sky, like a breath.

"He knows about us. He doesn't want me to see you anymore," she said.

"So you made a deal with him... is that what you're trying to tell me?"

"If he believes me, he'll leave both of us alone."

Joseph gave her a fierce look.

"No one can stop us from seeing each other, you hear me. No one! I can protect you. Trust me."

"That's not all of it."

The girl paused.

"What else?"

"He told me that he already came to warn you."

"That's not true... Why would he say that? He had to know you would tell me."

"Maybe he thought I would obey him without question."

"Not likely."

A new fear lit up Anna's eyes as she realized just how deep perversion ran inside of Valette, a man she would refer to only as "him" from now on in a desperate attempt to condemn him to anonymity.

"Then you need to watch your back," she said.

"Don't worry. He'd better not threaten me," said Joseph, raising one fist in the air.

Anna felt exhausted. Great weariness settled over her.

"I need to get back," she said.

"I don't want you to go."

"I don't have a choice..."

"I won't be able to relax knowing you're there."

"I'll keep my guard up."

"You can never be alone with him... never. Promise me. Until we find a solution."

Anna stroked Joseph's cheeks.

"It's going to be fine," she said without much conviction.

"I need to think about it some more, but I swear..."

The girl kissed Joseph to shut him up. Noting that he was too distracted to kiss her back properly, she tilted her head back to look at him.

"I love you," she said.

"I love you, too."

"I have to go now."

"When will I see you again?"

"I don't know yet, but as soon as I can slip away, I'll come. For now, we have to be careful."

"I understand, but it can't go on too long. I won't make it."

They agreed to hide their messages in a crevice in a low wall along the path to Grands-Bois, close to the farm so Anna wouldn't have far to go. Then Joseph watched her leave. On either side of the path, tall umbellifers stood guard like soldiers at attention, their inflorescences resembling upside-down epaulettes. As the girl's silhouette dwindled and then disappeared in the quivering air, Joseph felt powerlessness and anger rise inside him like a cloud of cold ash. He made way for that dull hatred, but also for something else looming just beyond, a vague shadow clearly growing in size.

Joseph had stopped sculpting. Fear and hatred were consuming him like rust eating away at a scrap of metal. He knew he wouldn't be able to leave Anna within Valette's easy grasp for much longer. Thinking about the man putting his grotesque claw on her one more time, or worse, was driving him mad with pain. He suspected that Anna hadn't told him the whole truth, to avoid panicking him further, and, in those moments, his burgeoning anger threatened to overflow and rain down on the animals, or even his mother, who imagined a broken heart and said nothing to avoid worsening the situation, thinking time would suffice to soothe her son.

Waiting was torture to Joseph, but he hadn't figured out a course of action that wouldn't endanger Anna further. He snuck away from Chantegril every chance he got, to spy on the Valette farm, at least once a day, checking the hiding place first, where he found messages meant to be reassuring but that still didn't appease his fears. After reading, he would climb a tree in the copse bordering the farm, an observation post that allowed him to monitor all comings and goings. When he saw Anna crossing the courtyard alone, against his advice, an electric shock would run through his brain, and he would prepare himself to rush toward her if needed, not like a lover but a protector charged with braving a demon. And whenever Valette appeared, like an ogre out of a fairy tale from Joseph's childhood, he was seized by an irresistible desire to wipe him off the surface of the earth. To destroy the man.

It was six in the evening when Joseph climbed the ladder to the hayloft. A few rays of light had found a way to creep inside through some broken roof slates and around the frame of the two-paneled door at the rear of the building. As soon as his feet touched the floor slippery with scattered seeds and twigs, he began unpacking the hay, furiously tossing forkfuls in the air, which he then pushed toward the hatch that opened onto the barn. The cows lowed when they saw the fragrant dry grass raining down, extending their necks through their headstalls and ramming their oily horns to try to reach it. There was a strange noise, which sounded uncannily like the cry of a mad owl beneath the beams. Joseph paid it no attention and continued to drop armfuls of hay through the hatch. Then came a second cry, and this time, he instinctively looked toward the rafters.

Despite the gloom, he made out two legs dangling in the emptiness, which extended into an indistinguishable shape sitting on a beam. Joseph clutched the handle of his pitchfork.

"Who's there?" he asked.

"Did I scare you?"

Joseph recognized the voice immediately. The man leaned forward and his face dipped into a pool of light. Valette was perched on the joist, like a tall brigand preparing to leap into the hay at any moment.

"No need to be afraid," he continued.

"I'm not," said Joseph, his voice unsteady.

Valette smiled, shutting one eye at the same time, as though some dust had gotten in.

"Not the impression you're giving," he said.

"What is it you want?"

"To talk a little. It ain't often—"

"You have no business here."

Valette made a pained face.

"Well, I'll be. So that's how you thank me for coming all this way to see you," he said.

"You're welcome to knock on the door, just like everyone else."

"Where's the surprise in that?"

Joseph regained confidence.

"I could have done without. Anyways, I have no intention of talking to you..."

"But still, you do like surprises, don't you?"

"Why do you say that?"

"When you sneak onto someone's property, I can only assume it's to surprise them."

"I don't understand."

Valette's voice went from mocking to contemptuous. "Sure you do."

"I don't sneak around," said Joseph feebly.

"Don't take me for an idiot... I've seen you wandering round my farm like a thief."

"I'm not a thief..."

"So what are you, then, a spy? What are you after?"

"I'm not after anyone."

"I said 'what,' not 'who.' Which means you are after someone, if I follow correctly."

Joseph thought about Anna, about what Valette was putting her through, and nervousness gave way to anger.

"I know what you are," he said, stressing each word.

"And what am I, according to you?"

"A... monster."

"That all?" said Valette, as though he'd been given a compliment.

"Now clear off!"

Valette leaned over a little farther, ready to drop.

"Could it be that you're after a fine-looking girl?"

"And so what?" said Joseph defiantly.

"If I see you trespassing on my land again, you'll leave different than you came, believe you me."

Joseph thrust his pitchfork forward, keeping a firm grip.

"I'll protect her," he said.

"And what do you intend to protect her from?"

"You."

Valette stopped swinging his legs. He placed his hands on the joist, on either side of him, and leaned back. His face disappeared into shadow again, leaving a bright tunnel that immediately filled with speckles of dust.

"Anna told me everything," continued Joseph.

Valette began to laugh. A disembodied laugh that faded into the stifling silence.

"I'd love to know just what she told you," he said finally.

"You'd better stay away from her from now on."

"If you let yourself get reeled in that easily by every pretty young thing, you're gonna get walked all over plenty, you ask me."

"Why would she lie?"

"She's a woman," snapped Valette.

"I told you to clear off!"

Valette placed his hands on his knees without moving his chest, face still lost in shadow. He looked like a decapitated mummy, shrouded, with arms outstretched. He took a deep breath, giving the impression that the words he was about to utter needed to gain some momentum before they came out of his mouth.

"I don't think you've quite caught on, you little shit."

"You don't scare me."

"Yeah, you already said."

Valette swung back and forth a few times, then jumped from his perch, landing in the hay several feet below. Without breaking stride, he slid across the ground to Joseph, who was still brandishing his pitchfork. Not at all intimidated, Valette took a prerolled cigarette from his coat pocket and lit it.

"Put that down," he said in a calm voice that contrasted with the fury seeping from his eyes.

Joseph obeyed. Valette came closer and blew acrid smoke that reeked of garlic and alcohol into the boy's face.

"I would hate for anything bad to happen to you... Who knows what the war holds. Last thing your ma needs is to lose both men of the household. She'd probably never get over it... wouldn't be fair."

Joseph had nothing to retort. Valette tossed his cigarette on the ground, then placed his mutilated hand on the boy's shoulder, though there was nothing friendly about it. He withdrew it just as quickly and stepped back, staring at Joseph, who was crushing the cigarette beneath his shoe. Valette used his back to push one of the door panels and walked out, leaving it open, abandoning Joseph to his indescribable shame, feet poised on the perimeter drawn by the light streaming in, wondering if it had been a dream. But there was that dead weight on his shoulder, where Valette had placed his vile stump. That weight, and its imprint embedded well beneath his flesh.

In her last message, Anna had said that Valette was planning to go to Saint-Paul the following day to sell some livestock, which would take him several hours, given all the drinks he would knock back at the inn. She would meet Joseph at the hayloft, could think of nothing else. Upon reading those words, Joseph should have been overjoyed, but his body was too tense to let him.

When he saw her enter the barn, he approached shyly, mindful not to disturb the air, or upset anything in her vicinity, for fear of shattering the apparition and the shadow that preceded it. He couldn't think of what to say and even his movements felt stiff and forced. But the girl only wanted one thing, and it wasn't words, so she offered him her lips. Joseph would have liked to surrender to that kiss, to the embraces that would follow, but he couldn't. He delicately pushed Anna away, eyes devoid of all expression. She tried again, desperate almost, but still, he offered nothing in return.

"He didn't try anything else?" he asked.

Anna let out a long sigh.

"No."

"I saw you, all alone in the courtyard. That's not what we agreed."

"Nothing'll happen to me in broad daylight. Stop worrying so much!"

"It's eating me up inside, goddammit."

"Come here . . ."

Joseph appeared not to hear.

"Valette came to see me," he said.

Anna stiffened.

"He didn't hurt you at least?" she interrupted.

"He warned me not to try to see you again."

"That's all?"

"I told him he didn't scare me."

She expelled the air from her lungs, her shoulders slumping at the same time.

"Means he can't be too sure of himself, if he came here," added Joseph.

"What'll become of us?" she said.

"I'll figure it out."

She leaned back to better catch his gaze.

"Kiss me," she said.

"I can't not think about it."

Anna waited a beat. Her face hardened.

"Then it sounds like he's won," she said, as if she was placing weapons at his feet.

"What are you on about?"

"It's as if I was never here."

Joseph's eyes clouded with incomprehension.

"Don't say that," he said.

"You're even forgetting to kiss me."

"Don't talk nonsense. I'm thinking about how to protect you."

"Please stop treating me like some tiny fragile creature."

"That's not what you are."

Anna placed her hands on Joseph's chest.

"I want the Joseph from before."

Joseph pulled the girl toward him, and their lips almost touched.

"I haven't changed," he said, forcing a smile.

"Prove it!"

Anna ran one hand through Joseph's hair. He inclined his head imperceptibly, like an animal trying to prolong a caress.

"Thank God you're here," he said.

"Well, you're here too, aren't you . . ."

"Sometimes I wonder if you would look at me the same way, if there were other boys."

"What are you talking about?"

"I can't help it. When I see the way you are, and then, the way I am."

"Nothing would change, believe me," she said in a gentle voice.

"I think about your story with the parallel worlds a lot. I wouldn't like it if you ended up in one where I wasn't there to watch over you."

"I'm not planning to . . ."

"At least you'd be far away from that pig."

Anna rose onto her tiptoes.

"You're going to promise me something," she said.

"Anything you want."

"From now on, whenever we see each other, we won't waste another second talking about other people and things that don't exist, okay?"

"I'll try."

"No, you won't just try! Follow me."

Anna put one foot on the first rung of the ladder leaning against the wall of hay, without taking her eyes off Joseph, then began to climb. He followed, head down, silently pushing away the image of Valette from a few days earlier, in the same barn, an image he would have to vanquish one way or another before he joined the girl in the haystack where they had made love for the first time, knowing he would never again see her the way he had that day.

Anna was emerging from the Bois Noir when she heard cries coming from the farm. She began to run, thinking that Valette had returned earlier than planned and discovered her absence.

When she reached the yard, she found her mother alone and completely flustered. Face beaming, Helen noticed her daughter and ran to her, laughing, then fell into her arms and kissed her cheeks, still laughing, crying too. Holding Anna's hands, she wiped away her tears of joy, laughing even harder, and said, "Your father was granted a furlough."

Anna's face lit up. "When?"

"He's probably already on his way."

"So he'll be here soon?"

"No, not here. We'll go meet him."

A vertical groove formed between the girl's eyebrows.

"We're going home?" she asked.

"No, it's far too dangerous. We'll take the train to Aurillac and find a little hotel there."

"Why doesn't he come here?"

"It's important that it's just the three of us, as a family. You understand, don't you?"

Anna looked down at the cracks between the stones where tiny plants were emerging from winter.

"I understand... How long will we be gone?"

"His furlough is two weeks."

"And then?"

"As long as the war goes on, we'll keep living here. As soon as your uncle gets back, I'm going to ask him to drive us to the train station tomorrow."

Anna pushed her mother away and let go of her hands.

"Tomorrow!"

"Aren't you happy, darling?"

"Of course I am. I'm very happy to see Papa again, it's just so sudden."

Irene was watching the mother and daughter from the bottom of the ramp that led to the barn, as invisible and unmoving as a piece of granite in a wall. She hadn't missed a word of their conversation, or their shameless, unrestrained joy.

"Let's go pack our suitcases. There's no time to waste," said Helen.

As they made their way to the house, Irene walked up the ramp, keeping her eyes on them, and using both hands to hold the fold of her apron containing a dozen eggs.

"So, that's it, huh? Your Emile got his leave!" she said in a haughty voice.

Helen froze when she saw her sister-in-law.

"You heard," she said.

"Hard not to, what with all your hollering."

"I just found out," she said, as if in apology.

Irene gave Helen a hard look, but this time it was filled not with disdain, but with corrosive pity.

"Try to enjoy it. You don't know when the next one'll come, or even if there'll be a next one," she added.

"I'm sorry, Irene."

"What are you sorry about?"

"For Eugene . . . I'm sure your turn will come soon."

Irene stopped walking, speechless, then immediately composed herself to show no sign of the blow this woman had just unknowingly dealt her.

"Leave Eugene where he is," she snarled.

"I understand how you feel, you know . . ."

"If one thing's for sure, it's that you can't, otherwise you'd take care not to be showing off the way you are, little lady."

"I didn't mean to . . ."

"Shoulda thought about that sooner . . . Now, go on, let me by!"

Anna slipped out that same night to tell Joseph the news, torn between her joy at seeing her father again and heartbreak at being separated. He was happy for her, sincerely, and said as much, but as soon as she told him, he sensed another feeling deep in his gut, realizing in that moment that he would rather have her close, despite Valette's menacing presence, than know she was far from him, the risk being that she might never return. He promised to wait beneath the tall purple beech trees, just beyond the black rock, to bid her a final goodbye.

Preparations for the departure proceeded in silence. Irene hadn't uttered a word since the conversation in the courtyard, alone in her world, alone with her secret. In any case, she'd said her piece to her sister-in-law. What else could she have added? Valette was calmly eating a slice of bread with fresh sheep's cheese, which he salted before noisily shoving large pieces into his mouth. Helen was impatient, looking out the window at the harnessed oxen, who were shaking their massive heads to chase the flies out of their eyes. Valette stood up, still chewing. "C'mon, hurry up. I've got other things to do, you know!" he said as he folded his knife and slipped it into his pants pocket. Helen and Anna followed him outside, each carrying one suitcase, which they placed in the cart. The oxen snorted. Valette climbed onto the fold-up seat and grabbed the flexible rod underneath. The women got in the back, standing on the bed strewn with fragments of dried manure, holding on to each other.

"Neither of you wants to sit by me? It's more comfortable," said Valette, placing one hand on the narrow seat.

"No, we're fine," said Helen.

Anna didn't respond to the invitation.

"As you like, but you can't stick together like that, it throws everything off balance," he said.

Anna crossed the bed and gripped a railing with one hand. Then Valette ordered the oxen to advance. The ensuing jolt nearly knocked down Helen, who was already daydreaming about the reunion with her husband.

They took the road that went to Saint-Paul. The dog accompanied them at first, barking after the wheels, but gave up after a few hundred feet. Anna stared at the muddy ribbon unwinding behind the cart, at the distance unfolding and taking her farther from Joseph, but closer to her father. Valette was studying the tender grass in the higher pastures, which looked as if they were charging the mountain, though it wasn't clear who was leading the attack—if the grass was truly mounting the slope or if the stone was descending, a question he'd never thought to ask, seeing only the hay that needed to be brought in, and not the infertile rock.

"It'll be near time to cut the hay, when you get back. You'll need to put some elbow grease into it," he said, turning to give Anna a long, lewd glance, like a large storm cloud ready to pour down over the girl.

A pleased expression on his face, Valette clicked his tongue and tossed a few onomatopoeias at the animals, as well as a needless stroke of the rod that whistled through the air and landed on one of the steers' backs. He turned again, this time toward Helen, as if he'd just remembered something.

"You'll ask him if he's seen Eugene, you never know."

"All right," said Helen.

The forest came into view and the slope became even steeper. The thaw had left deep ruts in the ground, birthing new stones that jostled the already jerky cart each time its wheels got stuck in the one or stumbled over the other. Helen and Anna were holding tightly to the rails so they wouldn't slip, and Valette's head and chest lurched from side to side with each bump. Right before they entered the forest cover, a flight of wild geese pierced the blue sky in asymmetrical splendor, making beseeching cries as they made their way to the northern plains that they would also abandon when the light grew weak, before returning the following spring. Such was their life.

When they neared the black rock, Anna probed the underbrush for the spot where Joseph had said he would be waiting. And he was there, hidden by the beech trees overlooking the path, observing the procession advancing at the oxen's stubborn pace. He wished he could shout to Anna to jump off the cart and meet him for a kiss, stop time long enough for such a miracle, spend a few minutes in one of those parallel worlds she'd spoken about the first time they met, a detour that would allow for their embrace, nothing more. Anna discreetly raised one hand, and her face was troubled, grave almost.

As soon as the cart had passed, Joseph emerged from his hiding spot. Standing motionless amid the withered trees, he placed one hand on his heart, watching the small procession from above. The sight struck him as indecent, not only because of the man he hated more than anything, but also because of the two women he was leading like livestock to market, with just as little regard. Joseph felt a weight constrict his chest. He moved his hand to his mouth and clenched his jaws around it. His teeth tore flesh, hit bone. Blood filled his mouth, though the pain came from his chest, his heart trapped in a vise being tightened by a mangled hand.

Joseph couldn't summon tears—too much ice in his eyes. He looked away from the cart, only to immediately look back, hoping that it had vanished, abruptly dropped into the village, like a bad dream. When it was out of eyesight, he remained where he was, feet planted in moss strewn with leaves shredded by the passing of winter, his body already tortured by absence, unable to move from the deserted path and the vast shadow that had just been cast over it.

They could see the first houses now and, advancing in their direction, the postwoman, walking with the confident stride of someone who believes the world expects something from them, which might even be the only reason they continue to make their way through it. She had swapped her hat for her husband's postman cap, which gaped around her head, and which he would never need again since he had ascended to heaven in a large explosion before falling back to earth as rain. Valette pulled lightly on the bridle to halt the oxen a few feet in front of her.

"Oh, thank God. Now I don't have to go all the way up to your farm," she said, waving a piece of paper.

Valette held out one hand to grab it.

"The letter's for the lady," she said, as though she was scolding a child.

The postwoman made her way around the cart. She gave the envelope to Helen, who immediately unsealed it and unfolded the letter inside as the others looked on silently. Helen read, then let the piece of paper dangle from one hand, a tiny deciduous object seemingly ready to end its fall on the cart bed, but which she nonetheless gripped firmly as she wearily handed it to her daughter.

"Bad news, is it?" asked the postwoman, overly contrite.

Helen looked at the woman in her ridiculous getup but couldn't answer her question for fear that she might collapse, from too much water inside of her and too much salt on the open wound that was her heart. Anna read the letter, then crossed the cart bed and took her mother in her arms, and neither could hold back her tears any longer.

"They took two of mine, you know," said the postwoman, jabbing her thumb against her chest.

Seeing that no one was paying any more attention to what she said, she didn't linger and set out the way she'd come, grumbling. She'd have liked to know the contents of the letter, but she didn't want to hear it, not really.

"God have pity on us," she repeated as she made her way down the path.

Valette understood there was no need to make the trip to Salers. He asked what exactly had happened. Anna finally told him that Emile wouldn't be coming to Aurillac, that a new offensive was being prepared, and that all furloughs had been cancelled until further notice.

"Bad luck," said Valette before spitting to the side. "We wasted all this time for nothing."

He directed the oxen to turn around. No one noticed the deep wrinkles radiating from his eyes, the expression of a mix of spiteful thoughts that in no way saddened him, though he would have far preferred that his brother had been struck dead, or at least that a shell had deprived him of a member of equal importance to a hand.

So you thought God would spare you from tragedy because you're wellborn!" said Irene.

Seated at the table, Helen was lifting a cup of coffee to her lips when the words struck her. She stopped mid-motion, gaze sweeping across the room, unable to imagine they were addressed to her.

"Are you talking to me?" she asked.

"You see anyone else? Don't pretend. You heard me just fine."

"Do you think it's the moment to say such a thing to me?"

Irene poked one finger—like a small root capped with a thick nail whitewashed in spots—at Helen.

"The moment to set you straight, yes," she said.

"I've never thought what you're accusing me of."

"Well, you must have thought it was your due... that the good Lord would listen to you more than the rest of us."

Helen felt tears rising. She set her cup on the table, keeping her eyes on it. Her hands were trembling.

"Why are you so mean to me? I don't wish harm on anyone," she said.

"I'm bringing you back to earth, is all! You have to admit you need bringing down lately..."

Cut to the quick, Helen summoned her strength. She leapt up to admonish Irene, as though she was talking to a maid.

"Well, I'm back on earth now, believe me," she said, raising her voice.

"Easy, girl! If that was the case, you wouldn't be walking around with a face as long as a month of Sundays. You'd fight, like we do."

Helen's determination didn't last long.

"I do what I can," she said, her voice feeble again.

"What you can isn't enough. Gotta force yourself."

"You think it's so easy."

Irene's mouth twisted into a forced smile. She extended her neck, as if she wanted to loom over this woman for whom she felt such contempt.

"It's hard for everyone, but around here, we don't show it when things aren't easy."

"I'm trying. Can't you see that, at least?"

"You had best try harder, 'cause for now I haven't seen much. We can't keep feeding a mouth that's just a mouth . . . It's time to get cracking."

"We gave you money. If you want more . . ."

Irene thrust out her hand to interrupt Helen.

"Money . . . of course! Can't milk it, though, or plant it, or harvest it, far as I know. Thank God your daughter's of haler stock than you. I'd hate for it to rub off on her."

Helen swept one hand across her forehead, shaking her head.

"I don't know how you do it," she said.

"How I do what?"

"You never talk about Eugene."

Irene froze when she heard her son's name. Her hands began to twitch, and she dug them in her coat pockets.

"I make do with that too," she said, and her voice sounded like the hissing of a snake circling its prey.

"Not everyone can be as strong as you."

Irene clenched her fists, and two uneven dimples formed in her cheeks.

"And what about honor? Though I'm guessing you never learned that one, huh."

Helen wished she could leave the room, but all she had in her capacity was to remain seated, in front of her cup of now cold coffee. Then she shut her eyes.

It was rare to see an automobile in these parts. Though there was at least one, which belonged to the gentleman who lived alone in the manor along Route du Fau. Monsieur "de something." Once a month, in peacetime, he used to drive around the countryside with no apparent aim, simply to empty the tank, then go home. Everyone had wondered what he was searching for, since he didn't talk to anyone and had hardly anything left apart from an automobile purchased with who knows what money, a dilapidated estate, and a name with an aristocratic particle in the middle, like an old, jammed hinge. The townsfolk had stopped being afraid of the family going on two generations now, and even less so its most recent member. They made fun of him in fact, bowing exaggeratedly when he passed, the way sharecroppers used to when the "de somethings" owned the vast majority of land in the region and multiple properties. He never responded to the provocation, didn't seem to notice for that matter. People figured he must be a little mad, stuck inside a past of nostalgic glory, behind the wheel of his car, but no one knew what was going through his head; no one would ever know what was going through such a head. He'd gone off to war too, and nobody had heard from him since.

The De Dion-Bouton descended along the winding road from Salers, backfiring and smoking. It reached the village of Saint-Paul, crossed the bridge, drove along the cemetery tucked into the shadow of the black rock, ascended toward town, then stopped in front of the church with a shudder of metal. The driver pulled on the brake lever with two hands, then removed his leather cap and protective goggles, revealing a zone free of dirt around his eyes. He rose from the seat and looked around as he took off his gloves like the driver of a Roman chariot calling upon whatever god was most likely to lead him to a hypothetical victory. Who could have imagined that he was simply fleeing the worst of all defeats?

He opened the car door, grabbed a travel bag stuffed behind the quilted seat, and got out. He was young, average height, very slim, and his face absent the slightest hint of emotion. There was something regal about his fluid gait, old-fashioned even, as he made his way to the inn in the town square. Three young boys suddenly materialized, buzzing around the automobile in admiration. They waited for its owner to go inside before approaching the slumbering engine and stroking the burning-hot chassis.

Two old men turned toward the stranger as he entered the inn. He said hello and they returned to their drinks, exchanging a complicit look, without responding. A woman approached the man suspiciously, a pitcher in her hand. She looked him up and down, as though she could guess his whole story with a single glance, or more precisely a story she would be careful not to question. The years had dug hollows into her face, but she still seemed spry, judging from her movements and voice.

"You lost?" she asked firmly.

The visitor briefly wondered if it was truly a question.

"No, not at all," he said.

The two old men furrowed their brows in unison, as though they'd agreed not to speak in order not to miss anything of the conversation.

"There's a place up in Salers that I'm betting is probably better suited for you."

"Do you have any free rooms?" asked the stranger, ignoring her comment.

"All I got is free rooms!"

"Can I rent one?"

"You sure?"

The young man smiled at the innkeeper. She didn't repeat the question, walked to the counter and set the pitcher down. He followed.

"For one night?" she asked, opening a register.

"A few. It depends. I don't know how long I'm staying yet."

"You looking for someone?" she said, flipping the register so he could sign it.

The stranger didn't reply. For the first time since he'd arrived, his face relaxed, and he smiled at the woman.

"I'm on furlough," he said, writing down his name.

She flipped the register back and read the name to herself, silently moving her lips.

"Hard to pronounce... if it's all right with you, I'll call you Mr. Mathias."

"Yes, of course... I'm looking for someplace quiet where I can rest."

"You'll find plenty of quiet around here."

One of the old men raised his glass as high as he could.

"Get the soldier a drink, on me. And don't forget us either," he said.

"Thank you," said Mathias without looking at him.

The woman grabbed a glass from behind the counter.

"Wine or plum brandy?"

"The hard stuff!" shouted the old man before Mathias could respond.

She cast a weary glance at the newcomer and, seeing no reaction, filled his glass with brandy, then replenished the old men, who swigged their drinks, clicking their tongues, still in unison.

"Where you from, soldier?" asked one of the men, noisily setting his glass on the table.

"Ardennes."

"Is it true what they say?"

"What do they say?"

"That it's far from over."

Mathias contemplated his glass.

"It's war," he said.

"Yeah, but sounds like this one's hitting its stride."

Mathias raised his glass and brought it to his lips without drinking.

"Cheers!" he said.

"Cheers," the two men replied in chorus.

They drank.

"We know what the papers say. And the letters," continued the old man.

Mathias set his glass down without a word. The woman slammed her fist on the counter.

"Can't you see he don't feel like talking? That he's here to forget what's happening out there. Aren't you?!"

"Thank you for the drink, gentlemen. It was a long trip," said Mathias, abandoning his full glass.

He nodded goodbye and grabbed the room key the woman was holding out conspiratorially.

"Second floor, first door to the right," she said.

"Thank you for your hospitality."

"Don't mention it. I'll come up and make the bed later. And if you want to eat something after, not a problem at all."

"All right."

She turned toward the old men, face disdainful.

"I promise they'll be gone when you come back down."

The duo tried to protest, but she swiftly sent them on their way.

"Well, if that's how it is, see if we ever set foot back here again, huh?" said one of the men, taking his partner as witness.

"I'll light a prayer candle at church and hope you don't," said the woman.

"That's no way to treat loyal customers," said the other.

From the stairs, Mathias heard the conversation become heated, then hushed voices and chairs scraping across the floor. He entered an austere bedroom furnished with a brass bed, a nightstand, and a low one-door wardrobe, tossed his bag onto a mattress sagging in the middle, crossed the room, opened the window, and slowly pushed open the shutters. He saw the two old men in the street, talking and lurching slightly. Mathias stepped back so they were out of eyesight and the valley unfurled before him, followed by the mountains in the distance, just as beautiful as he had told him.

Almost one year had gone by since the conscription. Grass was cut from June to July, and the weather was forgiving. Crops were harvested the same as they'd always been, but with ever fewer hands, less dedication, less strength. The war dragged on far away, and yet remained a steady companion to the townsfolk of Saint-Paul, each time it took a son or a husband, sometimes both at the same time, sometimes more, or, when one came back, deprived of his human form or his mind. Now people knew the conflict would last, since, as it turned out, it wasn't being waged by soldiers, but by high-ranking officers who would never enter the fray themselves, apart from playing with models on mahogany tables. Little matter what they said. It was in all the letters, which were often censored to protect those on the home front from becoming too angry, too horrified, too hopeless.

So they shouldered, they toiled, they swallowed their tongues, secretly hoping to age even faster, to escape their own suffering the best they could. Everyone fought in their own way, clumsily preparing their weapons, futile twigs, fully aware that they were no longer part of a common fate, but that each family was on the path to a unique destiny well out of their hands. Seeking to attract the attention of a selfish god that most certainly didn't belong to all.

Life at Grands-Bois contracted, too. Singular survival of the kind practiced by herd animals who serenely watch another of their cohort die in the jaws of a predator, relieved not to have been chosen. Of course, there was little risk of being caught by an open predator in these mountains, though things were hardly better; the predators here were sly, lying in wait somewhere you would never expect.

Irene had become a stone wall, capable of saying fewer than ten words in the course of a single day. Now she walked, not that anyone noticed, exaggeratedly spreading her legs to distribute an additional weight that couldn't even be detected on her frame. Valette and she never spoke of what she was carrying. Since the night she had threatened him, he hadn't tried to force himself on her again. Sometimes he would stare at her intensely, as if he wanted to convince himself of a truth claimed by this woman, which he had never considered understanding, simply because he had never felt the desire. The only enviable truth about which he cared could be found in a glass of brandy, in the unlocked heat of his body, in the dikes that yielded beneath the flood of his accumulated frustrations and allowed him, for a time, to forget his self-loathing. At the least, alcohol had that unrivaled power, which no human being had ever been able to reveal. In those moments, his desire to lift his niece's dress grew, to finally see her pretty little ass, pale and firm and bouncing beneath the fabric, to split it in two like a ripe, juicy peach on a vine. He had decided to leave her alone, to rebuild her confidence. The time would come when she would realize there was no way out. Until then, he would patiently help her get used to the idea.

Helen, however, had sunk into a lethargic state, all the lightness in her being stripped away. She moved listlessly, troublingly so, as though she didn't care what happened to her and was merely going through the motions. The cruel reality of the war had entered her, passing through flesh and bone, down to the marrow. She had become permeable to tragedy. There'd been no news from Emile since she received the telegram delaying his furlough, and now Helen feared the worst. Never seeing him again. Even the harsh words continuously flung at her by Valette and Irene seemed to reflect off her like burning rays on a windowpane. A vague sensation of warmth, and nothing more.

Anna was worried at seeing her mother so apathetic. Whatever she said, Helen would agree, without listening. Smiling at times, most certainly at someone else.

Her rare meetings with Joseph were the girl's only respites from the oppressive mood at Grands-Bois. They continued to exercise caution, so as not to arouse suspicions in Valette, who hadn't brought up the matter again. Joseph had calmed over time but remained as vigilant as ever. Kept his guard up around the demon.

Their hiding spots were leafy alcoves guarded by thick shadows. There, finally reunited, Joseph and Anna found a kind of peace, which ignited their desire and surrender to the flesh. This was their strength—the ability to momentarily keep at bay the weight of their lives, to give in to pleasure, as naturally as you would shake out the pins and needles in a stiff muscle, forgetting the feeling of absence that awaited them behind a door as soon as they parted ways.

Hands in his pockets, Valette was discreetly looking out the window, squinting from the sun, twisting and cracking his neck.

"There's someone outside," he said.

Irene stopped churning milk and lifted her head, observing her husband but not seeing him, as if she was trying to summon a specific memory of him that time had buried somewhere within a large heap of trifles. She picked up the churn with both hands, set it on the table, wiped her hands on her apron, rose, and walked toward her husband, who was still glued to the window, slowing with each step she took.

"Never seen him," she said after a moment.

"Where's that damn dog? Never around when we need him."

"What would it change? Not like he's ever sent anyone running..."

"He's been standing there like a lemon for a while now."

"Maybe he's lost."

"I don't think so. I'd say he's looking for something."

"Maybe he is."

"Why doesn't he knock at the door, then?"

Irene shrugged.

"Just ask him," she said.

"Probably a vagabond who needs some work."

"Don't look like a vagabond to me," she said after another pause.

"I can't place him."

Valette scratched his chin, stretching his jaws.

"Well, he'll be on his way sooner or later."

Then, an image glided into Irene's head: the angel from her dream leaning over her son's corpse. The temperature rose in her body; her heartbeat quickened.

"Shall I go talk to him?" she said, composing herself.

"Tell him that we don't have any work for him, if that's what he's after."

Irene went outside. She leaned slightly to one side as she walked, a lingering effect of the position in which she'd been churning the milk, but also from the surge of emotion still hindering her movements. The young man watched her approach. He pulled a blade of grass out of his mouth with a firm tug and let it fall to the ground. Irene froze a few feet away from him and swallowed hard.

"What do you want?" she asked, thrusting her thin body forward as though she wanted to mark the space between them.

"Hello! Mrs. Valette, I presume?"

"How do you know my name?"

"I asked," he said, extending one hand toward her, then withdrawing it.

"We don't have any work round here, if it's about that."

The young man was calm. Every word he uttered seemed to justify the previous one.

"I'm not looking for work," he said.

"Then why are you here?"

"I wanted to speak with you, and your husband."

"My husband is busy, so say what you have to say and clear out."

Irene slid one foot backward across the parched ground.

"We haven't seen you round here before . . . Where are you from, anyway?" she said in an uncertain voice.

"Somewhere that leaves nothing to be desired. I'm on furlough for a few days and then . . . I'll have to go back."

Irene's attitude changed at the mention of a somewhere that apparently couldn't be named. She looked at this boy disguised as a man, sure that he would have swum in any item of clothing, unable to imagine him with a weapon in hand charging the enemy, except for those eyes, two pieces of gypsum that nothing could penetrate.

"I came here to talk to you about your son," he said, turning the palms of his hands toward the sky.

Irene swiveled abruptly, just long enough to make out the figure framed in the window. Then she turned back around and stepped to the side so she was squarely across from the young man, blocking him from her husband's line of sight, as well as any gesture that might have betrayed the reason for his visit.

"What can you possibly tell me that I don't already know?"

"It was me . . ."

Mathias paused, hating the silence he'd created, and looked down, gaze lingering on the six feet of distance between him and Irene.

"It was me who closed Eugene's eyes," he finally said in a hoarse voice.

Irene stiffened. All her flesh seemed to vanish beneath her worn clothes, as if there was nothing but bone left to keep her standing. She gulped air into her dry mouth without the slightest sound.

"All this way to tell me that."

"I wanted to see where he lived... I promised him."

"Well, now you've seen it, so go on!"

Mathias took one step forward. Irene swiftly moved back, so the gap between them didn't narrow.

"Can I come in for a moment?"

Irene raised one arm in dismissal.

"No, you can't."

"He didn't have time to suffer..."

"What matters is that he's dead and no one can erase death."

Another silence filled the air, and, in that silence, there were two distinct kinds of pain contained in the same grief.

"You planning to visit all the families of the boys you saw die? You some kind of priest, that it?" she asked.

"We were... friends. Me and Eugene."

The young man's voice cracked at the sound of the name.

"Off with you, now!"

"I didn't mean to make you uncomfortable. I just wanted to talk to you about him..."

Irene struggled to remain motionless, at the risk of shattering beneath an enormous weight.

"I don't wanna hear another word. How else can I say it?" she said.

"As you like. If you change your mind, I'm staying here a few more days. I got a room at the inn in Saint-Paul."

"You got nothing better to do than stay somewhere you're not welcome? Like see your family, while you're still alive?" said Irene with rage and contempt in her voice.

"It's important to me that I stay a little longer," he said.

"I don't ever want to see you again. Is that clear enough?"

Mathias extended his arm again. Irene looked at his hand in disgust, at his long, double-jointed fingers like an insect's freakishly long legs, which she imagined closing her son's eyes.

"Goodbye, Mrs. Valette. My name is..."

"I don't wanna know your goddamn name."

He went silent, taking in the farm one last time. A sad smile of consternation formed on his lips. He left the farm slowly, as though each step required overwhelming effort. A long trail of sweat down his back had glued the fabric to his body, leaving a dark, vertiginous stain. Watching him go, his shirttails floating on either side of his frail body, Irene was reminded of the wings of a clumsy bird, and no longer those of her dream-angel leaning over her dying son.

Then he was gone. Irene again felt the weight of Valette's stare on her shoulders. She turned around, furrowing her brows in an expression of incomprehension intended for her husband. A ray of light set the window ablaze, sparing the sash bars in the form of a cross, like the pitiless condemnation of a heretic that nothing in the world could have compelled Irene to challenge. This man whom she would have to spurn for the rest of her days. This man who had just escaped fire and was already walking toward her. This man on the outside, the son on the inside.

"What'd he want?" Valette asked.

Irene gave a cynical sigh.

"You were right," she replied without a beat.

"'Bout what?"

"He was looking for work."

"Took you an awful long time to tell him we had nothing for him."

"Well, next time you can handle it, if you'd rather..."

"That's not what I'm saying."

"He wanted to know if I could suggest other farms that might hire him."

Valette spat, then nodded toward an empty space between two piles of rocks, where the man had vanished.

"Where was he from?"

"I didn't think to ask."

"Odd," he said, after thinking for a moment.

"What's odd?"

"He really didn't look like a day laborer, dressed like that, and he's not young enough or old enough not to be at the front."

Irene swayed gently, shifting her weight from one foot to the other, as though pulling herself from sludge to find her balance on more solid ground.

"What do you think?" Valette continued.

"Well, go run after him, if you care so much," she said curtly.

"Odd, very odd," repeated Valette almost without loosening his jaws.

"Maybe we were both dreaming."

Valette swept his atrophied hand through the air, casting a cabalistic shadow on the ground.

"You're talking nonsense. We can't both dream the same thing..."

"What would you know?"

"Don't tell me you're losing your mind?!"

Irene shrugged her shoulders, and they dropped down just as quick.

"Wouldn't be the worst thing in the world," she said, walking back to the house.

Tom was rolling along the ground in the garden, burying his muzzle in freshly turned-up clumps of dirt, then pulling it out with an exhalation of wet dust. Mathilde was kneeling on a short plank, both hands around the stake that Joseph was hammering into the ground with precise blows, the last of twenty-five. When he was done, Joseph let the tool fall with a dull thud, the handle leaning against one thigh. He tested the stake's rigidity by trying to move it with one hand, as he'd done for the others. "All good," he said with satisfaction.

Mathilde grabbed a ball of cotton string set on the plank beside a pair of sewing scissors with corroded handles, and used the string to attach a tomato plant to the stake, making sure it wasn't too tight. Then she cut the string with the scissors and placed everything back in the side pocket of her dress. Her hands were stained with a yellowish green substance that gave off the distinctive smell of tomato leaves. She rose, lifting one knee after the other, picked up the plank, and ran the back of her free hand across her forehead.

"I hope we get some nice tomatoes this year," she said.

"Can't catch disease, is all."

"We'll put some copper wire in the stems when the plants are stronger, like your grandmother used to..."

"I remember."

Mathilde turned to the side.

"Beans'll be coming in soon. We should be able to sell some."

Joseph gave his mother a surprised look.

"I never saw Grandmother sell a single vegetable from her garden... She gave them away when she had too much."

"Times change."

"We'll offer some to Leonard first. Seeing how much he helps us."

"Leonard has a garden."

Joseph raised the mallet into the air with a single hand and slammed it down on a clump of earth, which exploded.

"Of course we'll offer him some," she said.

"Would you have thought to?"

Mathilde leaned down and placed one hand on the head of the dog sitting at her feet.

"We need to take advantage of everything we can," she said.

"Aren't we're doing that already?"

A slight quiver threw a corner of Mathilde's mouth off balance, a hesitation that stretched her lips wide, as though she was voluntarily splitting her face.

"The government's offering to help us," she said.

"What's the occasion?" asked Joseph coldly.

Mathilde gave a weak smile, but it couldn't hold back the sadness flooding her face.

"We could get one and a quarter francs a day, plus fifty cents for every child under sixteen. That's what the letter said."

"We got a letter saying that?"

"Yesterday."

Joseph destroyed another clump of earth with the mallet.

"I won't be under sixteen for much longer..."

"All we have to do is ask, and then we get the money."

"You're not seriously telling me we're gonna beg!"

"That's not what this is. And anyways, we're in no position to refuse," Mathilde said firmly.

"We don't have to refuse. We just don't answer."

Mathilde rubbed her stained hands together, and a sickly-sweet smell rose to her nostrils.

"It's not as simple as you say," she said in a softened voice.

"I'll work even harder, if I have to."

"That's just it. You wouldn't have to."

"Father always told me that a man's work should be enough to feed his family, otherwise he's not really a man."

"Your father's not here."

Joseph glanced around.

"You see any other man round here at the moment?"

"I could have made the decision on my own, without talking to you."

"So why didn't you?"

Mathilde extended one arm toward her son, then placed her hand on the stake.

"Sometimes, I tell myself that you're growing up too fast."

"And whose fault is that?"

"I don't want you to end up paying for it one day."

"Well, everything costs something, don't it... I think I learned that from both you and Father."

A long sigh emerged from Mathilde's half-open mouth, infecting the air between them.

“You never tell me anything,” she said, stressing the last word.

“That’s ’cause there’s nothing to tell.”

“That girl still on your mind?”

Furrows emerged on Joseph’s face, shadows nestled within them.

“ ‘That girl’ is really all you can say? She hasn’t changed her name, as far as I know,” he said in annoyance.

“I’ve got nothing against her. I thought I’d made that clear. You still seeing her?”

Joseph abruptly pushed away the handle of the mallet, which bounced off the ground.

“Leave Anna where she is, Mother, and stop pretending! You’re the one who never talks about anything important.”

“That’s not fair.”

“Things don’t go away just ’cause you don’t talk about them, least of all this damn war.”

“I simply want to protect you.”

“Protect me? You really think that’s what I need? I’m not a kid anymore, for Christ’s sake.”

Mathilde felt powerless before her son, who was in fact fighting that “kid” inside of him.

“I tried to do my best,” she said.

“You know I’m right.”

“Maybe,” she said to herself.

“Well?!”

“Well, what?”

“You gonna throw that letter into the fire?”

There was winter in Mathilde’s eyes, the winter gone by and all the others, too.

“Fine,” she said.

They stayed in the garden awhile longer, without talking, wondering who would leave first, the dog between them looking from mother to son, son to mother, as though hoping to reconcile two equally beloved enemies.

Valette hurtled into the kitchen. He planted himself in front of Irene, one fist in the air, eyes quartered by rage. She stepped back, raised her arms in a cross to protect her face, and closed her eyes, waiting for the blow. The blow didn't come. Her ears were buzzing as though a blue bottle fly were whirling inside her head. She heard footsteps and the sound of a cupboard door. She opened her eyes, lowered her arms, and saw Valette standing beside the sideboard, gulping down brandy, gaze fixed on her. He wiped his mouth with one shirtsleeve and pointed at her with the outstretched bottle.

"You lied to me," he spat.

Irene, petrified, didn't move.

"What are you talking about?"

"That guy the other day. He wasn't looking for work."

"How do you know?"

Valette took another swig.

"He's all they're talking 'bout down in Saint-Paul. A soldier on furlough who arrived in an automobile . . . staying at the inn."

"Did you meet him?"

"No. Apparently he spends all his time on the mountain."

"So? What difference does that make?"

"What difference?! Why'd you make up that story, for Christ's sake?"

"'Cause you gave me the idea, remember?" she retorted.

Valette took one step forward and slammed the bottle onto the table, still gripping it, fury again blazing in his eyes.

"Talk, before I really lose my temper. I won't ask you twice," he said.

"Eugene was killed."

Valette froze.

"Eugene is dead," he said.

He stared at the bottle, a stunned look on his face.

"Why didn't you tell me?" he finally asked.

"I wanted to, but I didn't have the courage, I suppose..."

"What'll become of us now?"

"I don't know..."

Valette slowly lifted his head and looked suspiciously at his wife.

"Normally they send a letter to announce that a soldier's dead, not a person."

Irene didn't reply.

"You're taking me for a ride... You knew already, didn't you? Otherwise you wouldn't have reacted like that when that fellow came the other day," said Valette.

"I'm sorry..."

"When'd it happen?"

Irene sighed, drawing out her breath just long enough to find her words.

"February. The eighteenth."

"February... you've been hiding it all this time? Are you mad?"

"Like I said, I couldn't..."

"You have some fucking nerve, you bitch!"

"I thought I'd be able to tell you, eventually."

"How could you act like nothing happened?"

Valette squeezed the bottle neck as hard as he could, his mind churning over this new information.

"I don't understand."

"What don't you understand?"

"Why'd that kid come all the way here when he had to have figured we'd received the letter?"

"Ask him yourself, if you like, but I told him not to come back. That I never wanted to see him again."

"So there's something else I oughta know, then."

"I got nothing else to say. You can hit me if you want."

"I've never laid a hand on you."

"Do what you want."

"What I want…"

Valette paused, hand trembling, giving the bottom of the bottle the freedom to start dancing a jig on the wood. All the strength inhabiting his muscles appeared to have suddenly vanished, his limbs incapable of even rustling the canvas and cotton of his clothing, incapable of any coherent movements. He looked at his wife with dead eyes, meeting her equally extinguished gaze, as a haunting noise echoed in his head, squealing, like nails desperately clinging to a smooth wall. Irene had never seen him so distraught, so disarmed. At this moment when he was realizing that the foundation of his entire life, everything he had tried to achieve through his labors and otherwise, that what past generations of Valettes had constructed at the cost of their lives, that the relentless determination with which they had built walls and cleared fields in order to pass down both, and not just, passing down the memories of those struggles, too, that all of it was pure deception, a pointless ruin in the making. And he, Valette, could do nothing about it.

Irene placed one hand on her stomach. She approached her husband, arching her back exaggeratedly, comically almost. He let her come, still broken, then composed himself.

"That won't change anything."

Irene stopped. Now a chair separated them. She slipped her hand down her stomach, extending it toward the web of destroyed flesh hanging at the end of her husband's arm, and her curved fingers seemed to have taken the fetus's imprint, a promise she'd have liked to make without needing words to express it, and perhaps even to this man, seeing as there was no one else to whom she could offer it.

"There'll always be wars to take them away from us," she said in a low voice.

"What are you talking about?"

"You know what..."

"Maybe it's not the worst thing... to die at war."

Valette's lips shook like logs tossed around by a river current, looking at his joke of a hand, to which she had believed she had offered the most precious thing in the world.

"I can't believe you lied to me about it."

Irene hesitated, then dropped her hand.

"Maybe you've been lying to me all this time," he added.

"Maybe, but in any case, you won't find the truth you think you will on the other side of my lies."

"The truth? What do you know about the truth?"

Valette tilted the bottle slightly to see what was left. He inhaled, and then drank until it was empty, keeping the bottle in his mouth. He could see it jiggling, and his eyes began to sting, like when smoke got in and he would let it. He set down the bottle with one hand.

"Drinking like that won't help you."

He brought the bottle back to his lips out of pure provocation, then, remembering it was empty, held it out to his wife, enraged.

"Maybe you'd like to stop me."

"It'll kill you one of these days."

"Even so. What do you care?"

"We're gonna need you."

"You've never needed anyone," he said, not noticing the "we."

Irene nervously placed her hand back on her stomach. Valette waited, still holding out the bottle, this time like an offering, thinking she was going to say more, some words that would erase, in part, their conversation, or, appease their fire somewhat, but she maintained her silence, slowly stroking her belly.

Joseph had grown five inches in one year, with the muscles to match. He had hardened. Any lingering carefreeness gone. He tackled his physical labors with unusual aggression, exerting far more energy than needed, believing that one day or another he would have to defeat Valette, and preparing for it.

Leonard had noticed a change in the boy's demeanor, going on a few weeks. The old man wished Joseph would tell him what was going on, for he sensed some inner struggle. He might even have been able to help him, but Joseph revealed nothing, confided nothing, silent as the grave.

They'd gone out to chop beech trees into straight bolts that they would use to make calibrated fence posts. Joseph handled the axe with precision. First, he felled a young tree and removed its branches, then cut it at a spot whose diameter was still sufficient, without wasting too much wood. Next, he piled up the branches, always in the same direction, to dry them out for faggots come winter. Meanwhile Leonard would drag the bolts to the wagon, two by two, one beneath each arm, as if he were pulling a travois, then push them into the cart, widest ends first.

Once he determined the load sufficient, Leonard rolled the bolts to wedge them into place, so they wouldn't move during the trip. Joseph was still sending up large chips of white wood, circling around a young beech until it was left standing by the most miraculous of holds. He kicked it and the tree fell with the sound of ruffled feathers, as if a flock of wood pigeons was skimming the treetops above them.

"You can stop now. We've got enough," said Leonard.

"One more, while I'm at it."

"That's it, then. The cart's already plenty heavy for my mule."

Joseph chopped down one more tree, even more vigorously than the previous times, and loaded it onto the cart himself as Leonard warily looked on.

"Looks like you got energy to spare," he said, rolling the final bolt against a side rail.

To Leonard, Joseph, standing square as he was, holding his axe with both hands, looked like one of those ancient warriors who crossed the seas and violently conquered new lands. And now that the boy had nothing against which to direct his aggression, Leonard told himself it was time to lay their cards on the table.

"What exactly are you mad about?" he said.

"Job needs doing, don't it?"

"That's certainly one way to go about it."

"I don't know any other..."

"The way of a man in a rage."

Joseph wiped bits of bark off the edge of the blade, running it several times between his thumb and index finger until it gleamed with sap.

"Sounds like you know more 'bout it than I do," he said.

"I see what I see."

"Even if I am angry, as long as I'm directing it against the trees, no harm done," said Joseph provocatively.

Leonard tapped a bolt with the flat of his hand, as if he were petting an animal's rump.

"They don't protest, that's for sure," he said, emphasizing the first word.

"Say what you have to say and let's be done with it."

"Don't let your anger drive you. You might regret it for the rest of your life."

"I might just as easily regret keeping it inside."

Silence settled in, interrupted by the clicking of the mule's bit and the cry of a jay from deep in the forest. The old man continued, "Well, I've never met that kind of man."

"Maybe you haven't known that many after all."

"Maybe. But the men I did know wouldn't have told you different."

Joseph angrily tossed the axe into the cart.

"Turn the other cheek and all that bullshit. Is that what you're suggesting?"

"Usually keeping your distance is enough."

"Wise words," said Joseph disdainfully.

"I'm no wise man."

"Kind of, to hear you talk."

Leonard nodded and sent a jet of saliva out through his teeth.

"You weren't in the mood to hear all that."

"I wasn't in the mood to hear anything, if you want to know the truth."

"I'm just offering some advice. I can't stop you from doing what you feel is best."

Joseph, still annoyed, asked, "What are we really talking about?"

Leonard removed his hat with one hand, scratched his head with the same hand, then put back the hat, without a word. Joseph watched him, visibly calmer.

"You really like observing people, don't you?" he said.

"Not all of 'em, and it's already backfired on me."

Joseph let Leonard's words clear a path to him with machete strokes, which left room for Valette to make an appearance. Because it was Valette, after all, who had come to the barn to provoke him, whereas Joseph had always maintained his distance.

The old man was standing in the forest shade, a dark form speckled by dots of light piercing the leaves, chipped in spots, one hand around a tree trunk as though he wanted to crush it, all his impotence revealed in that grip, persuaded in that moment that the boy wouldn't turn the other cheek, much less back down.

"I'd hate to disappoint you," said Joseph.

Leonard walked around the cart to the mule, grabbed the bridle on her neck, and passed it under her head, turning his back to Joseph.

"It ain't easy being the man you want to be . . . None of us ever truly get there," he said.

Then Leonard nudged his mule to follow him. The axletree groaned a complaint well-known to men and forests. Joseph waited a few seconds before walking after them, eyes on the old man. Never had the hump on his back looked so prominent.

The news had traveled through the town and beyond. Imagine! A soldier on leave, who arrived in the backwater town of Saint-Paul from God knows where, driving an automobile... It was improbable, mysterious really. The word "deserter" came up in one conversation at the bar, but it remained to be proven, and the sympathetic innkeeper immediately rebuffed the suspicious party, saying that she knew more than she wanted to share, that he wasn't that kind of man, definitely not, not that kind of man at all. People insisted; they wanted to glean some understanding into the strange young soldier who spent his days roaming the mountain. Nothing doing. She would keep his secret, obviously. When one curious individual or another, out of desperation, tried to find out more by questioning the stranger directly, nonchalantly, as he was heading out on one of his long walks, he would politely skirt the conversation, impatient to set off. Though who could have blamed him for seeking some solitude after the hell he'd lived through, and to which he would return? Didn't seem much like a deserter, in the end.

Mathias was drinking coffee alone at a table. The innkeeper was washing glasses behind the counter. Each time she placed a glass dripping with water upside down on an immaculate rag, she would look over at Mathias, though there was nothing inquisitive about that look, more a mix of curiosity and tenderness.

"Can I ask you something?" he said.

"Of course," said the woman in surprise.

"I spotted a few farms on the way up to Puy Violent..."

"And you want to know who they belong to, that it?"

She slowly set down the glass she'd been washing and held on to it for a moment before letting go, the way she might have applied a cupping glass to skin to extract the humors of a diseased body. Then she walked over to Mathias's table, sat down, and, as she spoke, ran two fingers across the table's veined surface, tracing a road.

"First is the Valette farm. There's four of them up there. The son went off to war, so it's just his parents, their niece, and her mother. A little farther up, it's old man Leonard's farm, with his wife, Lucie, and farther still, the Lary farm. There's just two of them, the mother and son. The dad's at the front too, and the grandmother died this winter. Beyond that, there's nothing but a little shepherd's hut between you and the peak."

She tapped the destination point represented by a join in the grains of wood, a sheltered spot between two rusty nails shiny with wax. Mathias smiled at her.

"Thank you."

"You're looking for someone, aren't you?"

"No."

"If you want to know more about them, all you have to do is ask."

"I'm not looking for anyone, I swear."

"It's your business," said the woman, mildly offended by what she took as a lack of trust. Then, seeing that Mathias remained silent, she nodded and rose.

"I'm not the kind of person who spouts nonsense, you know," she added.

Mathias merely smiled again. He finished his cup and then stood in turn.

"I won't be back until this evening."

"You ought to wear a hat. You'll end up catching heat-stroke otherwise, with the sun beating down like that."

She walked away without waiting for a response and returned a moment later holding a straw hat as round as a colonial helmet. "Here."

Mathias hesitated for a second, then grabbed the hat without putting it on, and thanked her.

"Just don't lose it, you hear."

"Don't worry."

"It belonged to my husband, but he hasn't needed it for, well, exactly ten years now..."

"I'll take good care of it."

Wanting to avoid this kind of conversation at all costs, Mathias walked out of the inn, leaving the woman to the memories she would have happily shared with this stranger. He left town. And this time, all the people he passed seemed to have collectively decided to go no further than a sideways glance.

Once through the forest, the smell of burnt hay filled the air and the heat became more oppressive. Mathias barely felt it. He avoided the Valette farm and made his way to Leonard's. It was quiet apart from the sporadic lowing of cloistered animals and the clucking of a few hens, weak voices prostrate in pockets of shade. Mathias walked around the fenced buildings, without crossing a soul, then knocked at the front door. Forcefully. No one answered.

He decided to try the last farm the innkeeper had mentioned. When he reached its outer buildings, he heard a dull noise repeated at regular intervals. He paused for a moment, trying to identify it. He couldn't. To his ear, each space between the sounds wasn't composed of silence, but of an echo announcing the next, and which revived a stabbing pain inside of him. Mathias entered the farmyard. He found two men occupied with a strange task beneath a massive chestnut tree. With an axe, Joseph was blunting a stake set on a chopping block while Leonard burned the tip carved from another in the embers of a low fire.

Joseph saw the man first. He paused, and then Leonard lifted his head. They exchanged an incredulous glance.

"Is this the Larys' farm?" Mathias asked affably.

"Maybe. What do you want with them?" Joseph asked coldly.

"The innkeeper in Saint-Paul told me how to get here. That's where I'm staying."

"You didn't answer the question."

"I'm out for a walk, is all."

Leonard straightened up to face the stranger with an air of seeming indifference that always prompted people to say more than they would have imagined sharing.

"You're out for a walk, huh?"

"I'm on furlough."

"I heard as much."

"I came over because I heard some noise. But I'll be on my way, I would hate to be a bother."

"No bother at all. We were just about to grab a drink, weren't we?" said Leonard, giving Joseph a conspiratorial glance. "If you'd like..."

"Why not? It's hot."

Joseph planted his axe vigorously in the chopping block and, without a word, grudgingly headed to the house. After a few minutes, he returned with a jug of cider, which he gave to Leonard. The old man removed the cap and extended the jug to Mathias.

"Guests first," he said.

Mathias looked at the jug, unsure how to grab hold of it. Joseph was observing the stranger's movements with amusement verging on disdain.

"Round here, we don't bother with cups," he said in a provocatory voice.

"It's fine," replied Mathias, grabbing the jug with both hands.

He took a swig. Cider dripped down either side of his mouth, and he bent forward and spat.

"Go easy, if you don't want to hear about it from this one," said Leonard, chuckling at the stranger's clumsiness.

Joseph unceremoniously grabbed the jug from Mathias.

"More about not wasting," he said.

He wiped the lip with the back of his sleeve and took a long gulp, then passed the jug to Leonard. The old man put one foot on the chopping block, lifted the edge of his hat, drank, and then set the jug on his thigh.

"Where you from, anyhow?"

"Ardennes."

Leonard bobbed his head.

"Where are you really from, is what I meant."

"Paris."

Leonard took another gulp, then clicked his tongue before shoving the cork back in the jug using the flat of his hand, with one hard tap.

"A Parisian . . . Why on earth would you come all the way out here?"

"I was told it's a nice place."

"Depends on what for, I guess . . . And how did you hear about this 'nice place'?"

"Someone told me about it."

"'Someone' who?" interrupted Joseph, as though Mathias's words had pried open a jammed mechanism deep in his gut. What if this "someone" was his father? he thought.

Mathias paused and quickly glanced at the entrance to the farmyard.

"Eugene Valette. We were at the front together."

Leonard saw Joseph's shoulders slump and disappointment encrust itself in his eyes like dust.

"He didn't get a furlough, too?" said the old man.

"No," replied Mathias, surprised at the question.

"So you're not in the same regiment, then?"

Joseph didn't give Mathias time to respond.

"Do you know Victor Lary? He's my father."

Mathias paused again before responding.

"No, sorry. Never heard the name."

Joseph stared at Mathias, as if he was expecting a denial, or at least another hesitation.

"I'm guessing you stopped at Grands-Bois before coming here," said Leonard to change the subject.

Mathias dropped his gaze.

"I bet you weren't well received."

"I don't blame anyone."

"The war has nothing to do with how they are."

Mathias looked up at the old man, the irises of his eyes the purest of blues, as if frozen around a ring of cobalt.

"Did you know Eugene well?" he asked.

"A brave kid . . . I hope he makes it out."

Mathias removed his hat. He wiped the sweat off his forehead with the back of his hand. They were clearly unaware of Eugene's death.

"I won't give you any advice, but you'll gain nothing by sticking around here too long. Your family must be waiting for you," said Leonard.

"My family . . . it's a little complicated."

Leonard whistled air through his teeth, eyes still on the stranger.

"That's why you and Eugene get along so well, I imagine."

Mathias smiled sadly, then turned to Joseph.

"I hope your father returns soon," he said, his voice shaking several times as he spoke.

Joseph grabbed the axe and moved the handle forward to pull it out of the block.

"Yeah, we're praying for the same."

Mathias said goodbye, and they watched him walk away.

"Odd fellow," said Leonard, turning toward Joseph.

"It was like he wanted to pry something out of us."

"I don't think so."

"Says you!"

"Well, I saw a man who'd have liked to trade everything he owns for nothing at all in exchange."

"What do you mean?"

"That he didn't come looking for something someone could give him, and he knew it before he got here."

"Why?"

"No one can truly understand a man's heart. Whatever he's feeling belongs to him and no one else . . . Anyway, let's get back to it!"

Anna entered the bedroom and was chilled by the sight that greeted her. Her mother had taken every item of her clothing out of the wardrobe and spread them across the room. She was seated on the bed, fiddling with a dress like a child whispering to their teddy bear. Her lips were moving, her words devoid of sound.

"Mother!"

Helen didn't react. Anna went closer and kneeled in front of her.

"What are you doing, Mother?"

Helen looked up at her daughter, dazed, as though she had only just noticed her presence.

"Darling," she said, forcing a smile.

Anna gestured to the clothes scattered around her mother.

"We need to be ready," Helen said confidently.

"Ready for what?"

"For when your father comes back to get us, of course! He'll be here soon enough, I just know it."

Several seconds went by, during which Anna attempted to clearly identify what she was about to say and do. Then she lightly tugged on the dress, which prompted her mother to clutch the garment even tighter.

“Mother, let me do it.”

Helen rose, her face harsh.

“I know what you’re thinking.”

“I’m not thinking anything, Mother.”

“You think I’m crazy, is that it?”

“No, I’ve never thought that.”

Helen collapsed on the bed, overwhelmed and confused. She began to sob. Fat tears crashed onto the light dress, instantly forming small, dark halos.

“Go on. It’ll do you good to cry,” said Anna.

“I’m not crazy, you know.”

“I know, Mother, I know…”

“I can’t bear it here anymore. I thought I would get used to it, the way you seem to be.”

“We just need to hold on…”

“Irene’s right. I’m not strong enough.”

“Of course you are. You’ll see. This will pass.”

Helen gulped the excess saliva in her mouth.

“Just look, you’re comforting me, instead of the other way around.”

“I’m sure you’ll do the same, if ever I need you to.”

Helen delicately mopped her eyes with the edge of one sleeve of the dress, which she placed back over her knees, sniffling. She tenderly stroked her daughter’s hair with one hand, her eyes wide.

“I hope I’ll be here,” she said.

“I don’t doubt it for a second.”

Helen gave a vague, fleeting smile, then looked around the room, as though she was noticing the mess for the first time.

"Would you help me clean all this up?"

"Of course."

Helen cautiously lifted the lower folds of her dress and let them drop.

"They're so different."

"Who?"

"Emile and his brother."

The mention of Valette unleashed a torrent of disgust from Anna's throat to her stomach. Helen's fingers tensed on the dress, then she said:

"He's a brute... the complete opposite of your father."

"As long as we're together, he can't hurt us..."

"And then there's Irene under his thumb, always ready to humiliate me. I hate them both."

"Listen to me. We can't give in. If one of us stumbles, the other one will be there to pick her up."

"You're probably right," said Helen without much conviction. "We don't have a choice."

Anna wrapped her hands around her mother's fists and brought them together.

"We'll write to Father to convince him to come here as soon as he gets his furlough, okay?"

"That's not what he wants."

"Maybe, but I think it would be the best way... for him to leave us alone. We'll tell Father everything. He'll know what to do."

"I'm not sure that will suffice. They'll just keep making life hard for us once your father leaves."

"We have to try, Mother. And anyways, as long as Father's there..."

Anna paused. Helen was breathing hard, lost in thought.

"I think you're right after all. I'll write him," she said, as if an obvious solution had just struck her.

"We're going to be just fine, Mother. And you'll see, once it's all over, how quickly we'll forget."

Helen gave a weak smile, which immediately faded.

"I hope you're right," she said, pulling her hands from her daughter's grasp and slowly folding the dress.

"Vic-tor, Victor."

Mathilde felt an itching sensation on the surface of her skin, as though she'd just walked naked through a field of nettles. There wasn't a breath of air in the sweltering courtyard.

"Hel-lo Vic-tor, hello-hello-hello."

Fists clenched, she walked toward the barn gable.

It just kept going. "Vic-tor Victor Victor Victor... Hello-hello-hello."

The rasping voice was coming from the cage barely visible beneath an ample wisteria whose clusters of white double blossoms served as upside-down flashlights amid the building's gloom.

"Hel-lo Vic-tor, hello-hello-hello."

Mathilde was at the cage. Unclenched her fists. A jay hopped from its perch to the corrugated iron floor with the sound of a gong, then from floor to perch, incessantly, simultaneously uttering the words Victor had patiently taught it. A bird that had fallen from its nest five years earlier, which he had healed, fed, and eventually tamed. The bird's parents had flown around the cage for days. Victor, afraid they would poison their imprisoned offspring, chased them off by hanging garishly colored ribbons. They gave up in the end. The bird learned quickly, demonstrating an exceptional talent for imitation, capable of whistling and coughing like a human being, then, later, of reciting the names of every family member. But now, seemingly hatching a plot of terrible revenge, it could remember only one name. "Victor," which emerged from its black beak in endless repetition.

"Vic-tor Vic-tor Vic-tor."

Goddamn bird!

Mathilde slapped the outside of the cage with the palm of her hand several times. The bird froze on its perch, tilted its head toward her, aigrette raised, staring at her with a round eye that resembled a cup of black coffee on a white saucer.

"Hel-lo . . ."

Mathilde hit the cage again, harder, and the more she hit it, the louder the jay performed its exuberant litany. "Hello-hello-hello . . ." She pulled her hand away. The bird unfurled its wings, whipping the air in shimmers of lapis lazuli, folded them, and resumed, again and again.

"Victor Vic-tor."

The incessant provocation was more than Mathilde could bear. She hated this bird still staring at her with one black pupil in which her own image was reflected as though on the dark surface of a pond. She could have run away, so she didn't have to hear its voice, but she knew that wouldn't suffice. Asked the jay to shut up one last time, hitting the cage hard enough to scrape her hand. *Satan's spawn!* Why was the bird trying to torture her? Why "Victor"? How could such an ordinary bird be capable of such madness?

"Vic-tor hello-hello-hello Victor."

"Let the devil have you," she said, turning away from the cage.

Mathilde crossed the courtyard. Gnats collided with her, then bounced off. A fat horsefly landed on her shoulder and dug its stylet into the sunburnt flesh. She stopped when she felt the bite and crushed the insect with her hand; a cherry red stain appeared on her skin. She stamped on the fallen insect and resumed walking. Once past the gate, she thought she saw an animal the size of a wildfowl scurry across the path. Then she reached the last tree in a hedge beside the path, the one that wasn't a cypress but had the same willowy shape, though darker green in color. A yew. She picked a handful of orange berries blotched by ripening and returned to the cage in which the jay was still putting on its show. Threw one of the poisoned berries inside and waited for the bird to finally shut up.

"Mathias!"

"Yes."

"You promised."

"I promised what?"

"You told me you would take me to the sea."

"I always keep my promises, remember?"

"You're gonna have a hard time keeping this one."

"Stop talking, you're tiring yourself out for nothing."

"You know what I'd really like . . . after?"

"After what?"

"Stop it, please."

"Okay, tell me."

"I'd like it if you went for a walk in my mountains . . . while you thought of me . . . I'd like it if you did that."

"We'll go together, for Christ's sake."

"I can see my father's face from here."

"Who cares about your father."

"You'll do what I'm asking, right?"

"I will."

"You know everything about me, about my life . . . my family. And now I realize I don't know anything about you."

"What do you want to know?"

"Everything."

"The best part of me is my heart, and my heart belongs to you."

"Smooth talker."

"Beautiful angel."

"In the end, it doesn't matter. What I know about you is enough for me to love you."

"You should save your strength."

"It doesn't hurt so bad."

"That's a good sign."

"You're the most wonderful thing that's ever happened to me, and it's thanks to this war . . . Almost makes you wanna laugh, doesn't it?"

"I love you, too."

"Then all is well . . ."

"Exactly, my angel, all is well."

"You shouldn't be sad."

"Why would I be sad?"

"You know what I mean. Don't pretend, please."

"Do you want a drink of water, or something else?"

"No, I'm gonna close my eyes and rest for a bit . . . You'll stay here?"

"I'm not budging."

"Mathias!"

"Yes."

"I see it . . . you kept your promise . . . I see the sea . . . it's everywhere . . ."

The sun had scaled the entire sky, a perfect disc now grinding the blue to dust. Mathias had decided to leave the next day, but first, he wanted to go back to the mountain one last time. To *his* mountain.

He walked briskly, due west, stopping frequently to contemplate the majestic landscape, in those moments removing the hat lent him by the innkeeper to expand his field of vision, then putting it back on his head before continuing. His shadow was long behind him by the time he reached the river. Kneeled on the pebbled bank, placed his hat on the ground, splashed his face several times, and dampened the back of his neck and his hair, which he then slicked back in a fluid movement. He placed his lips on the water's surface, simply for the feeling. Drew back. The river-mirror was reflecting an unrecognizable image of him, a man absorbed in introspection that wasn't his. This gregarious river drowning out birdsong and even silence. "I'll take your sea and raise you a river, my angel," he said. He leaned over again and submerged his hands to the wrists, resting them on pebbles covered by slimy algae and swarming with caddisworms. Mathias recited a few verses in his head. He had read the poets, read their grand words expressing the echoes of the soul, which, in his mind, were wrongly confused with simple repressed feelings:

. . . the dead are no bother at all
They marry well with Mother Nature
See how they blend into the landscape
under the trees and beneath the grass
as if in the vastest of regions
stretching from the horizon to the sky's edge.

An echo of Mother Nature, capable of defying time, liberated of the burden of emotions, like a walnut its impermeable shell, finally ready to germinate.

Mathias let the light enter him, in order to receive what Eugene had received before him—this magistral beauty penetrating their beating hearts. For he had the power to grab the light from the air, but also from the water, the surface of a rock, and that light was music being composed, a grouping of sounds played out of order. He straightened up, withdrew his hands from the river, rubbed his face again, and lifted his head.

A man was observing him from the opposite bank. Mathias recognized him, though he'd never seen him before. It was the man Eugene had described to him on the front, the father he was forced to hate from afar, and maybe even in his eternal slumber.

Valette crossed the river with a determined stride, splashing his pant legs and his shirt. He kept his arms outstretched to keep his balance on the slippery stones. Mathias, still on his knees, watched him approach. Soon, the man would be right in front of him. Valette paused, the current swirling around his calves, measuring the boy up, as though he thought he could find the explanation he was looking for without having to speak. But clearly failing, he shouted, "Stand up!"

Mathias said nothing. He slowly stood, keeping his eyes on Valette.

"So it's you."

"You followed me?"

"Nothing in these mountains gets by me."

Valette emerged from the river. He was a half head taller than the young man.

"Do you know who I am?"

"I hadn't guessed that he looked so much like you," responded Mathias calmly.

"Why did you come to my home the other day?"

"Your wife didn't tell you?"

Valette haughtily lifted his chin.

"What would she have said?"

Mathias let his gaze slide along the river, on the surface of which trembled a scattering of light.

"That I was at the front with Eugene."

Valette betrayed no emotion.

"She made it sound like there was more than just that."

"He died in my arms."

Valette absorbed that detail, thinking about the letter Irene had hidden from him all winter, the one announcing his son's death. She had lied to him for more than five months, making him believe, without his prompting, that Eugene was sending news regularly. He could see her now, probably unfolding the same piece of paper each time without him realizing, her face impassive, inventing words, then folding the paper again before putting it back in her pocket. Valette paused for a moment, long enough to compose himself, then said: "I'm sure you're not telling me everything."

"What else would there be?"

"All this way to tell us something we already knew... It don't make sense."

"A promise I made to Eugene."

Valette clenched his fists. He took a step forward, now only a few inches from Mathias, menacing.

"What promise?"

Mathias didn't look down.

"I think I'd better be going."

"You're not going anywhere, goddammit!"

Valette was exactly as Eugene had described him to Mathias, but he wasn't intimidated. There was a long silence. A wide smile formed on the young man's face, which wasn't intended for Valette.

"There's still time, Mr. Valette."

"No, there's no time left at all."

"If that's what you want."

Mathias took a deep breath.

"I loved your son and he loved me," he said in a clear voice.

Valette blinked and took one step back.

"You what?"

"We were in love."

Valette's shoulders slumped miserably. He brought his ravaged hand to his mouth, then let it drop to his side.

"Can't be," he said.

Mathias stared curiously at the distraught man.

"Tell me it can't be," added Valette.

"Your son was the most wonderful man I've ever met."

"Don't you talk about him. Don't you dare talk about him, you little shit!"

Valette's voice scrambled, as though he'd dipped his head underwater, then he cleared his throat and spat at Mathias's feet.

"It's not true, I know it."

"I warned you, Mr. Valette. It's too late to go back now."

For a fleeting moment, Mathias had the wild impulse to place his hand on Valette's shoulder, to touch this man who despite everything remained Eugene's father, not to make any sort of amends, but simply because his lost love had come from this flesh and blood. Except that there was nothing paternal about Valette. Mathias decided to leave.

"Goodbye," he said.

"Don't you move... No Valette man could be what you're saying!" shouted Valette.

Mathias, ignoring the command, began to walk away, lighter and more peaceful than he had been since Eugene's death, as Valette screamed at him.

"No wonder we're losing this war with pansies like you in the ranks... Stop there, I won't say it again!"

Mathias could feel Eugene's hand in his, guiding him. He heard running footsteps behind him. Didn't turn around. A violent punch landed on the back of his neck. His legs wavered. He fell to his knees but stood up quickly, pushing off the ground with both hands. He kept walking.

"Stop, goddammit!"

Mathias's breath was mottled with pain, which felt like a blessing, an approaching of sorts. *So this is it.*

A second punch to the same spot, hard enough that Mathias fell flat on his stomach, face against the parched ground. He breathed in dust, particles sticking to his lips and some entering his mouth with a taste of iron. Then he rolled onto his back. Valette was towering over him, a parody of a devil whose silhouette was fragmented by the sun, and brandishing like a stake the whetstone he'd just pulled from his sheath, which he always kept on his belt during reaping season.

"Admit it. Confess that it's not true, and I'll let you go. You have my word."

Mathias spat out dust, and his mouth twisted into a half smile.

"Confess? I'm not guilty of anything."

"You forced him, didn't you? Is that it?"

"I didn't force anyone..."

"For fuck's sake, don't you understand this is your last chance?"

Mathias was contemplating the sky now, indifferent to Valette's words, summoning a memory, as though embarking upon a path that would lead him to Eugene's soul. Then, in a peaceful voice, he said, "If you only knew how much pleasure he—"

Valette didn't let him finish, mobilizing all the power of his good arm. He smashed the whetstone against Mathias's forehead, and it broke in two. The young man, smile still on his face, immediately lost consciousness. Valette dropped to his knees, grabbed Mathias's head with both hands, and crushed it into the pebbly ground with all the strength he had in him, then again, and again, and again, until there was nothing left to crush but a bloodied pulp of flesh and bone and hair. Then, he stopped, still breathing as hard as an ox on the plow. He spat on the ground to get rid of the metallic taste filling his mouth and let Mathias's limp head fall, still kneeling beneath the inert body that now resembled a lump of soiled rags.

"You'll never tell your lies about Eugene again, you little bastard."

Valette looked around him. With one bloody hand, he picked up the two pieces of the whetstone and slid them in his sheath. Blood had spurted onto his shirt and pants, forming constellations of motley stains soaking into the cloth. Calm reigned on the mountain. A large bird of prey was keeping guard in the sky, and its shadow slid slowly across the ground like a small angel on the road to perdition. Valette stood, walked to the river, and washed his hands. When he bent over, he saw his slightly blurred reflection: shirt caked in impure blood poisoned by an evil that had contaminated his own son, who, Valette suddenly thought, may not have been his own blood at all. He ripped off his shirt, as if it was burning his skin, plunged it in the river, and began scrubbing the dark stains. Seeing the blood spread instead of disappear, he quickly gave up. Not once did he consider putting the garment back on. Returned to the corpse, dragged it by the feet a good way upstream, and hid it behind some large rocks.

For a long time, Valette remained still, chest bare, the muscles on his pitted and bulging body tensed from the exertion, staring at the half-submerged corpse, not knowing if it was the sight itself that disgusted him the most, or the reminder of his son's shameful flaw. His unacceptable shame. "Rest in peace, if you can," he snickered, defying the corpse to provoke him one last time. The blood that had spilled from multiple wounds gave the young man's face a waxen quality, like a mask of wood lit up by large blue eyes that remained strangely expressive. Valette used his shoe to close that troubling gaze but managed only to leave a boot print on the soldier's face. So he spat on the body, and then spat again, until he didn't have another drop of saliva to spit. And then he left.

Irene buckled over at the first clap of thunder, though the storm had nothing to do with it. She spilled the bucket of milk. The thick liquid spread across, and between, the stones of the barn floor and blended into the slurry. Pain was eating at her from the inside. She placed her hands on her stomach and focused on her breathing, gradually calming herself. Once she felt she had the strength, she cautiously made her way to a small mound of straw that had long occupied a spot at the rear of the stable, tensing her jaws with each step so she wouldn't cry out. Then, back against the wall, she slowly slid down onto the straw, far from the door, so nobody would suspect she was there.

Little rascal... He was coming early. No matter. Irene would bring him into the world alone. Didn't need anyone for that, and certainly didn't want help. Her business. This miracle conceived to redeem one body and bring another into being.

Irene felt warm liquid flowing between her thighs. She leaned back and lifted her dress, then wriggled her hips to take off her underwear, which she managed to slide down her legs and over one sock. The piece of fabric twisted around one ankle like a sad, dirty brassiere.

The small piece of sapwood Irene had been safekeeping in her pocket for this miraculous day. Hands shaking, she put it in her mouth and bit down, summoning all the force of which her jaws were capable. Her water broke, the child pounding against her uterine walls with his fists, his feet, his head, impatient for freedom, clearing the path whatever the cost, like a soldier in the choke point of a trench. The image came to Irene in that moment, without sadness.

She knew the mystery of birth. Had already paid double the price. Bent her knees and spread her thighs, her shoes slipping on the golden straw whose points were leaving tiny red stars on the pale sky of her skin. She flexed her feet to reduce contact between her soles and the straw, her feverish gaze no longer able to distinguish anything other than the bony hills of her knees draped in the black fabric of her dress, like a tarp hanging over two poles, designed to protect her from God only knows what bad weather this time. Irene didn't care, for the child was coming and that was the only thing that mattered to her. Jaws still tensed around the piece of sapwood, corners of her mouth spouting grayish foam. An enraged animal, driven by instinct. The fleeting moment when Irene couldn't help herself from cursing the small being for making her suffer, the voice of pain. Crushing strands of sharp straw between her fingers. Drops of sweat formed, like needle heads, but didn't fall. She cursed the almost-born again in her head, and somewhere in those curses, there was always the name of God lingering, for her suffering was nothing more than human suffering, which brought her immense pride. This sacrifice wasn't in vain, and would never be. At no moment did it occur to her to hate Valette. He didn't exist, no longer existed, had only ever existed to plant this seed of life inside her womb. His role was coming to an end, one way or another.

Outside, bolts of lightning pierced the night and the sky gave way in the same second. Irene heard nothing. She was crying, begging for deliverance, using all her strength and will to bring this baby into the world. Another storm inside of her, far more powerful than the one raging outside. Biting down, exhaling spit reddened by the blood on her gashed lips. She felt her body close to liberation. Released her fingers gripping the blades of straw, rubbed her palms on her dress, sat up as far as she could so she could place her hands in a circle around her swollen, sticky vulva. Her heart was pumping blood in rhythm with her frenzied breathing.

She thought she heard sounds from above. Then noticed a new light spreading through the stable, and hay dust dancing on the surface of that light, like tiny, curious fairies swirling around her.

And he came. Finally. Little Moses tearing the maternal banks with his head, and that head alone represented the world reinvented in Irene's hands. Suddenly there was no more suffering inside her, and no more hatred, amid the intense release that followed, simply endless love for this child that made up for the loss of another, because this new life was the considerable payment made in exchange for a considerable loss.

The child was here. Whole, in Irene's hands, expelled from his cozy crevasse, still roped to the breached wall, his assailed lungs already taking in bursts of air perfumed with the smell of cows and manure that would never leave him. Her vision blocked by the swath of her dress, she felt him without seeing him. Immersed in her sheer joy, she didn't hear the dull thud behind her, like a sack of grain hitting the ground.

Irene spit out the blood-streaked sapwood and began to slow her breathing. She pulled her son onto her stomach and stretched out to stroke him. A silent chuckle emerged from her throat, a laugh well beyond happiness, a laugh drowning in madness. "My little boy," she said, now that she was holding her son tightly in her hands so he didn't slip, stroking his mucus-covered head and his body. Holding the child with renewed amazement in her eyes. She slowed her hand, then stopped moving it. No longer laughing. Still holding. Holding even tighter. Panic in her eyes replacing amazement. Holding so tightly. Until she couldn't feel the small creature anymore. Couldn't feel anything anymore. Not even this son, borne like a redemption for the sufferings of the world. Then a cry rose in Irene's throat, and emerged, as if she were expelling the flames of hell through her mouth, when she finally became truly aware of her hands clasped together, in which there was no one.

A warm wind began to gust, and this wind was like an invisible rope being pulled from the valley by an age-old and battle-hardened power, and this power was moored to vast clouds that reassembled large, dark rocks that had wrested their freedom from the mountain. Long lightning bolts streaked through the indigo air before disappearing in the quarries of the sky in a dull explosion.

Mathilde rushed outside, leaving the door open. Hunched over to resist the wind, she advanced slowly, her dress clinging to her tensed body, her long hair floating behind her. At the washing line, she began to unpin the dry laundry cracking on the rope and muffling the noise of the distant thunder. A sheet slipped from her hands, flew away, and wrapped itself around a stake: a ghostly apparition. Mathilde hurriedly grabbed it, then took down the remaining laundry. Arms full, she returned to the house, this time the wind pushing at her back. Before going inside, she turned around and called out to Joseph a few times, but he didn't answer. She assumed he couldn't hear her over the uproar in the sky, that he had certainly taken shelter when he heard the approaching storm, but still, a somber premonition was niggling at her.

She nudged the slightly open door with her foot, entered the house, threw the laundry untidily onto the table, then went to the window and pressed her face to the glass to watch for her son's eventual return. She started at each thunderbolt, her body instinctively moving back as if jostled by the boom, before returning to the window. Artificial night was settling over the farm at dizzying speed. A few seconds later, Mathilde saw large drops of water explode as they hit the ground, scattering dust like a herd of invisible horses galloping through the courtyard. Then a liquid wall came down, annihilating all hope of distinguishing anything whatsoever through the windowpanes, and filling Mathilde's heart with profound sorrow.

In truth, the "worst case" was leading the waltz in Joseph's mind. He thought incessantly about the pervading danger threatening Anna, his angel, convinced he wouldn't meet another for the rest of his life, that this was his chance, and could also become his loss, if he didn't take things in hand. He had heard that angels were never far from God, but Joseph didn't owe that supposedly benevolent god anything and had stopped counting on him once his father left. No, he didn't give a damn about God, certain as he was that he couldn't lose his father a second time. There was nothing he could do to help him. But he was the only one who could save Anna.

Knowing the kind of man Valette was, Joseph was sure that if he didn't act, his neighbor would do something irrevocable. It was a matter of time. And if tragedy did strike, he would never survive it. He could no longer put off going to Valette's farm and bringing her back. He would inform his mother after the fact.

Outside, dull rumblings shook the air, the sky growing darker by the minute. The storm was nearing. For a brief moment, Joseph thought about his grandfather, about everything he had promised his grandmother, then closed his mind to those memories so he didn't fall down a rabbit hole of doubts. He wouldn't find a better time to put his plan into action.

Starting in that moment, Joseph moved through the future like a ghost. Birds were fleeing the storm, carried along by the wind, the vegetation was blending into the inky sky, and the certainty in Joseph's mind grew the closer he got to Grands-Bois. He knew that the act that would sprout from that certainty would liberate him from the evil thoughts eating away at him, whatever it cost. For unless he acted, his body would remain the receptacle for contradictory impulses that could never mix: frozen water beneath a thick layer of oil. Sheer hatred preventing the purest of love from running freely through him. But for now: hold on to the hate and the anger. Cold, rigid, blinding anger. Hold on to it for the confrontation that was coming.

From all his spying on Valette's farm, Joseph knew its every nook and cranny. Impervious to the storm's growing fury, he stationed himself at the corner of the pigsty, waiting for the beast to emerge. After a few minutes, Valette came out of the house. Standing in the doorway, he flung his head back and, for several minutes, watched the sky thick with heavy clouds descend upon him, lightly swaying, sniffing the air like an animal evaluating danger. Then he swung his head forward, spat, and began to walk, nearly falling in the process, staggering from the clear influence of alcohol. He headed toward the barn, still wobbling, and hesitated before the closed door. For a second Joseph was afraid he would walk his way, but Valette decided to go around the building on the other side, disappearing from his field of vision. The young man walked along the gable to the opposite corner, where he saw Valette enter the hayloft overhanging the barn. Fat raindrops crashed intermittently onto the ground. Joseph walked to the heavy double doors that had been left ajar. He glanced inside. Valette was standing with his back to him and appeared to be struggling, bracing himself more than usual as he used a pitchfork with four curved prongs to toss small clumps of hay through the hatch. Joseph slipped into the hayloft without opening the doors any wider.

He heard a strange noise distinctly coming from the barn below, a sort of moan embellished by the thunder and raindrops now pounding the roof. Valette appeared to hear it too; he stopped tossing hay and pricked up his ears. The moan, or whatever it was, stopped. Valette shook his head and resumed his task. The smells of buried summer assaulted Joseph's senses, a fragrance that reminded him of Anna, her beauty, their embraces, their love. Watching Valette, Joseph wondered what beauty might mean to such a man, perhaps because he wanted to delay the confrontation, or fortify his hatred. *Beauty.* A word whose true meaning Valette surely didn't know, not even on a tiny scale, like the river of golden straw streaming through the hatch in the incandescent air, catching shards of light on its path to the darkness below. Of course Valette was incapable of imagining such a miracle. To him, hay served only to feed his cows, and air to fill his lungs. Valette was a monster capable of debasing everything he looked at, that he touched, a monster guided by his most primal instincts, a monster who took what he wanted without asking, things or people, made no difference. Joseph felt his resolve strengthen even more. He clenched his fists before he spoke.

"Valette!"

Valette dropped the handle of the pitchfork in surprise, and the tool disappeared through the hatch. He almost fell trying to grab it. Once he'd regained his precarious balance, he turned around, boots slipping on the glistening floor. Joseph was standing at least fifteen feet from the monster. He could make out red eyes buried in their sockets as though they'd been eaten away by a powerful acid. Valette shrank, his neck swallowed nearly whole by his shirt collar. Arms dangling, his alcohol-poisoned body began listing from side to side and he tilted his head, eyelids frantically blinking.

"What the hell are you doing here?" he asked without raising his voice.

Even diminished by alcohol, Valette still intimidated Joseph. The young man jumped when a lightning bolt filled the barn with blazing light, transforming Valette's silhouette into an even more monstrous apparition. Then the ghost turned back into the vulnerable man who could barely stand upright. Joseph summoned his courage and took a deep breath.

"I'm here for her."

Valette's eyelids stopped blinking.

"For who?" he said, his chest now swaying back and forth.

"Anna . . . I'm here to get her."

"You've got some nerve, kid. You think you can come threaten me on my land and just walk away?"

Valette flung out one arm as though he wanted to hit the boy, far away though he was, and almost stumbled from the momentum.

"Clear the hell out!"

Joseph didn't move.

"I don't think you're in any position to tell me what to do."

"Even drunk, I can crush you like the little shit you are, if I want."

"I'm not scared of you…"

Joseph took one step forward. Valette flinched back. No one had ever provoked him like this.

"I'll kill you, you hear me… If you don't clear off, I'll kill you," he said in a stammer that was difficult to hear over the rumbling thunder.

As he spoke, Valette looked for something he evidently didn't find, an object to defend himself with: the pitchfork that had fallen into the barn. He stepped back instinctively, turning at the same time, and found himself at the edge of the hatch, gasping. Eyes wide, he began waving his arms wildly, like such a trick could propel his body back to safety. Joseph watched. A simple flick would have been enough to make the monster fall. He did nothing. No need. Valette tottered, then tumbled. Legs swallowed by the void, he tried to grab the edge of the hatch. His bad hand. Slipped, screaming, dragging the grass scattered along the floor with him. He landed on his back twelve feet below. The sound of a long wheeze echoed through the barn, melting into the noise of the rain and thunder, and soon it was impossible to tell one from the other. Joseph slowly approached the hatch. Shaking, he saw Valette lying on a blanket of hay too thin to soften a fall. Stalks of grass were strewn across his face, and a foul gurgle rose from his contorted mouth; his legs weren't moving. Joseph observed the scene with curiosity, and also a degree of pride, as if he had pushed Valette himself, as if he had wanted to with all of his being and that had been enough to make this definitive action occur. He didn't feel an ounce of pity as he stared into the dumbstruck eyes of the monster, who was now a grotesque figure pitifully pinned to the ground forever, since it appeared obvious that he wouldn't be getting back up. That all that remained was for him to die.

Valette's trembling gradually slowed, then stilled. He desperately tried to use his elbows to sit up but quickly realized the futility. Managed only to lift one arm into the air, at the end of which was set his abominable hand like a rotten stump ripped from the earth, and which he extended, not as though he was beseeching help, but as if he wanted to strangle the boy whose face was framed by the hatch, strangle the very sight of him, which he was just as powerless to reach. His arm dropped, the hand left his field of vision, and maybe Valette had only dreamt that he saw it, maybe he hadn't had the strength to lift it. But he could still make out Joseph's hated face, it was all he could see, in fact, eyes glued to the individual responsible for his pain, or, more precisely, for the absence of his pain, since he felt none, which was the worst pain of all—to not feel anything. By chance, he had barely avoided the pitchfork, but when he slammed onto the ground, something had broken, something that was precisely keeping him from feeling any pain, something fundamental, irreparable, preventing him from moving or even speaking. Then he understood. He begged for death to take him at once. He began to weep, imploring Joseph with his eyes to climb down and finish him off.

Joseph cast a final glance at the inert body below, then he left the hayloft, closing the large double door behind him. It didn't matter what happened next. The important part was over. The monster had been vanquished.

Valette wished for death so hard that he thought he saw a pale humanoid form emerge from the rear of the barn, moving on four legs, like a demon emerging from hell to accompany him there. But it wasn't a demon that approached, then paused for a moment above him, looking at him, then the pitchfork, and back again. It wasn't a demon but someone who knew him, and who would deliver him. They had to deliver him. Valette closed his eyes and waited. He felt nothing when Irene sat beside him, lifted his head, and placed it on her bare thighs stained with dried blood, nor did he feel her hand stroking his forehead. He simply heard her voice, the nursery rhyme she used to sing to soothe her child, the only one she had ever learned. Death didn't deign to come that day. And so Valette would continue to wish for death during every moment of a last gasp that lasted eighteen years, watched over by a madwoman.

Wind-driven torrents were battering down outside. Joseph could hardly see through the thick veil of rain intermittently streaking the sky. He waited a moment beneath the eaves, not because he was scared to brave the storm, but simply because his mind was racing, wondering where he should go now and what he should do. The gutter was overflowing, unable to contain the water streaming down the roof as if spat out by an army of frogs. Little by little, his eyes grew accustomed to the darkness, and he thought he could make out a figure in the distance.

Then, nothing.

A blazing ball hurtling toward the earth tore through the clouds in its path and crashed into the ground as if, from the infinite depths, God himself was pointing a finger at the target to be destroyed. His judgment was irrevocable and merciless. Joseph fell. Instantaneously cast out of the world in which he had changed, through will alone, the destiny of one man, the worst of monsters though he may have been. The craftsman of a vengeance so ardently desired that it had come about in the end, and which Joseph fully assumed, even if he now had to pay the price. He could no longer feel his body. His head was filled by the explosion's thundering echo, and his ears buzzed with atonal music. Stripped of his senses, he had the painless, almost pleasant sensation of fluid trying to leave his body by any means, and it didn't occur to him to try to hold it in. He thought about his grandmother, about the question that had struck him at the moment of her death, about the exact instant a life ends. Now that instant had arrived for him. He thought about his grandfather, and the story that was forever repeating. Accepted his retribution by lightning. His legacy.

Then, nothing.

Head now empty, Joseph could hear the distant rumbling of thunder, the pattering of rain falling steadily, without interruption, pealing against the flagstones, as though it wasn't the Joseph he had known receiving this information, but another, detached from the former. The Joseph from a parallel world. The figure appeared again, the vision he'd had before the lightning. A body also splattered in mud, an adored body, loved more than anything. Her. Anna. A vision that would never leave him, wherever he found himself, for he wasn't yet sure whether he had entered the kingdom of the dead, if he had made it out, or was simply at its door. Eyes shut. Face pressed against the ground, ready to endure all punishments, knowing that he would never renounce the image emerging from deep in the earth, rising toward him. Revealing itself. This figure he was molding out of clay with his eyes. His masterpiece. Anna. The magistral perfection of an image that had become a body and a soul. All at once. Anna, now so close he could keenly sense her warmth. And when he rose, finally opening his eyes, he saw her.

Then, nothing.

How many days did the car remain in its pride of place in the town square? No one could say with certainty. Seven days. Some were interested at first, then, as they became overwhelmed by the tragedy in their lives, curiosity and envy turned to such indifference that in the end, everyone, except her, stopped seeing it, a part of the scenery that had always been there, in the same way that, later, people would stop noticing the monument whose future placement the vehicle had innocently heralded.

The papers wrote of the battles. But journalists had been ordered from on high not to describe too much of the horror, to avoid sapping the morale of families and yet-to-be-mobilized soldiers. In Artois, in Champagne, little matter where on the front, solders were buried. Victor had dug graves before, like the others. He knew how. Usually to bury an animal dead from disease, an accident, or old age, but never human bodies. The world upside down. On the surface, there was no more grass, no more trees, nothing but rats, corpses, and iron: nothing worth bringing back up. And yet, Victor had no choice, a new offense was being planned soon.

In the village, the Brousse family was grieving.

She was worried. Mathias had left town the night before and hadn't returned since. The two drunkards' resolution never to set foot back in the inn hadn't lasted long. They were surprised not to find the young man. She snapped that he did as he liked, that she wasn't on his back watching him, to which they looked at her suspiciously, the way you might someone who knows things and doesn't want to say them. She couldn't have cared less what they could have been imagining. She was worried. Her first thought was an accident, but the young man had taken enough long walks to start to know these mountains, and what kind of accident could have occurred at this time of year? She remembered the look in Mathias's eyes before he set out, determination making them darker than usual, and she suddenly grasped what had happened, why Mathias had spent his days roaming the mountain, so far from home, and what he had tried to convey to her the previous morning, without a word, simply with a look and a smile. The complicity between them. Shelter, a refuge to escape the war. That's what he'd been searching for. Because anything was better then returning to the hell blazing in his eyes, even dishonor. The end of his furlough must have been approaching. Mathias most likely wouldn't return, and if that was the case, she wouldn't report his disappearance, for fear that the police would go after him and shoot him as a deserter.

Only the townspeople knew that he was here. She left the two drunks, went into the young man's room, and, as a precaution, packed up his belongings, the few there were, which reassured her that he had taken his most important items. Then she hid them in her own closet, before returning to the room to tidy up. As for the car, the idea struck her as obvious as she made the bed: she would say that it had broken down and that Mathias had been forced to make his way to the Salers train station on foot so as not to miss roll call, that he would be back to get it on his next furlough, or else after the war, or maybe never. No one would ever think to check if the car worked. She would have it towed behind the inn, cover it with a tarp, and everyone would forget about it. Except for her. Simple as that.

When she returned downstairs, the old men were drinking in silence. She calmly walked to the entrance. The front door had been left open. For a moment she observed the automobile floating in the vesperal light, then went back inside the inn, and her eyes landed on the coat peg, on the exact spot where her husband's hat was no longer hanging, which no one would ever notice, except her.

Epilogue

Stricken with heat, the flock advances in a ripple of thick wool. A tide of sand-colored coats from which occasionally escape specks of dust instantaneously destroyed by the sun's rays. A horned ram in the lead, agilely navigating the rocky terrain, the procession squeezes onto a narrow, gently sloping path, followed by the shepherd and his obedient dog.

The shepherd squints as they descend toward a liquid horizon, glistening like diamonds hurtling down the mountain neck, momentarily slowed by a ledge. The animals don't need to see, their gaze fixed on the ground left to cover. They sense the water, delicate hooves picking up the pace, bells chiming, and bleating even louder. Then the flock breaks apart, scattering along the riverbank in an order that appears obvious to all. They drink, lift their heads, and immediately plunge their mouths back in. Drink their fill.

The dog strays toward the river and begins to eagerly lap the water, sending up large splashes and occasionally lifting its head to monitor the sheep. The shepherd unhooks a goatskin flask from his belt and takes small sips of lukewarm water, uses his shirtsleeve to wipe away the drops trapped in his beard, and closes the flask. He watches the flock for a few moments, then lets his gaze wander. Notices an object on the ground some sixty feet away, which resembles a large parasol mushroom. He walks over and bends down to pick up the hat, which he cautiously turns around in his hands. It's nicely made, compared to his shabby, sweat-stained hat, which he removes to try on this new one before folding it and slipping it into his haversack. Pleased with his discovery, with no thought to its provenance, he sits beneath an ash tree to enjoy some shade and the cool river breeze, to rest. The current is purring, the water jangling intermittently across the largely nude rocks. The shepherd slowly sinks into a peaceful daze, eyelids heavy. He lies down, places his head on a root, and tips the hat over his eyes. Dozes. Time, also stricken by the heat, rests too.

After several minutes in the sultry quiet, the shepherd is started awake by his dog barking. He couldn't say how long he slept, or even if he truly fell asleep. Curses the animal, which points its muzzle upward and snarls. The shepherd removes his hat, stands, shades his eyes with one hand, and looks at the sky. Something is spinning like the spoke of a wild wagon wheel. It ends its fall in a sheer canyon upstream. The dog continues to bark, still staring at the sky. "Cállate!" yells the shepherd, in vain. High in the sky, a bird of prey begins its descent, majestically carried by its wide, dark wings, the rest of its body a flame.

The shepherd recognizes the bird, knows what it dropped from its beak and what it's now hunting. Soon, he sees it disappear behind the rocks and puts the hat back on. He joins his dog, strokes its head a few times, and commands it to lie down and wait for him there. It watches, whimpering, as its master climbs the mass of fallen rocks that leads to the canyon.

After a few hundred feet, the shepherd flushes out the bird, which flies away and lands on a rocky peak a little farther on, keen eyes observing what it reluctantly abandoned. The shepherd notices a shape stuck between two rocks planed down like old molars, which is diverting the creek. He approaches hesitantly, the water hitting his shins, and gets close enough to distinctly make out the dike of fabric, which is in fact a disjointed body, partially consumed by vultures and crawfish. Blond hair and scraps of clothing float in the shallow current, offering glimpses of bones that resemble the creeping roots of a poplar tree. The body is so ravaged that the shepherd can't tell if it's a man or a woman. He tries to identify from where the person might have fallen, but there's no visible spot that would be high or close enough to cause death.

The shepherd takes the few steps remaining between him and the corpse, then leans over its face, whose empty sockets seem to be blaming him for arriving so late. A trickle of acid rises in his throat. He looks away from the horrific image before him. Legs wobbling, he makes his way several feet upstream, to a flat rock where he spots the object that fell from the bird's talons: a broken bone full of marrow. He carefully studies the fragments as though he had the power to glue them back together. Then he leans over the river, splashes water on his face with both hands, soaks his handkerchief, and presses it to the nape of his neck as he gazes at Puy Violent, which in that moment looks to him like a gigantic tombstone surrounded by yellow grass sprouting from the rock face.

The bird hasn't moved from its perch. The man casts a final glance at the corpse. All he wants now is to return to his animals and leave this place of death.

The dog is curled up in the shade of the ash tree. The shepherd whistles to order it to gather the flock, which it does, diligently. The sheep quickly fall in line to cross the ford and join the narrow gully leading to his hut.

After a few minutes' walk, the shepherd hears a long cry, turns around, and sees the bird of prey scale the sky, as if mounting a spiral staircase to challenge the sun, its body shrinking and flickering in a burning ether thick with silence.

The shepherd looks down, suddenly dizzy. Tiny particles flutter against the dark outline of his shadow stretching along the path. He stops for an instant, gathers himself, then quickens his step to catch up with the flock.

The path widens below, leading to a vast fir forest. Some of the trees are covered with caterpillar cocoons, tiny sails frayed to near transparency.

Two hours later, the flock reaches a stone cabin, its roof shingles ballasted with large pebbles. The animals rush to a trough dug from a tree trunk, clumping together like kernels of corn on a cob. The shepherd sits down on a log in the shade of the wood shed. Takes a lighter and his tobacco pouch out of one pocket, sticks a sheet of rolling paper between his lips. His fingers tremble as they shake sprigs of tobacco onto the paper that he seals with saliva. Then, he brings the cigarette to his mouth, spins the lighter wheel a few times with his thumb until a blue glow emerges, takes a long drag, and exhales the smoke with a sigh. He can't get the image of the corpse out of his mind. Won't ever.

Animals' thirst sated, his cigarette smoked, the shepherd steers the flock into a log corral, then returns to his cabin. Standing before the closed door, he shakes his head, as if reproaching himself, and sets out toward the village, thinking that surely people would want to know, and that, perhaps, his sharing this discovery will make them accept him more easily. Him, the foreigner. The village where he hasn't set foot in months, where the women and old men wear black. Where the children will soon do the same. Where the men have disappeared for a war that isn't his. And so he slows down. He stops to contemplate the mountains and the valley that are home to people to whom he owes nothing. He makes an about-face and returns to his impassive animals.

Maybe another time.

In memoriam of
the children of Saint-Paul-de-Salers
who died for France

Maurice PIONIER 8/20/1914
Jean AUBERTY 8/22/1914
Louis ROCHE 9/4/1914
Joachim THERS 9/16/1914
Paul JOANNY 9/17/1914
Joseph CHAMBON 9/26/1914
Georges JARRIGES 9/27/1914
Pierre BORDES 9/29/1914
Jean CHAMBON 9/30/1914
Pierre CHAUVET 11/12/1914
Firmin FAGOL 12/13/1914
Jean ANDRIEU 2/14/1915
Eugène VALETTE 2/18/1915
Firmin RONGIER 4/10/1915
Pierre BROUSSE 7/20/1915
Pierre BESSON 9/25/1915
Henri RONGIER 10/23/1915
Henri AURIAC 3/22/1916
Antoine BORNE 6/22/1916
Jean-Marie SENAUD 9/1/1916
Antoine RIGAUDIERE 9/29/1916
Antonin LAMOUROUX 11/5/1916
Pierre CHAMBON 5/2/1917
Jean-Marie BARRIER 6/3/1917
Gilles CAPY 4/11/1917
Joseph LIZET 10/5/1917
Jean-Marie CHANUT 5/11/1918
François DELTEIL 7/17/1918
Auguste MANAUD 7/23/1918
François CHAUVET 8/4/1918
Antoine JOANNY 9/26/1918
Louis APCHE 9/26/1918
Pierre FREYSSINIER 9/27/1918
Joseph LARY 9/27/1918
Léon JOANNY 10/5/1918
François RIGAUDIERE 4/30/1919

Acknowledgments

I want to thank Aurélie Janssens, for her sharp and discerning eye;

Sébastien Lavy, for his attentive reading, our long discussions, and the heavenly meals;

Léon-Marc Levy, for his support from the very beginning, his faith in *Clay*, and his invariably wise comments that helped me accomplish what I set out to;

Viviane Reyrolle, for her insightful clarifications on historical details (and well beyond);

Pierre Demarty, for his long writing paths, which I am never truly alone in taking.

About the Author

Franck Bouysse was born in France in 1965. He began his writing career in 2007 after working as a biology teacher. His novel *Born of No Woman* (Other Press, 2021) won numerous literary prizes in France, including the Elle Readers' Grand Prize, the Booksellers' Prize, and the Prix Babelio. His following novel, *Wind Drinkers* (Other Press, 2023), won the Prix Jean Giono.

About the Translator

Lara Vergnaud is a translator of prose, creative nonfiction, and scholarly works from the French. She is the recipient of two PEN/Heim Translation Fund Grants and a French Voices Grand Prize, and has been nominated for the National Translation Award. Her recent translations include *The Most Secret Memory of Men* by Mohamed Mbougar Sarr (Other Press, 2023) and *Demoiselles of Numidia* by Mohamed Leftah (Other Press, 2023). She lives in France.